A YEAR
IN THE LIFE
OF
ANDREA COE

LUCINDA E CLARKE

A Year in the Life of Andrea Coe

First Published 2020
Copyright © 2020 Lucinda E Clarke
Umhlanga Press
All Rights Reserved

Cover art and design by Sharon Brownlie
https://aspirebookcovers.com/

Compiled by Rod Craig
29/06/20

Also by Lucinda E Clarke

PSYCHOLOGICAL THRILLER
A Year in the Life of Leah Brand

FICTION
Amie – an African Adventure
Amie and the Child of Africa
Amie Stolen Future
Amie Cut for Life
Amie Savage Safari
Samantha (Amie backstories)
Ben (Amie backstories)

MEMOIRS
Walking over Eggshells
Truth, Lies and Propaganda
More Truth, Lies and Propaganda
The very Worst Riding School in the World

HUMOUR
Unhappily Ever After

CONTENTS

For Charlotte and Hermione

when you are a little older.

PROLOGUE

The young man hesitated outside the interview room. His palms so damp with sweat his hand slipped from the door handle. They never prepared you for encounters like this in law school where lectures were based on facts, precedents, arguments and dissertations.

The prisoner on the other side of the door had evoked feelings of sympathy on his first visit. The paperwork he clutched in his other hand, told him life had dealt her a raw deal. Now it was up to him to win her case or at least a reduced sentence.

He flung the door open with more force than he intended and marched into the bare interview room that housed three chairs and one metal table bolted to the floor.

He did not glance up as he pulled out a chair and sat down opposite her. The woman was raking her fingernails along the edge of the table. She was close to forty and in her youth, she would have been very attractive. She did not look her best today. Her greasy, tangled hair hung down to her shoulders, her cuticles were torn and bleeding, her eyes red and puffy, her face sullen.

He repressed his personal feelings. He was not here to admire her good looks but to discover the truth. He would need to earn her confidence. Could she tell how nervous he was? He hoped no one had told her this was his first case. He had been handed a 'no-win' scenario as his baptism by fire.

He glanced at his notes. She'd been here overnight and she had not uttered a single word, not to anyone. She was due to appear in court tomorrow and while he would automatically ask for bail, she would not be asked to plea until it reached the Crown Court. He needed her to talk if he was going to defend her. Premeditated murder carried a life sentence without parole, but she didn't look capable of killing a fly. He was young and naïve, but his instincts told him they had the wrong suspect.

The way she sat, perched on the hard, metal chair, displayed her anger and frustration. From his study of the case she had every right to do what she did, but the law didn't see it that way.

He pulled the file from his briefcase and opened it.

"I want to help you, but I need you to tell me everything. Do you understand?"

She nodded and moved her hands down to pick a piece of invisible lint off her dungarees.

"I need to hear the whole story, so why don't you start at the beginning?"

She walked her fingers up and down the crack along the edge of the table, looking down, not responding.

"Can I get you a coffee?" he asked. Someone had mentioned she was fond of coffee.

She nodded.

He left the room returning a few minutes later with a Styrofoam cup of pale brown, tepid liquid and placed it in front of her.

"Sorry, that's the best they have on offer." For a second, he thought she was about to pick it up and throw it at him, but she wrapped her fingers round it and gulped it down.

"Please, I can't emphasise strongly enough you need to talk to me." He paused. "Do you understand the charges against you?"

She nodded, playing with the empty cup, rolling it backwards and forwards on the table.

"And do you know what the penalties are if you are found guilty?" He persisted.

Again, she nodded.

"Then you need to help me. Start at the beginning and tell me your story, please."

JANUARY ANDREA

I gave a huge sigh of relief as Leah walked out of the café. She didn't suspect a thing. She was not even aware I'd been stalking her for weeks. Did I feel guilty then? Do I feel guilty now? No, not really. Life has always been 'dog-eat-dog' and life rewards those who claw their way to the top.

I peered out of the window to watch Leah disappear from view. She was hurrying home to make lunch for Bill, her live-in partner, and her stepdaughter Belinda. The perfect little housewife. There were days ahead when it would be hard to keep up the pretence of friendship.

In today's modern world it doesn't pay to be too timid. You need to stand up for yourself and give shit back to anyone who messes with you. But Leah is not like that. She's a left-over from the Victorian era, the quiet, submissive housewife who has yet to emerge into the 20th century much less the 21st.

It seems so unfair that she's the one with all the men, all the money, all the manners and graces, a husband somewhere on the run, and another man breathing down her neck, panting after her like a dog. She comes across as so needy, at a loss, unable to cope. So, what happens? Soft, daft people rally around and try to make life better for her. They feel sympathy and try to put things right any way they can.

She evokes the same feelings we experience when we see those cute little dogs on the television just begging for homes, or the little children who are starving to death in some far-flung African country. Many of us are already digging into our purses before the advert is even over.

Not me. Oh no. I have more sense. I know exactly what I want, how I'm going to get it and who I want to share it with.

I checked my watch. I would give her a couple of hours to feed the family before I phoned her. I might even wait until tomorrow. I still had a few supplies to buy and I needed to look up the contact name I'd been given. Evenings and late nights were the best times to shop.

I approved of Leah's choice of coffee shop and decided to have lunch here. I read the menu, and waved the waitress over and ordered a slice of quiche, a side salad and another coffee. I turned to gaze out of the window, to the wide mud flats exposed at low tide. Not a particularly pleasant sight.

It had been too easy to get Leah's new mobile number she'd lost more than one phone in the past. I already knew her address although I had no intentions of admitting it. In fact, my old friend would be amazed at how much I knew about her. I could have told her where she banked, the name of the book club she had joined, and the charity shop where she worked on a Tuesday morning. She was a member of the town library, attended a weekly swim session at the local baths with other amputees and occasionally volunteered at the hospital where she played with the children in the long-term care ward. The label 'Goody-Two-Shoes' described Leah to a T. She was just too good for this world. It's unlikely I can get my hands on her money without upsetting her but it remains to be seen how much fallout there is going to be.

I rummaged in my bag for a notebook and a pen. It was time to work out a timeline for 'the plan'. I was prepared for it to take a couple of months. I couldn't wrap it all up until I knew that Leah had received everything that was due to her. She would be amazed to discover that I knew more about the process than she did – the result of having a cousin working inside at the insurance company.

The waitress approached my table, balancing two plates and my coffee. As I ate, I stared at the blank page in my notebook. I didn't have a real plan at this stage and I hoped my absent partner could come up with something that would work. It wasn't fair to leave everything to me. But then it was going to be fun, and would certainly make life a lot more interesting.

The easy task would be to get Leah out of that stuffy apartment and to cement our friendship. I can always make her laugh and I'm savvy enough to see right through her insecurities – poor little church mouse. Nope, 'poor' is not the word for it. 'Rich' little church mouse!

Whoops, the waitress is staring at me. She probably wonders if I'm a little mad, giggling to myself. If she comes over all nosy, I'll tell her I'm a writer, planning my next comedy book. It's just so easy to fool the simple-minded.

I wish I had more patience. I know I should wait at least two days before contacting Leah again. It will be easier to manipulate her as she will be nervous if I've not been in touch. She might fret and worry and wonder if she imagined the whole thing. Did she notice I had not given her my new mobile phone number? But I have hers. That keeps me in the driving seat.

I have plenty to do of course. Now I have found her I must move down to Weston. Not too close maybe a couple of streets away, so I can walk to her flat. The first recce went well, lots of nice gateways and high hedges to duck behind. I'm getting quite good at this stalking thing, even if I do say so myself.

I pulled out my phone to message my partner, say I'd made contact with Leah and would update regularly. I had only just pushed the off button, and was putting it back in my bag, when Leah burst through the door and raced over to my table.

"I can't run the risk of losing you again. You are my best friend and the only person in the world who can reduce me to tears with laughter. Finding you again completes my world." She stood there with the broadest smile on her face.

I'd been planning how to worm my way back into her life, and she was making things so easy. I dropped my bag on an empty chair, stood up and embraced her.

"I can't believe it either Leah," I murmured in her ear. "I've never had a friend like you before." Well that was perfectly true, I don't usually do the 'best friends' bit.

"We have so much catching up to do, would you believe it's been a whole year? There is not a moment to waste," she added.

I laughed as I pulled away and held her hands. "What do the young kids say these days? Best Friends Forever – BFF?"

Leah glanced at her watch. "As soon as I got home, I turned around and hurried back in case you disappeared again. I must dash back. Belinda and Bill will be home soon and they will expect their lunch."

"Of course," I murmured. I almost added 'the perfect housewife', but managed to swallow the words.

"So," Leah grabbed my bag and pushed it into my hands, "you're invited too. It's only toasted sandwiches today, but I'll make plenty." She paused looking at the food on the table. "Oh, I see you've eaten."

"I'm fine, I wasn't going to finish it," I glanced at the remains of the quiche and salad still on the plate. "I'd rather spend the time with you."

Leah smiled then she looked serious. "Come to my flat it's not far." She paused. "You are free this afternoon, aren't you?"

I laughed at the desperate look on her face.

"Of course, I am. I have the whole day free for you."

"That's alright then."

I knew exactly where she lived. I had been watching her flat for days, noting the comings and goings, her daily routine. Leah had no reason to suspect anything.

Holding onto my arm, Leah slid a twenty-pound note onto the counter as she swept me out of the door. The sharp wind blowing off the sea, blasted our faces as she hurried me along the sea front, past the elegant Victorian houses built of honey-coloured Bath stone, remnants of a gentler age.

"How far is it?" I asked, feigning ignorance as I pulled my scarf tighter around my neck.

"Just around this next corner. We have a first floor flat, but it's really huge. That's the beauty of these old buildings, space for the family and, I guess even some staff, in the olden days."

"For those who could afford them of course." I glanced up at the two and three storey houses once elegant and desirable residences now carved up into small flats for the requirements of the modern age.

Leah dropped my arm as she dug into her handbag to retrieve the front door key. "I can't wait to see their faces when they walk in and see you."

I smiled. I had no need to fear any of the people living in this house.

We took the lift to the first floor. The flat was larger than I expected. The lounge, off to the left of the hallway had a huge bay window with panoramic views of the Atlantic Ocean in the distance and the mud flats stretching from the promenade at low tide. It was furnished simply but in keeping with the age of the building with comfortable sofas in chintz covers and a modern touch with the fake gas-fired stove and radiators against the walls.

"We have three bedrooms. The main one is en suite and this other room, doubles up as a kitchen, dining room and a TV lounge."

"It's lovely. How many of you are living here?" As if I didn't know.

"Just Bill, Belinda and myself."

"Three bedrooms? You have one spare?" Might as well get the sleeping arrangements sorted out.

"Yes. You never know who might turn up," Leah

smiled as she pottered around the kitchen collecting ingredients for the lunch.

So, she was sleeping with Bill.

"Why Western-super-Mare?" I asked as I leant against the fridge watching Leah slice the cheese and tomatoes.

"Bill. They offered him a job at the technical college and he loves it."

"Of course, they closed our local library, didn't they? Bloody government cuts." I perched on one of the high stools I dragged from under the counter.

She buttered eight slices of bread. "I was devastated. It was my only refuge, somewhere to go when I was too scared to go home."

I walked over and put my arm around her. "Leah darling you went through shit. Anyone would have freaked out with furniture moving, noises, voices from nowhere..."

"Especially that blue rabbit." She paused waving the knife in the air. "I would never have believed that a cute cuddly toy could appear so evil and so threatening."

"But it's all over now so you can relax."

"Well no, not exactly..."

Leah was interrupted by the front door slamming and Belinda barrelled into the kitchen, dropping her schoolbag on the floor. She stopped and stared for a moment then gave a shriek of delight and launched herself at me.

"I don't fucking believe it," she shrieked, enveloping me in a bear hug. "Where did you come from? Where have you been? How long are you here for?" The questions flew thick and fast.

"Whoa!" I couldn't help but laugh. "What language lady, but it's great to see you too."

Belinda took a step back. "Language? What? Oh, you mean fuck?"

"Yes. Not nice."

"Andrea, get with it. Everyone uses it these days. All the time. I've heard you use it! Hypocrite. It's just another word."

"I do keep reminding her," Leah butted in. "But she takes no notice."

It's amazing isn't it that a small exchange like that can tell you so much. Despite all the years Belinda had lived with her stepmother, she still had little or no respect for Leah, despite the woman giving her a roof over her head, when to all intents and purposes both parents had deserted her. Without Leah, the only person she could turn to was her brother Leo but he could not be relied on, not for anything. I wondered if Leah was also supporting Bill. I have no idea how much college librarians earned but flats this size, close to the beach with a sea view, don't come cheap.

A few minutes later, Bill walked into the kitchen. He gripped Leah gently round the waist and gave her a long, lingering kiss on the lips.

"How's my favourite lady?" he asked before nibbling her earlobe.

"Oh, for fuck's sake, you two at it again? Like bloody rabbits." Belinda made a grab for the first two sandwiches out of the toaster and perched on a kitchen stool.

Leah drew back sharply, putting distance between herself and Bill. It was obvious that Belinda made her feel she was doing the wrong thing.

"Belinda, you know I hate that language, please don't use it in the house."

"What? Fuck?"

Leah cleared her throat. "Yes the 'f' word. There are numerous other adjectives in the English language, thousands in fact."

"Yeah, well maybe, but it's the one we all use now. Yer gotta get with the programme."

"Actually, I don't," Leah snapped back. "I'm sure if I can find other words to use, you can too."

Belinda grabbed a second sandwich off the plate. "Whatever floats your boat," she mumbled with her mouth full.

I caught a look of sympathy from Bill. It looked as if he never interfered. Belinda was no relation to him, but I thought that poor Leah could do with some backup. I remembered how often her stepdaughter had reminded her that she was not her real mother and it was not Leah's job to tell her how to behave. No, of course not. But it was fine for Leah to cook and wash and clean up after her and provide her with clothes and spending money and meet her every need. Yes, all that, but on no account could she tell Belinda, what to do because she had not given birth to her.

Poor old Leah was between a rock and a hard place, I thought as she liberated the last four sandwiches from the toaster. It couldn't be easy anticipating Belinda's moods. One day she would be a charming young lady, sensible, easy to talk to and fun to be with. The next, a raging virago, swearing, sarcastic, rude and objectionable. I would have picked her up and shaken her until her teeth rattled, and if it had been me, a certain young lady wouldn't be able to sit down for a month.

Of course, kind and gentle Leah would never dare. It

looked as if she was still learning to be assertive. She'd spent hours studying the Great Dr Cromptom's book on how to be a complete, mature adult who knows his or her place in the world. I reminded myself to ask her if she had brought his book with her when she moved down to Weston from London. It promised the answer to all life's woes but, I could see now, that Leah's problem had not disappeared.

Bill caught sight of me and I could read the question on his face. Did he know me? Had we met?

I had told Leah I'd traced her through Bill, but that was not true. I hoped she wouldn't notice the slip. I did need to be more careful.

Actually, Bill we haven't. Once they packed Leah off to that mental hospital, I made myself scarce. I decided to put him out of his misery.

"Bill, I'm Andrea. I've heard so much about you that I feel I already know you."

He turned and smiled and offered his hand. "Pleased to meet you at last," his grip was firm and confident. Of course, Leah has mentioned you as well. You're the lady who made her laugh."

Bill turned to wash his hands in the sink. "So how was school this morning?" He smiled at Belinda.

"What's it to you? You *really* want to know? You don't need to pretend you're interested."

"Belinda! That's way out of line. Apologise to Bill immediately." I could almost see Leah's blood pressure rise.

"Whatever." Belinda grabbed another sandwich off the plate, stalked out of the kitchen and slammed the bedroom door behind her.

"Bad day?" muttered Bill.

"Yes," replied Leah and then she remembered I was still leaning against the kitchen counter and she smiled. "No, not all bad."

Bill hung around for a while after lunch then rushed off for his afternoon stint at the college. Leah brewed up our favourite coffee and we went through to the lounge chattering non-stop.

As irritating as she might be, Leah was a sweet kind little thing. She was so easy to like and so relaxing to talk to. It was hard to hate her. Well, maybe we would leave her a little of the money to scrape by on if things went to plan.

Across the corridor, a door banged and footsteps thudded towards the front door.

"On your way back to school?" Leah called out.

"Yeah, whatever," was the abrupt reply as the front door slammed shut behind her. Out of the corner of my eye, I noticed that Belinda's school bag was still on the floor exactly where she'd flung it earlier, so I guessed afternoon school was not on her agenda.

"You poor thing," I reached out and squeezed Leah's hand. "She's still a pain, giving you a hard time?"

"Yeah. There was a brief spell when I got out of the mental asylum," Leah shuddered. "I really thought we had turned the corner. She can be charming and good fun and even sensible. She was quite excited about moving down here next to the sea."

"Go on, be honest, you bribed her with tales of gorgeous lifeguards, muscles rippling over their six packs strutting up and down the sand."

Leah burst out laughing. "No, I wish. You should have seen that creep she had sleeping over at my mother's house. He made my skin crawl."

"Oh dear, we are sounding old. Can't be having that now darling. Young at heart. I'm a mature snowflake and I'm proud of it."

"Andrea you were middle aged when snowflakes were born!"

"Nonsense! You're only as old as you feel, or as the bit of manhood you can feel."

The tears ran down Leah's face as she hastily put her coffee down before she spilt it. "I've not laughed like that for weeks!"

"That's why you need me darling. To share the lighter side of life."

"You have no idea how glad I am to see you again Andrea."

'Welcome to my parlour said the spider to the fly'.

By the end of that afternoon we had slipped back into our old, comfortable friendship. So far, so good.

Several cups of coffee later and I took the next step.

"Where are we going tonight?"

"Tonight? I don't have any plans, though there is a good drama on Channel 4."

"Darling!" I threw up my hands in horror. "A good drama on the telly. Has it come to this? I told you I was here for a few days so we are going to paint the town red."

"Oh, I don't know."

"Of course, you do, we're going to have a great time."

"But what about Bill?"

"What about Bill? I'm sure he won't mind a little 'me' time on his own and he can fill you in on the plot in this famous drama."

"Andrea, I live a quiet life now and…"

"Balls to that Leah! You mean a boring, everyday life living in sin with a man you are not married to, a teenager who won't give you the time of day and a missing husband on the run somewhere in, where is it, South America? Who also, by the way, tried to have you committed or sectioned or whatever they call it these days? You call that a quiet life my friend?"

Leah giggled. "Put like that it sounds decadent."

"I can't see your mother approving, can you?"

"Mother never approves of anything. I could have Olympic medals on the mantlepiece, next to a Nobel Peace prize and she still wouldn't be satisfied."

"Yeah, you've had a shit life but it's all changing from now. I'm here and I'm your fairy godmother. So, where can we go in this town for a bit of fun?"

"They have tea dances at the Pavilion and there is a cabaret club on the outskirts of town I'm not sure where exactly."

"Lose the tea dances, far too staid. The cabaret it is then, and I hope they have dancing as well. I'm in the mood for a wriggle on the dance floor."

I watched Leah's face change. For a moment I had forgotten about her leg. Still it wouldn't stop her dancing, not if I had my way.

I gave her a playful poke and bashed her over the head

with a cushion. "Where has my friend gone?" I laughed at her and then jumped to my feet. "Right I'm out of here." I watched her face fall, like a kid whose ice cream has landed on the pavement. "But," I continued, "I will be back at eight thirty sharp knocking on your door, so I expect you to be ready." I walked into the hall to collect my bag and coat. "Plenty of time," I called back over my shoulder, "for you to cook up a storm for your family and let them know you'll be out having a ball with your best friend and you'll see them when you see them. Tell Bill not to wait up."

I flung on my coat and scarf and opened the front door before Leah could say a word. I wasn't going to give her a chance to back out or change her mind. I gave a little wave as I disappeared onto the landing, closing the door behind me.

Back at the hotel I rummaged through my suitcase discarding one outfit after another until I settled for a simple black cocktail dress with a few sequins around the neck. I planned to arrive back at the flat a little earlier than eight thirty; it might catch her off balance.

I connected my tablet to the internet and searched for a suitable venue for drinks before we got to this nightclub. I'd better get her a little tipsy before we hit the dance floor.

I kept exactly to plan and had the Uber waiting outside the gate where it could be seen from the lounge window. I kept my finger on the outside doorbell and chirruped into the intercom. "Here I am, all ready to party. Do I have to come and drag you down or are you coming down by yourself?"

I could hear a metallic giggle from the other end.

"I'm coming to get you!" I squawked. "Are you ready?"

"Andrea you are such a drama queen," Leah laughed. "I'll be down in a minute, but…"

"No buts! I'll wait in the car." I released the button on the intercom and backed off down the path and jumped into the back seat of the taxi. There was a definite chill in the air, and I wrapped my coat tightly around me. I kept my eyes on the door, but nothing happened.

The taxi driver turned and stared at me.

"You want to wait?" He drummed his fingers on the steering wheel, and kept glancing in the rear-view mirror, probably worried he was double parked and obstructing the road.

"Yes, my friend won't be a moment, she's on her way." I gave him my brightest smile and he smirked back at me. Huh, he should be so lucky.

It seemed an age before Leah finally opened the outer door and hobbled down the front path. I wondered if the damper sea air was good for her leg? I must talk to her about that. While she had a family around her now, I was going to destroy that. I wanted her to rely on me, and only me. *One step at a time Andrea, one step at a time.*

I got the taxi to drop us off at the bar, close to the night club, and asked him to return in an hour. That should be enough time to pour at least a couple of drinks down Leah's throat.

We found a seat and a young girl approached our table to take our order.

"Two gin and tonics," please. "Large ones."

"Andrea, what are you thinking? I hardly ever drink and a large gin…"

I patted her arm. "Sweetie, you deserve it. You are much too hard on yourself. You need to relax more and enjoy life, especially now. And who better than your very best friend here to help you do just that?"

I put my arm around her shoulder and gave her a hug as I encouraged her to drink.

Leah giggled. "It's so hard to relax. I can't believe that life can be this good again."

"Are you still sad over James and the kids?"

She nodded. "I know it sounds soppy, but we were soul mates. I've told you what a bitch my mother was and the abuse she threw at me as I was growing up. When I escaped and started nursing, I had so much freedom and then to meet a man who was so kind and loving, it was the answer to a prayer."

"Yes, I can imagine that." I took a small sip from my glass. I had no intention of getting drunk.

"Meeting James was like a fairy tale come true. Did I ever tell you that we met when he was a patient in hospital?

"Yes, you did, several times."

"Sorry, I must bore you."

"Darling not at all. I'm happy to hear it a million times, that's what friends are for."

Leah picked up her glass and took another gulp then turned to me. "Andrea, you know all about my life, the babies, the car accident, losing James and my leg, meeting and marrying Mason and most of what happened after that."

I nodded.

She continued. "But I know hardly anything about you.

You never, ever talk about yourself. I was in such a state most of the time, always talking about myself and selfishly never asking you about your life."

"There's so little to tell. Nothing very interesting. Lived in a small village in the south of England, Kent, then school, followed by secretarial college and then I met my husband. He died in a plane crash as you know. You and I met when we became neighbours. So now you know it all."

Leah nodded and took another gulp of her gin. I could feel she was still nervous, but hopefully not curious. I had not told her the whole story, in fact most of it was pure fiction. However, she could surprise me at times, and she didn't let this go.

"Are your parents still alive?"

I paused, hoping she would think I was composing myself. What could I tell her? Whatever story I made up I'd have to remember, and my memory is not what it was.

"Both deceased," I mumbled hoping she would not pursue it. She didn't but then stumbled onto more dangerous ground, all the while gulping down her drink. I signalled to the waitress to bring her another one.

"You, uh, told me earlier in the café that you'd had a fling with Mason before I married him."

"Uh, yes."

"When he was still with Caro?"

"Yes."

"How long did that…?" she paused, embarrassed.

"Ah, only a few months, if that. It was one of those lust things. I was unhappy with Ronald and Caro was giving Mason a hard time. We sort of drifted together. You know how it is?" Leah didn't look that convinced. I could never see her actually cheating on Mason, well not before he disappeared and vanished to some undisclosed location overseas.

"How did you meet?"

I thought rapidly. "He was walking Zeus."

Leah laughed. "The nemesis of my life."

"Frankly I never liked that hound either. Mason was besotted with him, wasn't he?"

"Yeuk. Not my kind of dog at all." She tossed back the last of her first glass and picked up the second without seeming to notice what she was doing. "I still have teeth marks in my leg."

For a horrible moment I thought she was going to pull up her long skirt and show me but instead she concentrated on her drink.

"Leah darling," I turned the conversation back to her. "I can sense you're not happy. Share with me?"

She snapped out of her funk and stared at me. "Maybe another time, not now. You told me we were going to paint the town red. So, let's paint."

"You're right. Finish your drink, our ride will be here in a moment. We don't want to keep him waiting."

Leah rose a little unsteadily to her feet and made for the rest room. The moment her back was turned I poured the rest of my drink into a convenient potted plant next to the wall. Tonight, I needed to keep a clear head, timing was everything.

The nightclub was humming by the time we arrived. The

dance floor was crowded, but I managed to steer Leah to one of the side tables and found us both a seat. I ordered more gin and tonics, it seemed Leah was getting a taste for them. I watched her as she looked around in amazement.

I patted her arm playfully. "Don't tell me this is your first visit to a night club. It is isn't it?"

She grinned and nodded.

"Such a sheltered life," I teased her. "Now I'm here I'm going to change all that."

"Are you staying?"

"What?" I'd been distracted a rather handsome man who was eyeing us out from across the room.

"Staying. Are you staying here, in Weston?"

"Oh, now there's a thought." I just had to play along. I pretended to think about something I'd already decided days ago. "Hey! Why not. You have the best ideas Leah."

She took another gulp of her gin and grinned. "Just now and then."

The band on stage finished their set and retired and the DJ took over. He began with some softer, less manic music and the dance floor cleared. Patrons made for the bar or the restaurant.

The guy who had been watching us for the last half an hour came striding over. "Ladies, may I interest one of you in a dance?"

"No, no thank you," Leah's response was immediate. She looked terrified.

"That's very kind of you," I replied, "maybe later. We've not been here long and for now we'll just enjoy the music."

He nodded and backed away.

"I'm not sure what Bill would say." Leah muttered so quietly I had to lean over to hear her.

"Leah, there's no harm having a dance with a member of the opposite sex, even if you were married to Bill, and you're not. This is the twenty-first century, darling."

"I'm still married to Mason…"

"Sweetie you can't be serious. He ran out on you for f's sake. He could be anywhere in the world, heck, he could even be dead or remarried."

"Dead?" The idea had obviously not occurred to her.

"I'm not trying to be dramatic, but it is a possibility isn't it?"

"I never…"

"Either way you are your own woman. Independent, mature, grown up and, I hope, becoming more assertive."

Leah grabbed a few nuts out of the bowl on the table before answering.

"I'm working on it."

Not hard enough, I thought.

As soon as the DJ had spun his last record, the band shuffled back on stage, picking up their instruments, twanging guitar strings and adjusting microphones. They began to belt out *Dancing Queen* and the crowd raced back onto the dance floor. I have yet to meet anyone who can ignore ABBA's music. I grabbed Leah's hand and pulled her to her feet.

"Come on, there's no way you can sit this one out."

She resisted at first but then allowed me to guide her into the throng on the floor where we weaved and swayed to the beat. I watched and waited for my opportunity. As the music stopped, I lifted my foot catching Leah's right leg just above her ankle and sent her crashing to the floor.

JANUARY LEAH

Dear Diary.

I can't believe my life is finally turning around. Andrea, my best friend 'eva', has walked back into my life. She is the one person who can make me laugh until I cry. I can cope with Belinda, her moods and her rudeness. She's just a teenager after all. I'm sure she'll grow out of it. And I have Bill, the sweetest man. I can talk to him about politics, the state of the world; we agree on so much. But not about woman stuff of course. That's why we all need that special girlfriend. Tonight, we are going to hit the town, although I won't make a habit of it. Andrea is single and I can understand she's probably in hunting mode, but just this once, to celebrate our reunion.

FEBRUARY ANDREA

The door creaked and swung back at me as I tried to manoeuvre the wheelchair into the ward. It was the first time I'd ever come close to one of these contraptions and they are not easy to push or propel or whatever you call it, the wheels go in all directions.

I paused at the end of the room and looked for Leah. I noticed the bunch of fake flowers on her locker and a couple of 'Get Well' cards.

I was intercepted by a nurse who hurried over. "I'm sorry, but it's not visiting time for…" she glanced at her watch "another hour and a half."

"I am so sorry, but I understand my friend is being released today and Dr…" I took a moment to think, "was it Doctor Wilson?" I said the first name that popped into my head. "Something like that."

"And your friend is?"

"Leah, Mrs Leah Brand."

"Her doctor is Doctor Miller."

"Ah, close enough. Anyhow…" I pushed the wheelchair closer to Leah's bed, "… I was informed I should come and collect her, so I've brought this in case…" I indicated the wheelchair.

"I can assure you that Mrs Brand is not due for release

today." The nurse dropped the attitude and smiled. "I guess it won't hurt if you visit her for a moment." She pointed to the wheelchair. "Don't leave that where anyone can fall over it and break something."

"No, no of course not," I murmured, suppressing a smile.

The damage had already been done.

I thanked her profusely and keeping a sedate pace, walked up to Leah and patted her on the shoulder. She opened her eyes, smiled, rubbed her eyes and struggled to sit up. I put my arm around her shoulders to jam a couple of pillows behind her.

"Andrea, how nice."

"You remember me, you've not lost your memory then?"

"Of course not. All I remember is being in that nightclub. We came off the dance floor then I was flying through the air and next thing I woke up in hospital."

I dragged a plastic chair over to the bed and took her hands in mine. "You have no idea how worried I was about you. They were very efficient the ambulance was there in no time and then they whisked you away. I didn't even hear which hospital they had taken you to."

"I'm in Weston General, aren't I?" Leah didn't look very alert. I noticed her eyes were a little unfocused.

"Yes, you are darling. I've had such a problem finding you. They tell you nothing if you are not a relative. Friends, it appears, count for nothing. We both know, friends are so much closer than family. We choose the friends who really care about us." *Don't overdo it Andrea.*

"How did you find me?"

"I went around to your place of course. Bill was a little reluctant to tell me much, but Belinda was a lot more helpful. We've always got on well. I'm very fond of her. But, enough of that. How are you? What do they say is wrong? Why are they keeping you in?"

"Whoa," Leah paused then winced. "One thing at a time."

"Sorry darling. Tell me first what the damage is."

"I've broken my good leg in two places and smashed up my false one at the same time."

"That's awful!"

"That's life." Leah smiled.

For such a timid, often pathetic person, Leah could be remarkably stoic. I had to admit a grudging admiration for her. There were times I wanted to shake her and tell her to be more aggressive, not assertive, but aggressive.

"How long are they going to keep you in this place?" I looked around at the beds, each housing a prone body, some asleep, others moaning, a couple lying back reading magazines. "It's a bit grim isn't it?"

"Not too long, but they say I was concussed and so they've been testing me to make sure my brain is okay."

"I can tell them it's perfectly fine. You recognized your best friend, what more do they want?" We both laughed.

Leah pointed to the wheelchair. "What's that for?"

"My entry ticket, nobody stops anyone pushing one of those." I dropped my voice to a whisper. "It's all part of the camouflage."

She laughed again. "I'll probably need that for a while. They tell me it'll be several days until I get my leg back, or maybe they'll give me a new one. And this one," she pulled back the blanket, "is all encased in a sort of strapped on plaster boot."

I leaned forward to give her a hug. "Oh darling, you poor dear. Never mind, I'm here to look after you. Men are useless and we can't rely on Belinda, now can we?"

"I'm sure Aunt Deidre will help out too."

"Who?" Alarm bells rang. Then I remembered. I had encouraged Leah to take a break and she had gone off to stay with her aunt-in-law. I'd forgotten she lived in Weston-super-Mare. Damn! "Of course. Has she been in to see you?" I glanced at the artificial flowers and the cards.

Leah shook her head. "No, she's away on a cruise. I think she gets back in a couple of weeks."

I picked up the cards. One was from Bill and Belinda, although I'm sure the writing was his. The other from Leah's aqua club. I guessed the grapes were from Bill.

"Have Bill and Belinda been in?"

"Uh, not Belinda. The message was that hospitals are not her thing."

"Typical."

"No one likes them," Leah protested.

I just shrugged and didn't reply. But then the nurse bustled over and told me my illicit time was up. I stood up, gave Leah a last hug and strict instructions to phone me the minute they said she could go home. I would also be back every afternoon for visiting time.

For a moment I thought Leah was going to protest but I put my finger to my lips and winked making her laugh as I waltzed out of the ward swinging the wheelchair from side to side and around in circles. I abandoned the wheelchair near the front entrance to the hospital, nowhere near where I'd found it, and walked out into the fine drizzle under a dark grey sky. I was fed up with living in this cold, damp country. I wanted blue skies, warm sun and gentle waves washing onto a pristine sandy beach. To get that I needed money, lots of it and Leah was due plenty of the stuff.

They kept Leah in hospital for a few more days. I had popped back several times at visiting time, only to bump into Bill on every occasion. He was always a gentleman, greeting me politely and offering to fetch me a chair, but I could sense a reserve in him. I didn't particularly care if he liked me or not, as long as he didn't get in the way of my plans for Leah. I did not need him whispering negative comments about me and putting doubts in her mind. To offset this, I was extra charming to him, thanked him profusely while smiling and patting his hand. I'm not sure he was that convinced.

I hovered, trying to be helpful, as the staff heaved Leah into a wheelchair to take her to the car. I had hoped that one of them would suggest I move in for a few days, but they didn't. Disappointing, but I would be popping in every day as soon as Bill left for work. I was going to make myself indispensable.

I stood by as Bill lifted her into his car and called out that I would see her later as I walked out of the hospital grounds. I'd use the time to look around for a place to rent. I'd also treat myself to more of that nice quiche they served in Leah's favourite coffee shop.

The rental prices were much higher than I expected, but then Weston is a seaside resort and very popular. I wanted two bedrooms, in the happy event that Leah decided to move in with me. That was the plan.

I was lucky to find a ground floor apartment a few blocks back from the sea but not too far out of town. It was also fully furnished, not exactly my taste, but it would do for now. My bank balance was dwindling rapidly and although I had put my London house on the market it had not sold. Prices in the capital had gone through the roof and it was almost impossible for young people to get a mortgage these days.

I made a flying trip up to London, packed a couple of large suitcases with clothes and personal items to tide me over for a few weeks. The first morning I was back I drove around to Leah's house and rang the bell. To my surprise Belinda opened the door. She looked quite pleased to see me.

"Andrea hi. Come in." She almost pulled me into the hallway and slammed the door behind me. "Have you come to play Florence Nightingale?"

I laughed. "Would that help?"

"You bet. It's not my scene to slobber over the disabled. And I'm stuck here running after her."

"What about school?"

"Yeah well, that's the only good thing about it. But now you're here, I don't have to be. That's neat. Come on, she's in here." Belinda pushed me into the lounge where Leah was sitting propped up in an Easy-boy chair with a blanket over her leg. "Look who's turned up? Best friend Andrea. I'm off for a while. Tell her what you need." She turned, grabbed her coat and bag off a chair and was out of the door before either of us could say a word.

"Do I have that effect on everyone?" I laughed as I went to kiss Leah on the cheek.

"Oh dear. Poor Belinda is not nurse material I'm afraid. I doubt she's gone to school though."

"What can I get you?"

"Just something to laugh at," Leah sighed. "I thought you'd gone back to London."

"I did, but it was just a flying visit. I'm staying here in Weston for as long as you need me. So, Madam, order your genie to get you anything you desire, and your wish will be my command." I gave a graceful bow and Leah chuckled.

"First order, a cup of coffee."

"Of course, I should have guessed. Coming right up."

Leah's new coffee maker was a different make to her old one and she shouted instructions through to the kitchen as I wrestled with the pods and I found out where the mugs lived and where to place them on the machine. I had brought some of Leah's favourite biscuits and carried it all through to the lounge.

"Oooh, custard creams," she exclaimed "You remembered."

"Of course. Now, tell me why so sad. Are you in pain?"

"No, thanks to the pain killers, but this cast boot thing is uncomfortable and weighs a ton. I hate not being able to get around."

"How long?" I pointed to the white contraption on her leg.

"They say maybe six weeks, but luckily both breaks were clean."

"Can you hobble around with those?"

"The crutches? A little. And Bill also got me that walker over there as well. I feel like a geriatric."

"But not in mind, darling. Give it a few days and you'll be hopping around like a one-legged bunny."

Leah shivered. "Don't mention rabbits please. I still have nightmares about them and they are always blue."

I could have kicked myself. "Oh, my angel I'm so sorry, I never thought. But I'm here now and Saint Andrea will protect you against all wildlife. I've brought my weapons, look." I whipped a pen out of my bag and waved it around like a sword.

Leah burst out laughing.

"So, tell me what else is getting you down besides the broken leg?"

"I feel so ungrateful complaining, when there are so many people in the world much worse off than me."

"But you are you and you shouldn't apologise for feeling as you. Come on, spill the beans. I'm all ears. Is it Bill?"

"Yea and no." Leah paused.

"That's what I like a straight answer," I parried.

Leah grinned. "He's a wonderful man. So easy to talk to and we have so much in common, but I sense that's he's not happy either. He's old fashioned and I think 'living in sin' is not for him."

"Divorce is easy these days, so why not cut ties with Mason and then you're free?" I knew the answer before she told me.

"You can't divorce someone without telling them and I don't know where Mason is, or, as you pointed out, if he is even alive."

"How long do you have to wait?" I knew the answer, I'd done my homework.

"I have not taken legal advice, but I Googled it and it's a long process. It could take years."

"Hmm, and you think Bill might take off before then?"

"Oh, I'd not considered that." Leah looked down at the blanket she was twisting between her fingers. "He's so loyal and attentive. I think he really loves me, but then I get the feeling that his conscience is bothering him."

"What does he say? Have you talked about it?"

"Oh no. I'm…"

That was so Leah, running from something she didn't want to face. She had such little confidence in herself. First, there was her mother, always putting her down. Then her adventurous siblings moving to far-flung countries, the accident, Mason's bullying and all that followed on from there.

"Maybe it is a little early to bring all that out into the open, so that's the problem then?"

"And there's Belinda of course."

"Is she still being a difficult teenager?"

"I think it's more than that."

"Like what?"

"She's rude, which is normal I guess, but she's also really moody. Goes into her bedroom for hours, and won't speak to me and then wanders around the flat in a daze."

"Drugs?"

"Oh no, I don't think so."

"Why not? Lots of youngsters get hooked on drugs. I hear they have a problem in most schools."

"But where would she get the money?"

"Bill?"

"I hardly think so. Neither of them has ever mentioned it."

"Mason?"

"What! You don't think she's talking to him? Knows where he is?"

"Probably not, but anything is possible."

Leah looked visibly upset. "Do you give her an allowance?" I asked.

"Yes, but drugs are expensive, aren't they?"

"There's only one way to find out."

"How?"

"Search her room. She doesn't keep it locked, like she did in the old house, does she?"

"No, but I want to respect her privacy."

"You don't do that, darling, if you want to protect your children and then help them, do you?"

"Do you think so? I'd not thought of it that way."

"I do Leah, that's the only way to think of it. And there is no time like the present."

"What now!" She looked alarmed, and sat forward spilling the dregs of her coffee on the blanket.

"No time like the present. Bill's at work, she's out who knows where, and I'm here to help. Tell you what, I'll do the looking and you just lurk in the doorway. Then you won't have violated her privacy and it won't disturb your conscience. I'll help you onto the seat on that walker and you can just observe. How's that?"

Before she knew what was happening, I had wheeled the walker over and helped her up and put her hands on the bars. She paused. For a moment I thought she was going to refuse. I urged her forward. "It's only a little way, across the lounge to the other side of the hallway." As I spoke, I gave her an encouraging push towards Belinda's room. Opening the door, I helped her turn to sit on the integrated seat and swivelled it around so she could see what I was doing.

Belinda's room was surprisingly neat and tidy, for a teenager. The bed wasn't made but how many youngsters bother to do that? I started just inside the door, prepared to work my way around the room. I was familiar with most tricks. The hollowed-out middle of books innocently sitting on the shelves. Shoe boxes at the bottom of the wardrobe that might look innocent until you looked under the shoes. Beneath the mattress and bed, with paraphernalia sandwiched between neat piles of clothes. If there was anything here, I would find it.

Leah watched in amazement as I went through the room with a fine toothcomb, becoming more agitated as each minute passed.

"Calm down Sweetie. She's not going to barge in through that front door any time soon."

"She might and if she catches you…"

"Relax, I'll take all the blame and then protest loudly that you were trying to stop me. My shoulders are big and broad." I stopped rummaging through the desk and looked at Leah. "She might even be impressed that we care enough to worry about her welfare."

"I don't think she'll fall for that for a moment. Maybe you should stop Andrea. I'm not comfortable with this and you're not going to find anything. Come."

I knew differently, in fact I was certain of it.

Leah struggled to stand, pushing her walker towards her chair in the lounge.

"Wait. Oh, no!"

Leah sank back down as she looked at me. "What? What is it?"

I turned to face her holding out a tissue wrapped around a pile of pills.

"What are those?"

I peered at them. "Not headache tablets not wrapped like this. And why put them at the very back of the bottom drawer of her desk if they were innocent?"

"I'm sure they're harmless. Belinda wouldn't be stupid enough to take drugs."

"Are you sure?" I walked over and handed her the pills. "How well do you really know her? You've not exactly bonded, have you?"

"Well no, but she's a sensible girl..."

I cut her off. "Leah, show some sense. She's had a few questionable boyfriends. You told me about the one she brought round to your Mum's house, a Neanderthal if I remember correctly? How sensible was that? Can you imagine what your mother would have said if she'd met him. Earrings, and a nose ring and more tattoos than skin?"

Leah appeared to shrink back into herself. She stared down at the white tablets, turning them over and over in her hands.

"What are these?"

"Xanax."

"How can you tell? How do you know that?"

"It's the only tablet that's long, in a bar shape and the name is printed on it."

Leah squinted at one of the bars and shook her head. She looked distraught. "I know nothing about drugs, nothing. What do these do? She may be looking after them for one of her friends."

"That's what most parents say, it's a common denial." I turned back to the desk and poked about in another drawer before pulling out two glycerine bags of white powder.

"Oh, for heaven's sake what's that stuff?"

I carefully pulled one open, sniffed then licked my index finger. "Not sure, but I think it may be Ket."

"Ket? What's that?"

"Ketamine. It's the current drug of choice among teenagers these days, or so I hear. Would you believe it's a horse tranquilizer, but kids snort it to get high and relaxed?"

"Not cocaine then?" Leah's face was white, and I noticed her hands were shaking.

I tested another grain of the powder. "No, coke has a slight numbing effect on the tongue, this stuff is glassy or slippery. You can't tell without a proper laboratory test of course, but I'm almost positive."

Tears began to run down Leah's cheeks. "What am I going to tell her father, how can I explain this? He'll blame me for not looking after her properly."

"Leah! Get a grip. He's hardly in a position to yell at you, even if he does turn up. And, have you forgotten that he's avoiding the law as well? Not everything is your fault. She's a strong willed, bloody-minded teenager who's behaving like most other kids her age."

I relieved her of the drugs and placed them back where I had found them after taking a photo with my phone. It never hurts to have proof.

"Come on, it's not the end of the world." Leah was staring into space, almost catatonic. "Maybe I should give you some Xanax? It's a benzodiazepine, a tranquilizer and the kids take it to keep calm. You know all the statistics coming out about teen depression and high suicide rates? They're worried about climate change, the lack of jobs after university, the horrors of living with mum and dad because they cannot afford their own place. So, the easy way out is to get high, or chill out for a while."

While I rattled on, I helped Leah to her feet and guided her back to the chair in the lounge. "Don't tell me you have never smoked a bit of weed at a pop concert or two when you were her age?"

"No! Never! I didn't even try one of my mother's cigarettes."

"Ah, silly me. No of course you didn't. Lots you missed out on my friend. All part of growing up. Not even one concert? Glastonbury?"

"No. Mother once said she might take me to see Tom Jones when he was at the Hammersmith Odeon but we never went."

"Oh, you poor darling. Tom Jones! When you were a teenager? Give me a bloody break." I gave her a hug before I went to make her another coffee and called back from the kitchen. "That's another generation back, you never had a chance to live, did you?"

"I had friends," she protested. "I guess I moved in

different circles to you. From school I went straight into nursing, and life was busy."

I rinsed the mugs and set one under the machine. "But darling did you ever have any fun?"

"Yes, of course I did. Even before we were married, James and I did lots together. A few weekends in the Lake District, a walking tour in Derbyshire and we even went to a couple of shows in London. But money was tight and he was studying to be a doctor and I was working extra hours to support us. There wasn't much time for fun."

"That's why fate has brought me into your life, to show you what you missed and catch up on a misspent youth. They say you have to experience every stage of maturity and you, my angel, missed out." I walked out of the kitchen holding two more mugs of coffee.

Leah giggled, then her face fell and she twisted the mug round and round in her hands. "What am I going to do Andrea? About Belinda I mean."

I pretended to think for a while. "I guess you can't ignore it. Those drugs are illegal, and they are in your apartment. At least we only found a few, it doesn't look as if she is dealing."

"Oh, my god, no!" Leah's hand flew up to her mouth. "Belinda! A drug dealer?"

"Highly unlikely. It's probably not serious."

"Maybe the doctor prescribed them for her, and she didn't want to tell me."

"Uh, no Leah. The Xanax, maybe, but not both together. I think you'll have to confront her."

"No, I couldn't. How can I admit I know she is hiding drugs in her room? No!"

"Then the next best thing is to watch her. Pounce if she appears drunk or spaced out. Wait, let me Google the effects so you know what to look for." I grabbed my tablet from my bag. "Here we are, have you seen any of the following? Sleeps for long?"

"Yes. She rarely gets up to get to school in time and stays in bed most of the weekend, before she goes out in the evening."

"Loss of interest?"

Leah sighed. "I can't remember the last time she was enthusiastic about anything."

"Irritability?"

"All the time especially with me."

"Preferring to be alone?"

"At home, yes, she's in her bedroom most of the time, but most teenagers are, aren't they? On the phone or social media?"

"That leaves us with aggression, hostility and appearing drunk."

Leah sighed. "Belinda is all of the above. What am I going to do? I can't cope with any more Andrea."

I leaned over and took her hand. "Whatever happens, we'll face it together. I'll be right beside you. That's what friends are for."

Leah smiled and squeezed my hand. "How can I thank you?"

"Just be my friend too."

"Of course, what would I do without you?"

What indeed I thought then smiled. "On the bright side it won't make you bankrupt. Ket goes for £20 a gram on the high street and Xanax for even less than that."

"Don't! We'll have to confront her, we must. You will help me, won't you?"

"Of course. Now, let's forget all this for a moment and tell me what you'd like me to get you for lunch. Is it just us?"

Leah nodded. "Bill has gone to Bristol for a meeting and won't be back till late."

"Perfect, so it's a girly day for us and we'll only think good things. Agreed?"

She nodded.

Not much else happened that month. I managed to steer Leah away from a confrontation with Belinda, there was time for that later. It wasn't too difficult. She was very hesitant about causing any unpleasantness and I ferried her to and from the hospital for her check-ups.

On the last day of the month, we went for a fitting for her new prosthesis. We laughed as we noticed this one had no bite marks on it Before he died, Mason's dog Zeus was known for attacking Leah's leg and got more than he bargained for, almost breaking his teeth in his frenzy.

It was a relief to hear Leah laughing again; it had been a while. I could tell she was still fretting over Belinda, and I guessed she had not discussed the problem with Bill.

Once the new leg was strapped on, Leah could now get around on crutches. I had once broken both legs as a child and had been confined to a wheelchair for several weeks so I could sympathize with her over her loss of mobility.

As the days went by, my resolve began to waver. Leah was a sweet, gentle soul and even I began to have a conscience. So, I was after her money, although it wouldn't surprise me if she handed over a chunk of it without me having to ask for a cent. But I couldn't take that risk, and my partner would go ballistic if I backed down now. He was funding me and I wasn't brave enough to cross him – not yet anyway.

For now, I did not have to make a decision. My contact in the insurance company kept me up to date with developments. It was a class action against the car manufacturers, a fault that caused the death of Leah's husband and young children. The figures mentioned were eye watering, but they were not ready to pay out just yet. It had stalled in the appeal court. In the meantime, it would do no harm to keep Leah dependent on me.

FEBRUARY   LEAH

Dear Diary,

How I hated hospital and was so glad when they sent me home. Belinda was supposed to look after me but she was worse than useless, even a little cruel; putting food and drink just out of my reach, not coming when I called her to help me into the bathroom. How humiliating, especially when I was desperate. She disappeared for hours on end. Bill of course had to be at work and if it hadn't been for Andrea, I'm not sure how I would have coped. She's been an angel. I can't wait to get back on my feet. Now I have the extra worry of the drugs Andrea found in Belinda's bedroom. What am I going to do? If I tell the police I can't imagine what that might lead to. Why does life have so many problems? The only light on the horizon is my best friend.

MARCH ANDREA

The month of March was cold. The wind continued to blow in off the Atlantic. It whistled through cracks, badly-fitting windows and doors. Living by the seaside lost much of its allure for me that month. Along with the wind, we suffered days and days of rain and cold, grey skies which seemed to hover just above head height. While I might have hinted that Belinda was depressed; I was tempted to reach for the Xanax myself.

Leah was still wearing her cast. No longer did they pile on liquid plaster of Paris over crepe bandages, but used a natty moon boot strapped on to keep the leg immobile. As she became more confident, she was able to hobble around, but with one false leg and the other in a mega-sized cast, she still relied on her walker or crutches.

I suspected Bill was spending more time at work than before. He no longer came home for lunch and the few times I ran into him, he appeared pre-occupied. Belinda was hardly ever around and Aunt Deidre had extended her cruise or stopped off with friends, I wasn't sure which. She'd written to say she couldn't face the tail end of winter in England and was planning to continue traveling, possibly to the south of France or Sicily to grab as much sun as she could.

This left Leah very much on her own which suited me

fine. She muttered something about looking for work, but that's pretty difficult these days if you have two working legs and Leah didn't even have one.

She attended her swimming session once a week with other amputees and she invited me along. I declined. Not my sort of thing at all. I have to admit to being squeamish and I don't like looking at Leah's leg – or rather, the missing leg – I prefer it when she wears trousers or a long skirt.

I tried to pry more information out of her but I had to choose my moment. Ask too many questions and it can sound like the Nuremburg trials. But since I saw her every day, we talked a lot. I learned that the insurance company was not keeping her in the loop at all. In the meantime, I had the inside information on the car crash claim. I didn't know what was going on in the life insurance claim. That was another chunk of money Leah was entitled to, but it was being handled by a different company.

James had invested in a huge policy not long before he died, and I know they baulked at paying out. Yet I guessed they must have given Leah something. After all she had moved down to Weston, was renting a flat and she wasn't working. She didn't appear to be worried about money, but then she didn't throw money around either and there was always the UK benefit system. She was bound to get some kind of disability allowance.

It's difficult to prise information about money out of the British. They will discuss a wide variety of subjects quite openly but when it comes to finances, they are super secretive. I reasoned there was one way to open the money door.

I rang the bell downstairs bright and early the next morning and breezed into the apartment giving her a huge hug. I was hoping that for once we could talk about something other than Leah's problems. She was obsessing about Belinda now. Like a dog with a bone she would not let go. 'What was she supposed to do about her stepdaughter? Should she ask her about the drugs I found in her room, or ignore the problem? Would it get worse? Who was supplying her with the drugs?' I wasn't going to answer that one, now was I? 'What was she going to do?'

I tried to deflect her but she kept dragging up the subject. Honestly, I'm not sure why she worried so much about that kid. It's not as if she was her real mother. Protect me from citizens who take their responsibilities so seriously. No wonder so many are stuck at the bottom of the pile.

When I went around this morning making myself totally indispensable, she greeted me for once, with a smile.

"I've thought of something I could do!" she said as she gave me her usual hug.

"Go on, share." I swept past her and plugged in the coffee machine. "Any of those doughnuts left?"

She had the grace to look abashed. "Uh, no I finished the last two after dinner."

"Naughty Leah. We'll just have to make do with the chocolate biscuits I just happen to have in my bag." I grabbed a plate and tipped them out. "So, what's this amazing idea?"

"I'm going to go to Belinda's school to talk to the staff."

I paused and took my time spooning sugar into the coffee mugs.

"Oh dear. No."

"Why? I thought you'd be pleased. I don't have to mention the drugs, but enquire how she's coping and if her work is up to scratch, is she in with a nice crowd of girls, that sort of thing."

I pushed a mug across the kitchen table followed by the plate of biscuits.

"Leah that is a terrible idea." I watched her face fall. I know her so well she is always so eager for my approval.

"But why Andrea? Isn't that what caring parents do?"

"Well yes, if they are the parents of course. But darling, think. Your relationship with Belinda is so fragile. She gave you hell in the early days and then for a while after you came out of that home, she was fine. She was, wasn't she?"

"Yes. I thought we had really bonded. We were friends. We had some great times together."

"But it didn't last did it? You moved down here and be honest, things went downhill again? And now there's a much bigger problem."

"The drugs."

"Yes. They are addictive; and things can only get worse. To be honest with you darling you're on a hiding to nowhere. A visit to her school won't help and if Belinda finds out, she's going to be furious. She may even get violent and..." I paused to stare at Leah's leg in the moon boot and the crutches leaning against the table. "...how could you defend yourself?"

Leah's fist hitting the table top, rattled the mugs and plates as she shouted. "I've made up my mind. I've thought long and hard and this is one thing I can do!"

I brought up every argument I could think of against her interfering but it made no difference. For once Leah was adamant and nothing, I said would change her mind. I'd have to go with her and direct the conversation as best as I could.

As we drew up outside the school gates, I reminded her one more time not to mention the drugs. We had only found a few of them and if she told the teachers they were bound to tell the police, then Leah herself would be legally liable though I didn't believe that for a moment of course. I argued it would backfire, alienate Belinda, and when Bill heard what would that do to their relationship? I think it was the last point that hit home. Apart from me, right now, Leah had only Bill to rely on. He made her happy and while I intended to break that up very soon, I could use it now as an indirect threat.

Walking into the reception area brought back bad memories of my own school days. Not a week went past when I wasn't in trouble. It hadn't taken me long to run my own gang and no one dared defy us. Even the teachers were scared. The final time they tried some gormless way of punishing us, we set fire to the stock room and since it was filled with paper, and tubs of glue and heaven knows what else, it went up like a rocket. Wasn't it a shame they could never prove we did it? We all had cast iron alibis – each other. We hid behind the bicycle sheds and laughed so loudly I'm amazed they didn't hear us.

Ah, those were the days but it didn't last of course. Once we were let loose on the world, tearing off our uniforms and flinging the text books into the canal, it didn't take me long to realise that to get on in the world, I needed money and the best way to get that was through marriage or crime.

I helped Leah over to the reception desk and the secretary directed us down a cream-painted corridor past badly drawn pictures of rainbows and kites floating in bright blue skies.

Mrs Grantham was waiting in the doorway, ushered us into a small room and waved at the two chairs the other side of her desk. She looked like a pleasant lady with grey hair scraped back into a bun wearing a twin set and tweed skirt. One of the old school, I could tell. She settled herself in her chair and peered at us over the top of her glasses.

"You're here to ask about Belinda Brand yes?"

I'd noticed the pair of sensible oxfords on her feet and inwardly grinned. This old battle-axe was easy prey.

"Yes." I answered before Leah could get a word in. "Belinda is Leah's stepdaughter, despite the same surname. My dear friend has only known her for a relatively short time."

"Several years now," Leah protested. "But I am concerned about how she's settled into her new school, made friends and if she's keeping up with her work."

"Belinda is not very communicative at home," I elaborated, only to receive a disapproving look from across the desk. Leah also nudged me, but I ignored both of them.

"We lived just outside London," I rattled on, "and it's so very different to living here in the West country, by the sea."

"Quite" said Mrs Grantham, cutting in before I could

say more. She looked down and leafed through the file in her hand. "It looks as if Belinda's work is quite satisfactory. She's not in the top tier, but she is coping. I would like to see an improvement in her marks. I think she could do a lot better."

"Oh dear," Leah spoke without thinking. If she opened her mouth now then she would also open a can of worms.

"Leah, that's great news," I squeezed her arm. "Now you can relax and stop worrying about her. Thank you." I began to stand up but Mrs Grantham's next words steered towards dangerous territory.

"I see she has had several days off. Has she been ill?"

Perfect. Youngsters on drugs often skipped school. Just as long as Leah kept her mouth shut. I rushed to fill the gap.

"She did have that bad dose of flu recently; don't you remember Leah?"

"I don't..." she began but again I cut her off.

"Mrs Brand had a bad fall recently and was hospitalised." I dropped my voice, leaned forward and directed my words to the teacher. "She's also been on strong medication."

Mrs Grantham looked alarmed. She glanced at Leah and shuffled the papers in the file in front of her.

Leah looked puzzled but I was saved by the bell which echoed down the hallways.

Mrs Grantham stood. "If that is all, unless you have a particular worry?"

"No. I'm sure your words have reassured us both. I'm also very fond of Belinda, but..." I hesitated "... we didn't tell her we were coming. You know how paranoid teens can be."

The grey eyes, which matched the hair, bore into me for a moment and I had the uncomfortable feeling that this elderly educator could read my mind. I stood up quickly, helping Leah to her feet and thanked Mrs Grantham for her time.

The moment we left the room, Leah turned and glared at me. "Honestly Andrea you took over completely I didn't get a word out. How could you?"

"But darling," I whispered as I steered her along the corridor, "be honest, you were about to mention the 'you know what' weren't you?"

She looked a little ashamed and her cheeks reddened as she shuffled along beside me, my hand propelling her under the elbow. "Well maybe. We can't just ignore it and do nothing."

"Best we handle this by ourselves. If the school gets involved then her career could go right down the tubes. It would be on her record, think of that. Her whole life destroyed before she has a chance to live."

As I settled her in the passenger seat, I pushed home the point. "The school might suspend her. Then Bill would have to know and what if he can't take it? He's such an honest and open character. Where would that leave you?"

I climbed in behind the steering wheel and pressed on. "Do you really want the police involved?"

Leah shuddered. I sensed there was something she hadn't told me. I had no idea why she was reluctant to contact them. Had she had dealings with them in the past? It wasn't like her to hold anything back. If it was me, I'd throw Belinda to the wolves without a second thought. She was

OK on a good day but I would not be putting up with her moods and rudeness for long.

When I dropped Leah off, she did not invite me in as she usually did and when I went to get out of the car, she told me abruptly she could manage and might see me the next day.

That was a bit of a blow but I knew how to bring her round. I'd let her stew for a day or so and then make a huge fuss of her. Maybe I could use her fear of the police to my advantage.

By the time I got back to my rented flat I had worked myself into a rage. There had to be easier ways to earn a fortune. I flung my bag on the table and sank onto the damp, lumpy sofa. The accommodation was not what I was used to. One lounge dining room, two small bedrooms, miniscule bathroom and a galley kitchen although I didn't plan on doing much cooking or entertaining. I didn't even want Leah coming round here, I'd need to upgrade if I was going to persuade her to come and live with me. I realised I was getting low on funds, very low. Even if the London house sold soon, it was mortgaged up to the hilt and I'd see little from that. My partner and I had put all our efforts into this venture, but the rewards would be worth it. Blue skies, gentle waves lapping on a white sandy beach, cocktail in hand as I laze under the umbrella shading me from the hot rays of the tropical sun.

The shrill sounds from my mobile snapped me back into the present. Scrabbling to release it from my bag I swore as I looked at the caller ID.

"What do you want?"

"What the fuck do you think I want Sis? Can you talk?"

"Yeah, for now. A progress report?"

"Bingo."

"I've nothing to tell you. Nothing new. I'm making myself indispensable, just as we agreed."

"Is she living with you yet? Prised her away from family and friends?"

"No, not yet. It takes time. I'm doing my bloody best."

"Well things are moving at this end and the pay-out is imminent. I can't hold it up for long."

"Can't you put her name at the bottom of the pile?"

"Already done that. If her surname began with Z it would help."

"Yeah, well it doesn't. Just stall as long as you can. I've got a couple of things on the go which should speed things up. Hang in there."

"Don't let me down Sis. I'm counting on you."

"That makes both of us. And don't call me Sis!"

He disconnected abruptly without saying goodbye. Things were moving so I dare not leave Leah to stew for days. I'd go and see her tomorrow but I had a few things to pick up first.

I rang the doorbell pulling my coat tightly round me to keep out the cold Atlantic wind. The intercom clicked.

"I have planned a very special treat, so hurry up and get ready we're going out." She buzzed to let me in and when she opened her front door, I was wreathed in smiles and carrying one of those helium balloons which said 'I'm sorry' on it.

Leah took one look and burst out laughing. "How ridiculous," she cried. "Andrea you never grow up."

"Whatever would I want to do that for?" I gave her a big hug. "And, as they say, that's not all." I marched into the kitchen and handed her a paper bag. "Look inside."

Leah pulled out two small teddy bears. Her face was a study.

"They were in the window and I couldn't resist them. 'Friend Bears' BFF, Best Friends Forever, I think that's what the youngsters say these days. See, one for you and one for me. Which one do you want?"

She stood and stared at them.

"Go on, which one?"

She picked up the orange one with the red checked feet, but I could tell she was reluctant to even touch it.

"Don't you think they are just too cute?"

"I guess so, but I'm not so keen on…"

"I didn't choose rabbits Leah. These are bears, quite different. We keep them to remind us of our friendship and how I'll always stand by you."

I swept the other toy back into the bag.

"And, I have planned a special treat for you. We're going shopping."

"Andrea, I can't. Look at me! I was about to clean the oven." Leah waved her rubber gloves at her apron, track pants and pointed to her uncombed hair.

"No problem, I'm not taking no for an answer. The oven can wait darling, it will still be here tomorrow. I'll just read a magazine until you're ready."

"But where are we going? What shall I wear?"

Good. First objective achieved. She was willing to drop everything and do as she was told. I laughed. "It's my treat. First a coffee at the Bistro, then let's raid Walker and Ling's and, I found the most delightful little boutique the other day I can't wait to show you."

Leah hovered uncertainly in the kitchen. She glanced at the oven and her yellow rubber gloves and then whipped them off and smiled.

"Why not? But it may take a while."

"I have the patience of a saint," I trilled. "Take as much time as you want, as long as we get there by lunch time. I even managed to park the car close by so you won't have to walk far."

"You think of everything! I'll be as quick as I can." Leah hobbled off into the bedroom and closed the door. As soon as I heard the taps running, I jumped off the couch and sneaked into Belinda's room. It was just as tidy as last time, but it wouldn't hurt to leave a few more little packets. Let her talk her way out of that. I was careful where I put them, I certainly didn't want her to notice. I'm sure the police know all the usual tricks and will find them quickly after the tip off.

Leah was much faster than I expected and I'd only just raced across the hall and fallen back on the sofa with a magazine before she appeared in the doorway. If she thought I looked flustered, she didn't mention it.

I stood up and smiled at her. "Right! Let's hit the streets! And the shops! And the lunch place too."

It began to drizzle as we left the house and it was a mission getting Leah and her crutches into the car. I dropped her at the entrance to the department store and rushed off to park.

By the time I returned she had hobbled inside out of the rain and was looking though the nearest rack. I grabbed her arm.

"No Leah, this is old fuddy-duddy stuff. We need to find something more modern, younger."

"Don't be silly Andrea I'm over forty and I'm not going to be mutton dressed as lamb."

I pretended to burst into tears. "Are you saying that I'm dressing like a teenager? Leah, you've wounded me to the core. My heart is broken" I clutched the right side of my chest before moving it quickly to the left.

Leah dissolved into giggles. "Don't be silly Andrea. You're sophisticated. Me, I'm just homely and I can't carry off those fashions the way you can. Jerseys and jumpers, and trouser suits in classical styles, that's more me."

I sighed. "That's why you need me as your personal dresser. Come, let's have a coffee here and then we're going to hit the boutique shop next door."

A light salad for me and two doughnuts for Leah later, I managed to get her as far as the doorway to Rosie's boutique. Seeing the mannequins in the window she shrank back.

"No Andrea, I'm not going in there. Can you imagine the prices? Not my scene."

"Poor darling," I opened the door with one hand and placed the other in the small of her back. "To look, costs nothing and that's all we're going to do. Look."

"But what's the point if we're not going to buy anything?"

I squeezed her arm and put my lips close to her ear. "That's the fun. We pretend, act as if you can afford to buy out the whole damn shop."

The boutique was small but screamed quality. I guess it was the most expensive dress shop in Weston Super Mare. There were a few dresses on display near the entrance then steps leading to two grey elegant sofas resting on the thick pile carpet. On the coffee tables in front, lay catalogues for clients to browse through. There was also a platform with mirrors on every side. Stands on either end of the sofas held jewellery, very expensive bling in a variety of colours, a tempting array of accessories for every occasion.

Leah gave a half-hearted embarrassed giggle as I manoeuvred her over to the nearest display. None of the dresses were priced but each one was on show with matching shoes, handbags and coats.

"I wouldn't even dare ask the prices," Leah whispered.

"Darling, if you have to ask how much it is you know you can't afford it. That's part of the fun."

I examined a cherry red cashmere dress and asked the assistant who glided over the deep pile carpet if I could try it on. She looked us up and down as if we'd arrived from the nearest homeless shelter, but she could hardly refuse my request.

"Of course, madam, but we only have this in size 10."

"Perfect." I replied before she could change her mind. It would be too tight, I'm at least a 12 on a good day, but I needed a reason to be in here for a while.

Leah was looking a little alarmed, but didn't say anything as the assistant took down the dress and asked me to follow her up the steps and into the dressing room. I nudged Leah. "Take a seat on the sofa and look through the catalogue. And do try and relax." She dragged her feet as she trailed behind us and I left her hovering by the accessory stand.

I swallowed hard to suppress the giggles as I squirmed into the undersized dress and then waltzed out to ask Leah how I looked.

She shrieked with laughter as the shop girl shot across the carpet lost for words. "Maybe Madam would like to try on something in a different size?"

"Are you suggesting this is too small?"

"I think it's a little tight in places."

I turned to Leah. "Be a dear and hand me that blue one while I try and get this off."

I spent the next hour trying on one dress after another until the young girl's eyes began to glaze over and Leah perched uncomfortably on the edge of the sofa, was about to nod off. I nudged her each time I came down to show her the latest creation I had poured myself into, swirling and twirling, waltzing around the sofas making her laugh despite her embarrassment.

Only one other customer came in to the shop while we were there. It took her a few moments to decide on a silk scarf, which was long enough to distract the assistant and for me to accomplish my plan.

"I can't find a single thing that I like," I moaned loudly as I threw on my coat, pranced down the steps and grabbed Leah's arm. "Come, let's try somewhere else." I glared back at the long-suffering shop assistant as I flung open the door and marched Leah outside.

"What a relief," she said as she hobbled along the pavement. "I'm not cut out for those kinds of places."

"Why ever not?" I turned and faced her. "You have every right to go anywhere you want."

"I don't feel comfortable. I prefer shopping in the chain stores on the High Street."

I shook my head and steered her towards a coffee shop, pushed her towards a table and went to the counter to order the drinks and pastries. I carried them back and slid the saucers and plates onto the table.

"Leah darling, you have to be more confident. You are still too self-effacing. Look what you've come through and what you've coped with?"

"I know, and I do now believe I'm sane as well," Leah gave a lop-sided grin. "But that doesn't mean I… oh I don't know. Andrea you know exactly what you want, and you're not afraid to say or do anything you like. I wish I could be more like you."

Not a chance, I thought. I smiled. "That's all part of your charm and why you are my best friend, my only friend really."

I sliced into my pie and licked the cool sharp taste of the lemon off my fingers. "They had some pretty fabulous stuff in there didn't they?"

"Yes. And the way they matched everything together made every outfit extra special."

"Did you notice the jewellery?" I asked.

"How could I miss it? Do you think those stones were real?"

"Hmm. Difficult to tell. Nothing had a price on it.

Easiest way to check for bling is to prise the diamonds out and try to cut glass with them."

Leah laughed as she dug in her bag for her purse to pay her share of the bill. She was good like that, more often than not she picked up the tab for both of us. I watched her carefully, as her face turned white and her lips trembled.

"Sweetie, what's the matter you look as if you've seen a ghost. What is it?"

"Look in my bag," she hissed as she thrust it under my nose.

Shimmering, even in the dim light, was a diamond bracelet.

I leaned across and lifted it out of her bag. "I noticed it in the shop. It's lovely isn't it? You bought something, after all." I examined it closely before passing it to her.

Leah sat frozen. "I... I... Noooo. I didn't buy it and I didn't take it. I would never, ever I mean..." she trailed off. She held it as if it was radioactive.

"Of course, I believe you sweetie but how did it get there? You don't think you were dreaming and dropped it accidently?"

"No! I don't remember even seeing one like this in there. But I didn't steal it. I swear I didn't."

I tried to look shocked. "What are you going to do?"

"I must take it back of course. Explain I've no idea how it got there. I'll do it now." Leah dragged herself to her feet.

"Darling, no, let me." I put out my arm to stop her. I wriggled my arms into my coat. "I'm better at sweet talking you know I am. Let me take it back and I'll make some excuse."

"No, I should do it. It was in my bag."

"You know you'll make a complete hash of it. You look so guilty and you've done nothing wrong. Here give it to me. It won't take me a minute." I whipped it out of her hands and slipped the bracelet into my coat pocket. "Wait here for me and stop worrying. Crazy Andrea will make it all right."

I ducked out of the coffee shop and along the street straight into the pawn shop on the corner.

The bell above the door tinkled as I walked in, tugging my hood forward to cover my hair. An elderly man shuffled out of the gloom and stood behind the counter. I didn't say a word as I handed him the bracelet. He turned it over and over in his hands before fixing an eye glass and peering at it closely.

"Not sure these are real diamonds," he said at last.

"Of course, they are. Do you think I'd try and pawn bling?" I snapped.

We agreed on a price and I gave him my name and address – Leah Brand, 44c Temple House, Willow Street, Weston-super-Mare. As I stepped back out into the street, I smiled. The bracelet hadn't cost anything, part of a heist months ago and I'd just made a tidy profit on it.

Leah owed me now. I was the best friend she could depend on to get her out of trouble. There was more than one way of skinning a cat.

Back in the café, I reassured Leah that all was well and told her to forget it had ever happened. I could see she was still nervous and at one point I had to hastily stop her from going to the boutique to apologise in person. I reassured her over and over that the sales lady quite understood and as it had been returned almost immediately, she'd hear no more about it.

I was at my wittiest and brightest as I helped her into the car and drove her home. I soon had her laughing again but it was forced and I could see she was shaken. I gave her a big hug and assured her I would always be there for her. She nodded as she hobbled up the short path to the outside door and disappeared inside.

I had just put the car in gear when a taxi pulled up in front of me and to my horror, Leo, Leah's stepson, got out, dragging a suitcase behind him. He strode up the path and rang the doorbell. I ducked down in the seat, hoping he wouldn't see me and waited until he had disappeared inside before driving away.

What was he doing here? That was not part of the plan. This was becoming a nightmare. I wish people would stick to what was agreed and stop improvising.

MARCH LEAH

Dear Diary,

This month has been both good and bad. It seems the school is happy enough with Belinda, although I can't stop fretting. There were very few tablets in her room, so I'm going to believe she is keeping them for a friend. I will keep a sharp eye open for weird behaviour, but since I see so little of her, I'm not sure I'll be able to judge.

The worst event this month was finding that bracelet in my bag. I guess I shouldn't even write this on paper, but, since my hero Andrea, smoothed things over and persuaded the shop it was a genuine mistake, it can't hurt to remember yet another debt I owe her. I will never go in there again, ever. It was so kind of her to give me that teddy, but it sent shivers down my spine. I have an aversion to any stuffed toys these days, they all remind me of the blue rabbit. I'll hide mine away in a cupboard and hope she doesn't notice. It's my imagination I know, but the one Andrea has looked quite sinister.

I can hobble around now, it's much easier and I'm hoping that next month they will take the boot off and I can get back to normal.

March ended on a high note with a visit from Leo. So glad to see him. He has been quiet for some time but I expect he's come to spend time with his sister and make sure I was being a good mother. The flat is getting quite crowded, but it's nice to be surrounded by family and I do enjoy cooking for them all.

APRIL   ANDREA

I'm fuming. When I phoned Leah this morning, she said she was sorry but she had already agreed to take Leo around town and show him the sights. Has she forgotten who her best friend is? How dare she dump me for her stepson who is certainly no friend. He's playing with fire if he thinks he's going to muscle in. I'll book an appointment for us at the local spa and insist she come.

To my relief she was waiting outside for me the next morning as I drove up. I put on my brightest smile, jumped out and ran around to help her into the passenger seat.

"Darling, I've missed you. How are you?" I inadvertently thumped her cast with the crutches. "Whoops sorry. Oh sweetie, I didn't hurt you, did I? I'm so sorry."

Leah smiled and shook her head as she wriggled into the car and allowed me to tuck her coat in and gently close the door. Was it my imagination or could I feel Leo's eyes bore into the back of my head from the window above as I flung the crutches onto the back seat? I refused to look up to see if he was watching.

I kept my voice light as I steered through the mid-morning traffic and turned out onto the Bristol Road. I brushed aside Leah's attempts to play down my missing her, it had only been forty-eight hours. She'd been coping well and I'd never believe who had turned up on the doorstep?

I began guessing it was Darth Vader, or Mickey Mouse, and a whole list of silly, impossible guests and I soon had her in fits of laughter. I could sense her relax. At last as we swept into the driveway to the spa, she told me Leo had travelled down from London for a few days.

As I parked the car, I turned to her and grabbed her hands. "Oh Leah" that's awful. What does he want? Don't tell me. He needs money, right?"

"No," Leah pulled her hands away. "It's nothing like that. He genuinely wanted to see me and Belinda."

"Simply hasn't got around to asking you yet, getting settled in first I bet." It was difficult not to sound vitriolic.

Leah looked genuinely hurt. "Andrea it's not like that at all. I have a lot to thank Leo for, getting me out of that home for a start. He's family."

"Only by marriage – to a husband who has absconded I might add."

"You never let me forget, do you? You bang on and on about how tenuous my relationship is with the only family I have."

I was immediately contrite. "I'm so sorry Sweetie, I'm just trying to protect you. Mason is god knows where. It looks as if Belinda is into drugs, and while Leo told you he was in Australia, I told you he had been locked up at Her Majesty's pleasure and that's why he wasn't around. What kind of family are we talking about Leah? Believe me, I'm your only friend. I'm the only one you can trust."

For a horrible moment I thought I'd lost her. She sat

chewing her lip, looking at the floor. "There's Bill." She said it so quietly I almost didn't hear.

"Yes of course there is, darling, and I'm sure in time you'll be able to rely on him as well."

"I can rely on him now!"

I didn't answer but shook my head slowly to show I was not convinced. Time to change tack as I hurried to help her out of the car.

I think I made good progress that day. It's often better to plant seeds, water them with the odd hint then stand back and let them grow by themselves.

We had a good time at the spa having our favourite beauty treatments and I was careful to stay away from topics relating to family and relationships. When I dropped her off later that afternoon, I didn't accept her invitation to come in and join them for dinner. I pretended I had another engagement. I could see the frown on Leah's face wondering who else I might know in Weston, but she was too polite to interrogate me.

The following morning, when I knew that Leah would be at her aqua swimming classes I went around to the flat. I parked a little way down the road and prayed that Belinda was out and Leo was in.

I breathed a sigh of relief when he answered the door.

"You alone?" I asked him as I brushed past him into the narrow hallway.

"Yes. No one here but me."

"And what the fuck are you doing here? You were supposed to stay out of sight in London."

"Yeah, well I got bored and, no one was keeping me in

the loop." He followed me into the lounge and as I turned to face him, he poked me hard in the chest. "Not a bloody word, not one. I thought you were supposed to report back every bloody day." He emphasised each word with his finger thumping my ribs. I stepped back to stop myself overbalancing.

"There is nothing to report," I hissed. "It takes time. I can't expect her to walk out on everything, not after a couple of days! I'm the one who's doing all the work. All you have to do is to wait patiently in London sitting on your fat backside. Malcolm's job is to shuffle paperwork and delay payment until we are ready and Mason lies low wherever he's decided to bloody hide out. He's a loose cannon, I don't trust him to go along with any of this."

"You stupid bitch! You told me he was on board with the whole thing! What are you saying now?" Leo was pacing the floor slapping the wall on either side before turning and striding back again.

"I was never sure. I didn't get much chance to discuss it with him. He was too busy having a fling with that actress. I'm not sure if he was genuinely worried about Leah going mad."

"He knew about the bloody money though."

"Of course, he did! Why else would he marry her in the first place? But when it turned sour with a couple of his clients, then he had bigger problems on his plate. No point in having a fortune in the bank if you're wearing concrete boots propping up a new carpark in south London is there? And now we don't even know where he is." He had me pacing up and down too. I was far too jittery to stand still.

"I think Belinda knows." Leo pulled out his cigarettes as he flung himself into a chair and played with his lighter.

"You can't smoke in here," I snapped. "Leah doesn't allow smoking in the house."

"She allows me. I'm her saviour remember?" The lighter flared and he lit up.

"Oh yeah, silly of me to forget that. None of that charade would have been necessary if you'd done your homework properly. 'Get her sectioned,' you said. Oh yeah brilliant idea until someone, like yours truly, bothered to read the small print."

"Yeah well we all make mistakes. What if she was let out, managed to prove she was sane? I mean all by herself. Time for her to go after the money, right?" Leo blew a smoke ring up to the ceiling.

"She didn't even know she was entitled to any bloody money! It was you with your big mouth Leo who told her about the insurance policies."

"Well, what other excuse could I use to put the blame on Mason? And you, you, silly bitch went and blamed me!"

I smirked. "I thought that was a masterstroke. Divide and rule. I've convinced her I can't stand you."

"Ah! That's another bone I have to pick with you. How dare you tell her I have been in prison."

"Well you have."

"She didn't have to know that. I was quite happy with the Australia story."

"You know she has a sister, Daphne, in Australia."

"It's a bloody big place. Chances of me ever meeting her are zero."

"Especially as you were never there."

"Yeah, well find out what town or city she's in and I'll tell Leah I was thousands of miles away on the other side of the continent."

I walked over to the drinks cabinet and poured myself a large whisky.

"Bit early for that isn't it?"

"I need to think." I tipped the glass and took a long swallow. "Wait! Did you just say that Belinda knows where Mason is?"

"Not sure. She was a bit cagey."

Tossing down the last of the whisky and pouring another, I turned to face him. "Can we trust her?"

"I wouldn't put money on it. She's always been a spoiled brat, but she is aware of what Leah's done for her."

"Yeah, little Miss Perfect. God, she drives me insane."

"Belinda?"

"No stupid. Miss Perfect Leah. How can anyone be so nice, so kind, so gentle, so loving?"

"For fuck's sake you're not going soft on her, are you?" Leo sprang to his feet and towered over me his face right up against mine. I took a couple of steps back but not before grabbing the whisky bottle. I managed to squeeze past him and stood in the archway to the kitchen.

"Of course, I bloody haven't. Weak people like her make me sick. Look we're wasting time." I filled the glass a third time before Leo marched forward and yanked the bottle out of my hand.

"Then stop drinking and focus. We need to reassess the damage so far."

I sat back on the sofa, turning the glass tumbler round and round in my hands. "You and I are still enemies. That would make sense yes?"

"We can hardly be friends all of a sudden, you warned her off me."

"Hah! I thought you were the one who was into war books. Never, ever let the enemy know who all the enemies are. So, for now, she trusts you and she trusts me, right?"

"Yeah if you say so."

"But she has no idea we are a united front."

Leo's eyes lit up as he walked over to grab another glass and pour himself a drink. He placed it on the coffee table as he lit another cigarette. "So, let's see if I have this right. We can work from two sides, unbalance her."

I sighed. "Honestly it makes more sense for you to disappear back to London. Lie low."

"What and miss all the fun? Fat chance."

"How stupid can you be. You idiot!" I screamed at him before realising the sound might carry to the next door flat. I lowered my voice. "It was agreed I would come down, alienate her from friends and family and get her to move in with me. Then, once under my roof we can immobilise her the moment the payouts are due. Simple eh? Except you're about to throw a spanner in the works. I can get rid of Belinda and Bill easily enough but then she would still have you. Now do you get it, you moron?"

Leo stared at the carpet for several seconds, tapping his foot against the leg of the coffee table. "Yeah, guess you're right. But..." he turned to glare at me, "...you better keep me updated, every day. And I bloody well mean every day. Hear?"

"Yes, and I'm sorry about that. I forgot."

"Well don't. Otherwise there will only be three of us sharing the spoils. Two if Mason keeps his nose out of it." He leaned forward invading my personal space again. His eyes bored into mine reminding me how dangerous he could be.

I shuddered. I knew Leo could turn very nasty and since his time in prison doubtless he had plenty of friends who would be only too happy to help him. Until we had our hands on the money, I was safe, but after that, who knows. I would have to watch my back.

We both jumped as we heard the lift whining. I rushed into the kitchen to rinse out the whiskey glass, slide it back into the cupboard and just had time to pop a mint in my mouth before Leah appeared in the hallway.

"Oh," she said looking startled to see both of us in her lounge.

"Leah darling," I rushed over to give her a big hug. "I forgot today was your swimming thingy. I popped round and he was here." I tossed my head towards Leo and pulled a face. "I was just leaving." I dropped my voice to a whisper. "Don't ever ask me to stay in the same room as him. He's poison. Don't believe a word he says. Don't forget he was in prison. I am so worried for your safety."

Leo must have heard the last bit, as a voice behind me said. "No worries, I'm going back to London first thing tomorrow."

Leah disentangled herself from my arms and hobbled across the room. "Oh Leo, it's such fun having you here. I'm sure Belinda appreciates it too."

"Really?" My voice dripped with sarcasm. "Don't tell me she stayed in last night and spent time with her big brother?"

"Well no." Leah bit her lip. "But I'm sure she'll miss him."

"She has other things to take her mind off everyday life, doesn't she?"

Leah knew I was referring to the drugs and turned pale. She turned back to Leo. "You must do as you think best." she said.

Leo put his arms around her and gave her a big hug tucking her head into his chest while poking his tongue out at me. Would he ever grow up?

I put my coat on, wound a scarf round my neck and grabbed my bag. "You know where to find me Leah. You have my number."

I walked out closing the front door firmly behind me. I was taking a bit of a chance, but I felt confident enough that once Leo was on his way back to the capital, Leah would be putty in my hands again.

I held two cards. My friendship with Leah and the contact with the insurance company and I was not about to share that information with anyone.

I stayed home for two days. It wasn't easy. I had no television or radio and I couldn't concentrate even when I tried to read the latest book I'd bought. It was tempting to go look around the shops, or stroll along the beachfront but I didn't want to take the risk of running into either Leah or Leo. He said he was leaving, but would he?

By day three I was getting jittery. Had I miscalculated? I didn't trust Leo and I had imaginary conversations in my head where he was bad mouthing me to Leah. I was pacing the floor, making half-hearted attempts at cleaning the flat by scrubbing the oven top, scraping off months of grease and dried fat. I shuddered to think who had lived here before me. I took the curtains down and washed them carefully by hand. I dared not put the thin fabric in the washing machine, it looked too fragile, the material was held together by the grime that had settled over time. The water turned a muddy brown as I rinsed them again and again.

I had just hung the newly washed curtains and was looking around for something else to occupy my time when my mobile rang. I lunged to pick it up and breathed a sigh of relief to see Leah's number on the screen. I counted slowly to ten to allow it to ring a few more times before pressing the green button.

"Hi."

"Andrea?"

"Darling who else do you think would answer my phone?"

Leah chuckled. "How are you? Are you still in Weston?"

"For now, I am Sweetie. I've been thinking about going back to London..." I let my words hang in the air.

"Oh…" there was a long pause before she added. "And what did you decide?"

"I have not made up my mind yet. I love the seaside and the fresh air, but… to be honest Leah, without my best friend it doesn't matter where I am." My own words made me want to throw up.

"But we are friends, aren't we?" I thought Leah was about to burst into tears.

"I thought so, but friends listen to their friends, especially those who have their best interests at heart and – well to be honest Leah I warned you about Leo. He's dangerous and I can't stand by and watch you get hurt. It would break my heart."

"He's not here Andrea. He's gone back to London. He left the next morning like he said he would."

"Are you sure?"

"Yes, I called the Uber to take him to the station."

"That is such a relief my darling. Now I know that you are safe I can breathe easy again."

"You really care that much?"

"Darling after myself, you are the most important person in the world to me."

Snuffles and gasps on the other end of the line, it sounded as if Leah was crying.

"How can I cheer you up? I know – a visit from your favourite person bearing doughnuts and custard creams."

The snuffles subsided and she gave a weak laugh.

"I'll be round within the hour." I hung up before she could say no. I gave a huge sigh of relief. All was right with the world again.

As soon as she opened the door, I gave her a huge hug, squashing the doughnuts in the process. I waved the bag around and blamed it all on her.

Leah gave her girly laugh, and walked into the kitchen to turn on the coffee maker.

"Whoa, let me choose my pod, I hope you have a good

selection. Any Java?" I kept my voice light while assessing her condition. She looked a little unkept. Her hair had lost its sheen, her track pants were sagging at the knees, and her baggy jumper was covered in fluff balls. In only a couple of days she had gone downhill.

"So, what's the latest news then?" While my voice was bright and cheery, I hoped the update was not good.

Leah sank onto a stool. "I don't know. Everything seems to be falling apart again."

"Oh darling." I finished making the coffee she had abandoned and pushed the mug towards her, even spooning in her two sugars. I slid the flattened pastries onto a plate. "Poor little doughnuts, I'm so sorry, did I give you a hard time? Never mind, Leah will eat you anyway."

She gave a half smile.

"Come on BFF tell me what's bothering you. Let Aunty Andrea make it all right for you."

Leah sank her teeth into the first doughnut. For several seconds she chewed while I guessed she was choosing her words. "You'll think me such a cow, but Belinda has been impossible."

She was interrupted by the slamming of the front door and the young lady in question barrelled into the kitchen.

"God you're eating again. Don't you ever stop?" She grabbed the second doughnut off the plate and took a huge bite.

"Uh how about hello Andrea, how are you?" Leah's voice wavered.

"Oh, hi Andrea, didn't see you there." Belinda laughed hysterically.

"I'm not that tiny young lady." I grinned at her.

"Lot smaller than she is," Belinda waved her index finger at her stepmother. "And if she keeps stuffing her face, soon she'll be the size of a house."

Belinda crammed the rest of the doughnut into her mouth and opened the fridge door. She grabbed the remains of an apple pie and poured a healthy dose of cream over the top.

"No school?" I kept my voice light.

"Nah. Well nothing of interest."

"Isn't it exam time soon?"

"Guess." She slammed the pie dish on the kitchen counter and glared at me. "Don't you start. She's bad enough. Always poking and prying and question after question till I wanna scream. If I'm happy to let her live her life with a man she isn't even married to, then she should let me live mine. Both of you, keep your nose out of my business. Anyhow think he's losing interest and fast. Think about that then."

She swept out and slammed her bedroom door behind her.

"That went well," I tried to lighten the mood. Leah looked as if she had been punched in the stomach. "No wonder you look down Sweetie, she's a handful, isn't she?"

"How does anyone cope with teenagers these days? They are a law unto themselves. I can't stop her going out, I can't make her go to school. I dare not even mention what you found in her room." Leah wrung her hands.

"I'm sure she's a good kid underneath. She'll come to her senses in a few months as long as the drugs…" I let my words hang in the air.

Leah covered her face with her hands and began to sob.

"Maybe tough love is called for. Maybe you should go to the police."

"Nooo. I can't get them involved. Don't ask me to do that please."

There it was again. She was afraid of the police. Why? I didn't think she was fretting over stealing the bracelet. She'd heard nothing more about it. I suspected she was afraid of Belinda too. Did that young lady have some kind of hold over her? I was itching to know.

I tugged her hands away from her face and held them between my own. "Leah darling, why are you so scared of talking to the law? Come on you can tell me anything. Talk to me. Why do you feel so threatened by them?"

"Don't waste your time Andrea." The voice behind me made me jump. "She's not going to tell you and I don't think I will either. It's none of your fucking business. Is it stepmother dear?" Belinda thumped Leah hard on the back as she crammed a pod into the coffee machine. "It's family business."

Leah's head whipped round and her eyebrows rose.

"What you're forgetting Belinda is that you can choose your friends but you can't choose your family." I snapped at her.

"Ain't that the truth," she agreed, opening the sugar jar. "And," she added spitefully, "I didn't choose her." She nodded towards Leah. "It was my dad's choice and I just had to put up with it."

"If Leah makes your dad happy why should you make her so miserable?"

"Well my dad ain't here or hadn't you noticed?" Belinda spooned three spoons of sugar into her mug and stirred it frantically. For a moment I saw how she was hurting. Both her mother and father had run out on her and left her with a stepmother she had little time for.

I noticed Leah staring at Belinda. So, those two had history together, well a secret anyway and it concerned the police. I was dying to know but now wasn't the time. I'd bring it back up and grill Leah the first opportunity I got. I couldn't even begin to imagine what it was.

Belinda was stirring her coffee so vigorously that it slopped onto the table. Ever the little housewife, Leah jumped to her feet, grabbed a cloth and cleaned up the mess.

"Go on then, haven't you told your best friend your exciting news?" Belinda urged.

"Oh, it's not that exciting, and I'm not sure I can even do it," Leah spluttered into her mug of coffee and her hands were shaking as she put it down on the counter.

"Come on then. Tell me. I'm all ears."

Leah hesitated. She stared at the last remaining doughnut as if it was a lifesaver.

"OK then let me guess. You won the lottery? No? Uh, you've been chosen as a political candidate for Weston-super-Mare."

Belinda shrieked. "Andrea get real!"

"Not that then. I know, a talent scout saw you and has offered you the leading role in his next Hollywood movie."

Belinda looked at me in disgust and marched back to her bedroom the coffee swirling dangerously in her mug as she waved her arms dramatically. But Leah was smiling.

"Nothing as grand as that. There's a group in town for amputees and they have asked me to speak to them about my experiences."

What a let-down. Although I guess this would be a big thing for my mousy friend.

"That's wonderful," I clapped my hands. "When? Tell me all about it."

"Next week, but I may not…"

"Of course you can and you will. Want me to come with you? Or maybe Belinda…?"

"Oh please! Can you see that happening?"

"Well no."

She smiled again

"She'd probably put you off by whispering rude words and coughing and stuff like that."

"And you won't?"

"Darling, you will give the best speech. Give them the best talk they have ever heard. You must do it."

"I'm not sure I have the confidence to stand up and face all those people. Maybe once, when I was younger when I was happy and had a career, before everything went wrong."

"But think of how it will help others who have lost limbs. They will understand and empathise with you. You can't not Leah, you must do it."

"I'm still not sure."

I stood up and marched round the small kitchen. "First point. Pretend they are all sitting in front of you naked."

"What?"

"It's the speechmaker's crotch, uh crutch so to speak."

Leah burst out laughing.

"Darling I promise you it's the way all these public figures start out. Now, if that's not enough, remember that everyone needs bathroom breaks. Now, that brings us down to the same level doesn't it? See them all, sitting on the loo?"

Leah hugged herself as she laughed. "Andrea you are impossible."

"It will only be you and I with our clothes on and I'll be there right beside you. Promise."

"But I don't know what to say."

"Simple, just tell your story. When you came round in hospital and were told they had removed one of your legs. How did you feel? Then explain how you learnt to walk again, the pain, the hard work and how it was all worth it. Today you are a confident, mobile and independent woman, living happily here in Weston. Then ask for questions. Simple."

While I'd been waltzing round the room, I kept glancing over at Leah. To be honest, she was hardly the model for a confident, mobile and independent woman. It was only a week since they had removed her boot and she still hadn't got into a normal way of walking. I'd caution her not to mention how she fell over so easily at the night club.

"You must also add the bit about Zeus attacking your false leg, it always helps to add some humour. Do you want me to help you write it, then you can practice it beforehand?"

"No, that I can do by myself. But thank you."

The following morning, I popped round to Leah's flat a bit

later than usual. I had run out of basic foodstuffs and made a run to the local supermarket. I was surprised when Bill answered the door.

"Ah Andrea, Leah's not here. Was she expecting you?" He made no move to invite me in.

"Uh, well no, but we pop in and out of each other's most days so…" Not strictly true. I had never once invited Leah round to my flat.

"Shall I tell her you called? Is there a message?"

I sensed Bill was none too pleased to see me. I hate it when people second guess me, or appear to read my mind. "Any idea what time she will be back?"

"I'm not sure, she wasn't specific."

I turned to go, then faced Bill before he had a chance to close the door. "I hope things are OK at the college? I mean you're usually at the library, aren't you?"

"Yes, but not today. And thank you Andrea but everything is fine."

I had no option but to bow out as gracefully as I could, taking the one flight of stairs to the ground floor rather than stand and wait for the lift.

As I marched off down the road, I considered my options. I could either make out that Bill was coming onto me and drop hints to Leah or, suggest that Bill had a thing for Belinda. Which one would work best? He would deny it of course, and it would be a 'he said, she said' scenario but it was best to keep it simple. If I'm honest I was a bit miffed that Bill didn't find me attractive. I'm intelligent, witty, and well-read even if my education was cut short and as far as the world knows, an independent and financially secure woman. But men don't change, do they? They always prefer to play the protector, relish the caveman approach to the cowering little woman and Leah fell right into that category.

When we walked into the hall Leah took a step back. I grabbed her hand and urged her forward. "You can't back out now," I hissed. "It's too late. Come on Leah, you can do it." I squeezed her hand.

She straightened up and gave herself a shake as a tall woman dressed in country tweeds with her messy, grey hair piled up on top of her head bore down on us.

"Leah I can't tell you how much we are all looking forward to your talk. I'm sure you're going to be a great inspiration to us all. Can I get you some tea?"

"Do you have coffee?"

For a moment the hostess paused. I could read her mind. *Didn't all British people drink tea all the time?* "Yes of course, I'll see what I can find."

I half expected Leah to start apologising and change her mind but she said nothing.

The hall was in an annex to the hospital. The audience sitting and waiting patiently was larger than I expected. Most were in wheel chairs, some were probably still in-patients. I fussed around Leah but she brushed me off, seeming to relate more to the crowd who were in the same situation as herself.

I hate hospitals at the best of times. I don't like to even think about the days when I am old and frail and dependent on other people. What could be worse than having your nappy changed by some callow youth who forgot to close the door and you are desperately searching for the right words to complain. No, hospitals were not for me. I was already approaching forty and if I was going to enjoy life while I was still active, I'd better get a move on.

Leah had not allowed me to help her to write her presentation but it was surprisingly good. She had put together slides on her laptop and explained in simple language how her prosthesis fit and to my horror, pulled up her long skirt and showed them. I closed my eyes. I'm not into such stuff.

There were tons of questions when she had finished, and listening to Leah's answers I realised for the first time what a trauma she had suffered, and the pain she had experienced when learning to walk again.

"Even now," she was saying with a laugh "I'm not too good on the dance floor, as my good friend can tell you." She looked across to me and smiled.

The applause lasted several minutes and the chairlady thanked her profusely for her time and her courage in sharing her story. She also reminded the audience that Leah had not let life get her down, that she'd picked herself up after her terrible loss and was now living happily in Weston and enjoying a wide range of activities.

One of the other amputees came over and gave Leah a hug. Well half a hug as she only had one arm. Leah turned to me. "Andrea, meet Rachel. We do the swim club for amputees every week. You should see how she streaks through the water. If she had both arms, I'd swear she'd be in the next Olympics."

I managed a weak smile as I shook Rachel's remaining hand, the left one.

"Are you joining us for coffee?" Leah asked brightly.

"I'd love to but I need to get the kids from playgroup. Another time?"

"Yes, for sure. After swimming next week?"

"It's a date."

Leah was beaming as we left the hospital grounds. The experience had boosted her confidence no end and I sensed she was about to share something with me but then changed her mind.

I steered her in the direction of our favourite coffee shop, and took her arm to steady her. The wind was blowing strongly off the sea as usual, but she pulled away and walked confidently beside me.

Once settled inside in the hot steamy warmth of the café and we'd put in our usual coffee and doughnut order, I took Leah's hands in mine and told her how proud I was of her, the presentation and the response and rabbited on about how much she had helped her audience.

"You were right," she said. "I can do it and you know, once I stood up there, looking at all those naked people sitting on the loo, I wasn't frightened anymore."

We both laughed.

"The organizer has asked me to give more talks, maybe even travel around the country. Andrea it's made me feel useful for the first time in ages. Appreciated even."

This was not good. It was time to throw another spanner in the works.

"Oh Leah, I'm so pleased for you. I know this is a lousy

time to tell you, but now you are so much stronger, I think it's only fair to tell you what has been going on."

"What? What is it?"

I could see the fear in Leah's eyes but we were interrupted by the waitress delivering our order. I purposely delayed as I slowly tore the paper sachet and poured the sugar into my cup. I added the milk and stirred the coffee slowly, pretending to hesitate.

"I've been afraid to tell you this for a while…" I paused.

"Tell me? Tell me what Andrea? What's the matter are you in trouble? Can I help?"

"It's not just me, possibly both of us."

"Andrea, spit it out. Don't keep me in suspense. What's this all about? Tell me."

"If you insist. It's Bill."

"What about Bill?"

"I always thought you were such a good match, and he was always so quiet…"

"Get on with it, Andrea. What exactly are you trying to tell me?"

"I'm not sure I would trust him Leah."

"Trust him? What's he done?"

"Please, please believe me I'm only telling you this because you're my friend, my best friend. But if it happened to me, I would want to know. It's awful to find out you were the last to know, and everyone else is talking about…"

"What?" Leah banged the table and people nearby turned to stare. "Just tell me, spit it out."

"Well, on a couple of occasions, Bill has come on to

me. At first, I laughed it off, thought he was just joking, fooling around. But then he became more persistent. When I popped round to see you the other morning, I quite forgot you were at your swim session he invited me in and then he, uh, forced himself on me."

Leah sat frozen in disbelief.

"I'm so sorry but I felt I had to warn you. Please believe me I never led him on, I promise. I'd never do that to you, Leah."

Tears ran down her face. She didn't bother to wipe them away and I watched fascinated as her mascara began to run.

"No," she murmured. "No, don't say that."

I leaned towards her across the table. "Leah, how much do you really know about him?"

"He's told me all about himself. He's been an open book. I had no reason to disbelieve him."

"But have you seen any proof? Any paperwork, other friends, social outings with his family?"

"Well no but then I wasn't expecting to. He's widowed and his children live overseas."

"So, you've not met them then?"

"Not yet but I'm sure I will one day."

"And his parents?"

"Andrea this is beginning to sound like the KGB. I've known Bill for almost eighteen months and I have no reason to doubt him. He also had a miserable childhood..."

"Just like you, how convenient."

"Andrea! That's not nice."

"I'm so sorry my pet but I'm not making this up. I'm

trying to save you more heartbreak. God knows how much I care for you."

Leah lowered her head, her words muffled in her sleeve. "I don't believe this. First Mason, then Belinda, now Bill, and I'm not supposed to trust Leo either. Who is left? Everyone I know makes me so unhappy."

"I'm left. You have me." I patted her arm. "Tell you what Leah, come and live with me. You know you can trust me. Let me take care of you. I'll not cause you a moment of worry and unhappiness. Who else can make you laugh like I do?"

For a brief moment I thought she was going to agree, then she fished in her pocket for a tissue and wiped her eyes. "Thank you that's so sweet of you, but I need to think about this. I need to make a decision about Belinda, find out more about the drugs. And, I need to talk to Bill. No, I can't believe he would do that. Not with my best friend. He's always been such a gentleman."

"From what you've told me, I believed that too. But all men are the same. They are always out for what they can get and I guess he's no exception."

Leah stood up abruptly, sending the plate of doughnuts sailing off the table to crash onto the floor. We were the focus of everyone in the café. I went to stand up but she glared at me.

"I need to be on my own. I need to think. I'll see you tomorrow Andrea."

She turned on her heel and stormed out of the café, ignoring the waitress and the curious crowd who all watched her leave.

I sat back and ordered more coffee. Once again, I had planted the seeds and I only had to sit back and watch them grow.

APRIL   LEAH

Dear Diary,

Just when I thought I was going to be so happy life has shaken me again. What am I doing so wrong? First it was Leo. I didn't tell Andrea, but I did a lot of checking on the Internet and found no evidence that Leo had ever been in Australia. Then I googled prisoners in the UK. It was easier than I thought. I'd expected all this privacy and personal data act to block such information but if you pay up you can find out if someone has a record. I found proof that Leo had indeed been inside. So, Andrea had told me the truth. Even so, I was quite sad to see Leo leave, I'd quite enjoyed his company, even though he had tried to borrow money from me. Andrea was right about that too. I wonder what he lives on as he never mentioned a job of any sort.

I'm still worried about Belinda. I can put up with her behaviour, just, but what am I going to do about the drugs? A couple of times I've hovered in the doorway to her bedroom but, unlike Andrea, I've not had the courage to go ferreting around.

And now Bill. Did he really make a pass at Andrea? More than a pass if I'm to believe her? I've wracked my brains trying to recall how they acted together to see if there was ever a hint. If there was, I missed it. I'm at my wits' end, again, just when I was feeling on top of the world after the presentation. Am I losing it? I'm still fretting about that bracelet. I've never stolen anything before, what's the matter with me?

I don't think things can get any worse.

MAY ANDREA

I left it a couple of days before I went round to Leah's place. I was curious to see if Bill had managed to convince her he was innocent. When I rang the bell downstairs, she let me in and as I came out of the lift the front door had been left open for me. I was relieved to see that Bill was out, but Belinda was there. I could hear Leah's exasperated voice coming from the kitchen. "I don't know how you can eat so much food. Please ask before you raid the fridge. That's the third time this week you've taken something I planned to cook for supper."

"Well how was I to bloody well know that? You should mark it or something. I gotta eat, you wouldn't want me to starve, would you?"

"I'm not going to spend my time labelling food in the fridge. All you have you do is ask. Is that too much to do?"

"Yeah, whatever. Prison camps are better than this joint."

"You wouldn't know, you've never been in a prison camp." Leah snapped back.

"Seen them on the telly, so I know exactly what they were like, so there. Our generation learns about stuff, not like in your days when you had no technology and were bumbling around in the dark."

"I know one thing. My generation never spoke to our parents the way they do today."

She was right. The things Belinda said made me wince. She didn't need to be on drugs to make her behave badly. I was hoping she would go out so I could quickly check her room to see if the hidden stash had been disturbed.

I stood by the kitchen door watching the pair of them. Had they forgotten I was on my way up? Neither of them noticed me.

Leah was rolling out pastry on the counter top while Belinda perched on a stool at the breakfast bar. I guessed she was deliberately trying to wind Leah up.

"Don't suppose you had all that much to learn at school, did you?" Belinda's voice was muffled by the pork pie she was chewing.

"Enough I guess." Leah sighed. "They say that knowledge doubles every ten years, so yes, there is more to learn, but we were also taught manners, how to consider other people, kindness, politeness and self-control. All of which are sadly lacking in today's world."

"I'm all those things to my friends." Belinda took another bite of the pie.

Leah paused. "Belinda, can't we just call a truce? I'm not asking to be your best friend or your mother or your jailor either, but can we be civil to each other? Stop this sniping and back biting. It's wearing me out."

"Yeah, whatever." The teenager turned and noticed me for the first time. "When did you creep in?"

"I've just arrived." I moved closer hoping to see if Belinda's pupils were a normal size. I wouldn't be surprised if she had taken a few drugs, most teens did these days they were widely available in school, the pubs, clubs and out on the street.

Belinda started to raid the cake tin. After cutting herself a large slice, and piling several biscuits onto her plate, she stalked out of the room.

"Darling, how are you?" I walked over and hugged Leah. She looked as if she had not slept the last couple of nights. "You look so tired, dark circles under your eyes and too many wrinkles for such a young woman." I ran my thumb over her cheek.

Leah brushed me off. "Ha, hardly young, but you're right about one thing, I'm not getting much sleep."

"Tell me all," I walked over to switch on the coffee machine, then paused. "No, on second thoughts wine. That's what we need." There was a bottle of white wine in the fridge door and I poured us both a hefty glassful.

"Bit early in the day," Leah protested.

"Nonsense, any time is wine time. Hey somewhere in the world the sun is setting."

Her mouth lifted slightly as she took a healthy glug.

"What is it sweetie? Belinda, or Bill?" I really didn't mind which one it was.

"Bill is away in Birmingham, a conference for college librarians. No, it's Belinda. She was out all last night."

"Where?"

"Who knows? All I do know is the police brought her home at six this morning blind drunk. Well I guess she was drunk she could have been drugged up to the eyeballs. I can't tell the difference."

"Oh, you poor dear. What did the police say?"

"Not a lot. They gave me a warning that if they pick her up again, they won't return her but sling her inside."

"Serves her right."

"That's easy to say but then she'd have a record and it's hard enough getting into college and then a job without that hanging over her head."

I lowered my voice. "Did you tell them what's in her room?"

"God no! As if I would? And land her in more trouble? She's a handful as it is."

"Leah, darling, she's sixteen now, she's an adult."

"Not as far as the law is concerned. She is legally entitled to buy cigarettes, get married, apply for benefits, drink in a restaurant and join a trade union. But she's not an adult yet."

"You googled it?"

"How did you guess? Oh. And she can also leave home."

"But she's not going to do that, is she?"

"Not a chance." Leah was rolling the pastry so hard it now covered the whole counter top and holes were appearing in the middle. She stopped her frenetic work and wiped the sweat off her brow.

I took the rolling pin out of her hand. "Come, sit. Relax. Here, have another slurp of wine." I put the tumbler in her hand.

She knocked back the whole glass and I was quick to refill it to the brim.

"Getting drunk won't solve anything."

"True, but it will make you feel better for a while."

She gave a half smile, brushed the flour off her hands, and went over to sit at the dining room table. "I can't throw her out Andrea, so don't even suggest it. I would never forgive myself if anything happened to her. She's my responsibility."

"Send her to Leo then. He must be living in his father's house. Put her on the train to London."

"I can't. She's in school. I guess she has friends here in Weston although I've not met any of them."

"Druggie friends most likely. She'd be better off without them."

"If she is taking drugs, she could get her hands on them more easily in the capital."

"What do you mean 'if'? Stop deluding yourself Leah, you saw what we found. What did she say when you asked her about them?"

"I haven't."

"You still haven't asked her?"

"Andrea," Leah began to get angry. "You know I've not said a word to her. Why are you questioning me now?"

I leaned over and gave her another hug. This adult babysitting was giving me a headache. I needed Leah and Belinda to have a blazing row and hopefully either the teen would walk out or her stepmother would throw her out.

Leah took a deep breath. "I have kept a careful watch and I've seen no signs of drugs. Yes, I know I said she was moody and rude and lazed around in bed half the time, but as you saw, she has not lost her appetite and if I stare into her eyes much more, she'll have me up for abuse."

I laughed. I couldn't help it.

I threw my arms around her and rocked her to and fro but we sprang apart when we heard Belinda scream from the bedroom. My first thought was she'd found the drugs I'd planted but I was wrong. All of a sudden Belinda flung open her bedroom door. She stood in the frame holding out her mobile. Her face was white and her hand trembled. She took one step towards Leah and stopped.

"It's Dad and he wants to talk to you."

Leah started and sat up. "Mason?"

"Yeah. You, not me." Belinda marched over and dropped her phone into Leah's outstretched hand.

I was disappointed when she grabbed the phone and stood up too quickly for me to stop her. She moved away and I was unable to hear both sides of the conversation.

She wandered into the hallway and into her bedroom where she closed the door behind her. I was itching to know what was said. I heard her say goodbye and then there was a long, long silence. I was holding my breath. Belinda was pacing around the kitchen. She walked over to the TV and switched it on, she channel hopped for a couple of minutes then turned it off, sighed and flung herself on the sofa.

I picked up a magazine and flicked through the pages. Matchstick models wearing beautiful expensive clothes, plastered in even more expensive makeup, manufactured at the expense of tortured animals. The bloody women decorating the pages would look a million dollars in bin bags. I flung it to one side in disgust.

Fifteen minutes later Leah walked back in and handed Belinda her phone.

"Hello? Hello?" She glared at Leah. "He's hung up! Didn't he want to talk to me? I'm his daughter!" She tried to call the number back but all she got was a disconnected signal.

"Sorry Belinda he was in a hurry."

"What did he want?" I couldn't wait any longer.

"Where is he?" Belinda whined. She was close to tears. "Is he coming home?"

Leah sat next to her on the sofa and would have put her arms round her stepdaughter but she moved away. "No dear. He's in Australia, well that's where he wants to meet. He didn't say he was there now."

"Is he in hiding?" I asked.

"Yes, I think so. He asked me not to discuss this with anyone."

"Then she shouldn't be here." Belinda poked me in the chest. "Tell her to go home."

"Belinda, Andrea is not going anywhere. Calm down."

"He wants to meet you? Where?"

"In Australia."

"I'm coming and you can't stop me." Belinda sprang to her feet, put her hands on her hips and leaned over Leah. "He's my dad and I have a right to see him."

"Even though he ran out on you?" I couldn't resist it.

"Shut up you. Button your lip."

"Belinda!" Leah's rebuke was half-hearted. Her head low, her hands twisted round each other, she looked bewildered. "I don't know what to do," she whimpered.

"Let's take this one step at a time. You're sure that was Mason on the phone?"

"Course it was," snarled Belinda. "Think I don't know my own father's voice. And he wanted to talk to her!"

"Belinda, I understand why you are so upset, but if your dad wants Leah to meet up with him in Australia then he would talk to her. You can't arrange all that can you?"

Belinda didn't reply but continued to pace around the room, her arms wrapped across her chest, the anger spilling out surrounding her like a vapour cloud.

"And Mason wants you to meet him? Did he say why?"

"To talk, I guess. He wasn't that specific."

"More wine. I might even let you have a glass too."

"Big deal."

"You probably had a lot more than that last night, didn't you?"

Belinda shrugged. "So, what if I did?"

I rescued the half empty bottle from the fridge, grabbed a second one and poured two large glasses and a half glass.

"Gee thanks, is this all I get?"

"Yes. For now. Think of it as a nerve tonic."

I was alarmed at how quickly Leah gulped down the alcohol. It dawned on me that I had not taken much notice of the cases of wine stashed in the spare room. Was Leah drinking in secret?

"I don't know what to do," Leah repeated.

"You have two choices. Either you go see him, or you forget he called. He must want something other than to talk, or he could have used WhatsApp or Facetime or one of the other apps. Did he ask you to take anything with you?"

I thought Leah was about to tell me but she pressed her lips together and didn't answer.

Belinda leapt to her feet and disappeared into her bedroom, and returned waving her passport in one hand. "Here, it's current so there is no way I'm staying behind. He's my dad."

"If I go then of course I will take you." Leah said and Belinda beamed.

"How soon do we leave then? Tomorrow? I'll go pack."

"Wait up. I've not decided yet."

"You have to go. We have to. My bloody mother doesn't care about me, and now you're trying to keep me away from my father too. You cow!"

For a moment I thought Belinda was going to attack her stepmother and I stood up prepared to pull them apart. At the last moment she thought better of it, but stood bending over the cowering figure on the couch.

"I guess we should," Leah said at last. "I'm not sure how much it will cost, flights are expensive and the bank..." She trailed off.

"It's only money," Belinda sneered. "And you have plenty of it, I know you have."

"And how would you know that?" I asked her. Had a payment come through I didn't know about? "Let's all go," I added. "That way, if your dad needs to discuss well, business with Leah we can keep each other company."

"This is family you nosy old bitch. You keep out of it. He's my dad and she's my stepmother."

I saw Leah's face brighten a little. Belinda might well suck up to her just to get on the plane, but on the flip side the trip might forge a bond of sorts between them.

"What do I tell Bill?" Leah whispered.

"Whatever you bloody well like." That was Belinda's contribution.

"Tell him you're traveling to meet your husband." I added.

Poor Leah, it was one thing after another. If she had more guts, she wouldn't be in such a mess. If I was her, I would have flung Belinda out onto the streets, dumped Bill for being such a milksop and given me, my marching orders.

But of course, she wasn't me.

"I'll have a think and let you know."

Belinda's face dropped. "But we must go!"

"I can't give you an answer Belinda. You'll have to be patient." Leah glanced at her watch and jumped to her feet. "Goodness, dinner is going to be late." She went to rescue the pastry, deftly folding it over and rolling it to the correct size for the pie dish she got out of the cupboard.

Some people relax with alcohol, cigarettes or yoga. Leah busied herself in domesticity. The payout would be wasted on her. What's the point of having a fortune unless you paid others to cook and clean for you? What would Leah do all day? She wouldn't appreciate it, in fact, she would be lost. I was really doing her a favour in relieving her of the problem.

I dithered for a while until it became obvious that Leah was not going to invite me to dinner.

I said my goodbyes, giving Belinda a brief hug before she could stop me. Never hurts to keep everyone on side and hurried back to my flat. It was time to update my partners.

I called Malcolm first. He was still at work but made the excuse he was going out onto the balcony for a smoke.

"What's up Sis?"

I ground my teeth. "Mason phoned Leah."

"What the fuck for?"

"He wants to meet up."

"Why?"

"I don't know and I'm not sure he told her. I have a suspicion he wants her to deliver something. If it was just to talk, then he can do that from a distance."

"Oh shit. This couldn't have come at a worse time."

"Agreed. But what can we do?"

"Go with her. Stick to her like glue."

"I tried but I don't think she'll have me along for the ride. But I have a better idea. Are you listening?"

"Go on."

"This is what I want you to do."

When I knocked on the door to Leah's flat the next morning it was to find her packing. For once Belinda was all sweetness and light. Teens always are when they're getting their own way. She greeted me like a long- lost aunty.

"Andrea, we're going to Australia and we'll be in the air for hours and hours and they have films onboard. We get to stop over in Singapore. I hear that's a really cool place."

"Don't get too excited, we'll only be sitting in the airport for six hours." Leah's voice came from her bedroom.

"Plenty of time for sight-seeing!" The teenager didn't have a clue.

"Mmmm. You'd better pack a jersey." Leah walked into the hallway.

"You're kidding. I'll only need my bathers and T-shirts and shorts," Belinda protested.

"Trust me, it's colder there than you think and they are going into winter now. Suit yourself but I'm not lending you any of mine nor buying you more clothes. I've heard Australia is expensive."

I didn't want to ask outright where they were flying to in Australia, so I made myself useful, topping up the coffee mugs while I scouted around checking to see where Leah had put the tickets. I was beginning to despair until I knocked some magazines off the coffee table and there they were. Of course, no one had proper airline tickets these days, they had e tickets printed off the home computer. London Heathrow to Perth Australia in two days' time. Leah had also printed out visas for both of them.

I made my excuses to leave. Now I knew where they were going, I could advise Malcolm. We had to know what was going on. We couldn't trust Mason and how he would react. I had got as far as the door when Leah came rushing up and grabbed my sleeve.

"Andrea I am so sorry. I was thrown off balance. I wasn't thinking, can you forgive me?"

I looked at her. "You have nothing to be sorry for. What are you talking about?"

Leah pulled on my arm and led me back into the TV area and pushed me down onto the couch. She sat beside me. "It was such a shock, hearing from Mason and I wasn't thinking of you."

"Me?" I had no idea where this was going. I fixed my eyes on the blank television screen in an effort to keep my face and voice neutral.

"Will you come with me?"

"But Belinda…"

"Forget Belinda. There is no one else in the world I trust and I think I'm going to need moral support. I can't do this alone."

This was so much better than I expected. I'd already planned to send someone to shadow Leah, now I'd be able to see first-hand what went down. "I, I don't know what to say." I didn't want to sound too eager.

"I know it's short notice, but it only takes ten minutes to get an online visa, I'll pay for it and I'll pay for your ticket as well. I'm sure we can get you on the same flight even. And," she rushed on, "I doubt if the hotel where Mason's told me to stay, is full, not at this time of the year. Andrea, please say you'll come."

I could see tears forming in Leah's eyes and she clutched my hand so hard it was beginning to hurt. She reminded me of a frightened creature caught in torchlight on a quiet country lane.

I said nothing for several seconds. "I'm very flattered Leah. I'm not sure I can help much."

"I know it's a lot to ask." She released my hand and heaved herself off the sofa. "Look, forget I asked, I will have Belinda."

It was time to jump in and reassure her. I sprang to my feet and put an arm round her shoulder. "Of course, I'll come, you idiot. How can I let you cross to the other side of the world and take the chance you'll get lost!"

Leah burst out laughing, the tension draining from her face. Hell, she needed a mother, not a friend. Giggling she said, "Difficult when I won't be flying the plane."

"How soon do we leave?"

"The day after tomorrow, is that enough time for you to pack?"

"Oh, for fuck's sake you're not dragging her along with us, are you?" Belinda stood in the doorway her face like thunder.

"It will be easier for all of us," Leah walked over to her to give her a cuddle but her stepdaughter ducked out of the way and walked round the sofa and glared at me. "Do you have to come? It's our family business."

"You can never have too many friends Belinda, not real ones." I stared at her. "And, there was a time when we were friends I seem to remember?"

For a brief moment Belinda's face lit up, then it settled back into her usual sulky look. "Yeah well, things change." She said nothing for a moment and then flounced off to her bedroom slamming the door behind her.

Leah sighed and shook her head as she went to turn the coffee maker on. "Do teens have to behave like that?"

"Of course, they do. It's written into the constitution. 'Thou shalt give parents and teachers a hard time from the age of thirteen to twenty-one or you will not be awarded the right to be a teenager'." I was on a roll. "It's called the teen charter. 'It is incumbent for thou to be rude at all times. Remain in bed most of the day, then rise, raid the fridge and go out and party until dawn. Thou must gather around you as many disreputable friends as possible and defy all rules and regulations and authority especially those who care for you and attempt to teach you at the labour camp otherwise known as school'."

Leah was crumpled up against the kitchen counter laughing with the tears streaming down her face as I flung my arms around like a town crier reading from an imagined proclamation sheet.

"Enough! I'll have an accident."

I changed tack. "Lights, sound, action! Ladies, do you experience those little embarrassing moments when you laugh or cough, or maybe when you're on the dance floor? It's quite normal, but we have the answer…"

Leah fled into the bathroom. I breathed a sigh of relief. I was back in the fold.

It took less than half an hour on Leah's laptop to register, pay for my visa and book the flight tickets. I wouldn't be sitting next to the Brand family but that was not a problem. What else do you do on long haul except eat, sleep and watch the movies? I was also looking forward to the stopover to raid the duty free at Changi Airport. I would pack earplugs not only for the flight, but to shut out Belinda's constant whining and complaining.

Besides acting as companion to Leah, I would have to work out a way to talk to Mason alone. What game was he playing and was he still on board or had he decided change sides?

MAY LEAH

Dear Diary.

I'm in such a whirl I don't know which way to turn. A call from Mason after all these months. At first, I was upset he'd called Belinda and not me, until I remembered that somewhere between that awful institution and moving house I'd lost my mobile and I had to get a new number. Stupid, I know, but it wasn't until later that I discovered I could have transported the same number with all the same contacts. My data is apparently lodged up there in a cloud but I wasn't going to bother. All I wanted to do was put my old life behind me and make a fresh start but it keeps bouncing back to taunt me.

I must be mad traveling half way around the world to talk to my husband. When I first heard his voice, I was tempted to say no, until it dawned on me that I could ask him for a divorce and make some kind of arrangements about his daughter. I find it very strange that he didn't ask me to bring her with me. I'm not sure how he will react when he sees her, but she is his flesh and blood and his responsibility.

I'm so relieved that Andrea has agreed to come with me. I'll need someone to keep me sane, especially if Belinda acts up. She never misses an opportunity to put me down, disagree, contradict, argue or brush me off. I had enough years of that with my mother and I don't need more. It's time I had a bit of peace. I also need time to mend fences with Bill. I feel he is drifting away and I've not had the courage to ask him about his moves on Andrea. That is so hard to believe, yet, she has never lied to me and I've known her a lot longer. I think when I get back, I will try and get him to introduce me to some of his long-time friends or family. You can tell a lot about a person from the contacts they keep over the years.

I can't believe that May is coming to a close and it will be June tomorrow. I must keep positive. One good thing is my leg has healed and the new prosthesis is a better fit and much lighter than my old one. And, there are no teeth marks in it to remind me of Zeus. There is always a silver lining.

I must keep cheerful and tell myself to remain positive and yes, even assertive with Mason. He has a lot of explaining to do.

JUNE ANDREA

I had heard Leah advise Belinda, that it might be cold in Australia at this time of year. I'd quite forgotten it was their winter in the southern hemisphere, so I packed accordingly. I doubted there would be much time for lounging by the pool on sunbeds and I checked out the average temperatures for June. Nineteen degrees Centigrade didn't sound that cold coming from England but there was likely to be rain, so I stuffed my raincoat into my case.

We had visas for a year, but return tickets for a fortnight. Leah was worried about Belinda missing too much school, especially as she would be taking her final exams next year. Pretty stupid, since I doubt that young lady walked through the school gates many times a week. I think the staff give up chasing kids who won't cooperate. I know I would if I was a teacher. If they don't want to learn then it's up to them – spoiled brats.

I ordered a taxi to take us to the station and when we drew up outside Leah's flat it was to see a very sulky teenager waiting on the pavement with the largest suitcase I have ever seen.

Telling the driver to wait, I hopped out and pointed to the bright orange luggage. "Just how much do you need for two weeks?"

"Don't you start too," Belinda glared at me and held on tightly to the handle.

"You'd never backpack round South America with something that size," I battled to keep my voice bright and friendly but I wanted to slap her silly face.

"We're going to Australia, not South America. Your geography's way off," she snarled.

I was about to make one of my famous sarcastic replies but Leah appeared and, slamming the door behind her, joined us on the kerb.

Not only was Belinda's case large, it must have weighed a ton as the taxi driver had trouble lifting it into the boot, and Leah and I had to sit with our cabin bags on our laps as there was no space for them in the back.

"How heavy is that case?"

"I have no idea, but she wouldn't listen to me. I told her it's not about the size, but if it's more than twenty-three kilos they'll zap her at the airport, maybe she will listen to them."

I patted her hand and winked.

The train journey passed without incident, although a kind gentleman had to heave Belinda's case onto the train. It wouldn't fit in the luggage area and she insisted in leaving it in the aisle and it caused chaos when people couldn't get past.

"I thought today's youth was supposed to be savvy," I whispered in Leah's ear.

She shrugged her shoulders. "I warned her I'd refuse to help her with it, so she needn't even ask."

"You don't think she's got, um, you know any…"

Leah's face went white. "Oh no, surely not? She isn't that stupid."

"I hope not, but they do have sniffer dogs at the airport, so maybe hand her her ticket and we'll keep our distance."

My friend looked shocked but didn't reply. I could see the worry lines on her face so I buried my nose in a book for the rest of the ride.

To my chagrin, at each stage of the journey, a friendly male popped up and assisted Belinda. She sailed through the train station to the airport bus and into the departure halls, without having to lift a finger.

I hung behind in the queue interested to see what would happen once the check in desk clerk noted the weight. I was looking forward to this but they took an aggregate of both cases and since Leah was taking minimal clothes, I watched as the giant suitcase disappeared on the conveyor belt and out of view behind the desks.

Belinda looked very pleased with herself as she waltzed over clutching her boarding pass. "See, no problem."

I managed to smile and approached the desk.

We'd arrived in plenty of time but decided to go through customs and immigration and wait in the departures area. I was behind Belinda as she approached the security metal detector. It rang loud and clear and she was told to go back and take off her coat and shoes. I would have thought she might have copied all the other passengers but no.

I waited while she threw them off and flung them onto the conveyor belt and tried again. The machine screamed a second time. She was instructed to take off her belt. By now she was red in the face and stormed through a third time. I could have jumped the queue but this was more fun, especially as there was now a long line of people waiting less patiently by the minute.

The machine still protested as she attempted to walk through and this time, they took her firmly by the arm and marched her off to an enclosed cubicle on the far side. I walked through with no problem and collected my tray. As I was re-packing my electronics, watch and coins, Leah came over looking troubled.

"Where's Belinda? She was right behind me a moment ago."

"Over there." I indicated the little box room, the door firmly closed.

"Why?"

"Whatever she had on her, set the alarm off, three times. Hey, Leah, don't look so scared, I'm sure it will be fine. They just need to check her out."

"If it's the 'you know what'." Leah was chewing her lower lip.

"Not a chance, it's metal that sets the machine off."

"We hung around for what seemed like hours, but was only ten minutes at the most, until she was released and a rather shamefaced Belinda joined us to rescue her tray of belongings and clothes. She was accompanied by an airport official who I'd not like to meet in a dark alley at night. Belinda had to open her carry-on bag, and empty out her coat pockets and the world contender for the woman's all-in wrestling team (my description) picked through the contents one article at a time.

Leah watched from the packing table as the official

rummaged through her stepdaughter's belongings and I noticed she was holding her breath. If only she could just dump the child with her father and be spared all this hassle.

At last they let Belinda go, and with a face like thunder she flung her carry-on bag over her shoulder and marched ahead of us announcing that she was going to get a coffee. We trailed behind her as she made for the nearest bar only to see her ordering a gin and tonic.

Leah rushed forward to try and stop her, but I held her back. "If she wants to get plastered it's up to her. Come, I think we could also do with something stronger than coffee."

We collected our drinks from the bar, but Belinda did not join us at our table. She was too busy chatting to some youth with a shaved head, a ring through his nose and long dangly earrings.

"Ignore her," I said. "Let's just enjoy ourselves."

Leah looked apprehensive, but she nodded. "So glad you're with me," she murmured.

When it was time to go to the boarding gate, we had to prise Belinda away from her rather unsavoury new friend, and she trailed behind us with Leah looking back to see she was still there.

The moment we were on the aircraft she announced she would not be sitting with her stepmother but would take the seat reserved for me, several rows back.

I think we were both relieved. We'd get a break for a few hours from teen angst.

I was disappointed to see we were no longer offered night shades or those dinky tubes of toothbrushes, toothpaste and eye drops. Just showed how long it's been since I travelled long-haul. At least we were not asked to pay for food or drinks and I wondered how many little bottles Belinda would order before we reached Singapore.

"What could be more fun that escorting a drunk teenager around Changi Airport?" I whispered to Leah. She didn't know whether to laugh or cry.

I managed to watch three films, have a good sleep, little keeps me awake, and I quite enjoyed the food. I could tell Leah was nervous as she couldn't sit still. I offered her my aisle seat so she could get up and walk around, but she declined.

By the time we landed at Changi, it was late in the evening and a few of the shops were closed. Belinda had calmed down and maybe because she was now far from home, seemed less confident. It was difficult to match the well behaved, pleasant young lady who walked round with us as we browsed in the shops. She persuaded Leah to buy her some perfume, a silk scarf and a book. She was happy to drink coffee and sit quietly.

While we were killing time, I remembered something Leah had told me ages ago. "Haven't you got a brother in Australia?"

"A sister, Daphne."

"In Perth?" I held my breath.

"No, Brisbane."

I breathed out. "Miles away on the other side of the continent."

"Two thousand six hundred miles, I checked it out. Three days by car if you didn't stop."

"We have no idea how big Australia is."

Six hours can seem like an age while waiting in a half empty airport, but just as I had dozed off on the hard, plastic chair, it was time to board for the last leg.

We landed in Perth in the early hours of the morning, just as the sun was appearing above the horizon. It was easy to get a taxi although I'm sure the driver charged us extra for heaving the overweight suitcase in and out of the vehicle.

The hotel was in the centre of town and it didn't look that prepossessing but the reception area was pleasant and the staff were friendly.

They took our passports and copied them and gave us our plastic cards for the rooms but as we turned to go, the young girl called Leah back.

"Mrs Brand. I have a message for you." She handed Leah an envelope.

We squeezed into the lift which took us to the third floor and Leah and I left Belinda to manage her suitcase by herself. We were curious to see what she'd brought but we were playing it cool.

I was also dying to see what was in the envelope. It had to be from Mason, who else? In the room, Leah put it on the shelf under the television set. I didn't take my eye off it for a moment.

"Oh gross!" We turned to look at Belinda.

"What's the matter?" It was a perfectly ordinary hotel room, and I was pleased to see there was a kettle and sachets of coffee on hand.

"Is this it? One room?"

"What did you expect, a suite?" Leah snapped.

"I expected a room to myself. Do I really have to share with you two?" Belinda flung her arm out indicating the double bed and the single on the other side of the bedside table.

"I'm not made of money," Leah sighed. It's only for a few days.

"Well, I'm not sharing a bed with you. It's incestuous and I'm not cuddling up to her either."

"I quite agree," for once we were in harmony. "I'll check downstairs, I'm sure we booked two rooms, didn't we?"

Leah ran her hands through her hair. She looked frazzled and I don't think she was thinking straight.

"Leave it with me, I'll sort it out." I picked up the phone to call reception. Naturally I would prefer a room of my own but I needed to keep an eye on Leah. I didn't want her sneaking out for private meetings.

The hotel staff were very accommodating and half an hour later, Belinda was bouncing into her single room and Leah and I changed to a double, with two single beds. If Belinda went AWOL for a while, I wasn't going to let that worry me.

As I unpacked and hung my clothes in the wardrobe, I was itching to ask Leah to open the letter and read it to me, but she ignored it. Wasn't the bloody woman curious? What was it with her?

I offered to make us coffee and as I put her cup down on the shelf, I knocked the letter to the floor. "Hey, you forgot about this," I said as I handed it to her. For a moment I thought she was going to put it to one side, but after staring at it for a moment she ripped it open and a key dropped onto the carpet.

I picked it up. It looked like one of those keys that opened the left luggage lockers at any transport hub in the world. I turned it over and over in my hand. It caught the light from the window and fluoresced the number 2406 etched in gold.

"Safety deposit box?" I asked, keeping my tone light.

Leah looked up from the letter and shook her head. "Train station."

"Cloak and dagger, real spy stuff," I laughed and hummed the Pink Panther theme.

It was not enough to make Leah laugh. She folded the letter and pushed it back in the envelope and put it in her bag. I had no option but to hand her the key as well which she also tucked into the side pocket of her handbag.

"I don't know about you, but I'm going to take a shower. I need one after all that traveling." It was hard to sound casual, but I consider myself a pretty good actress. I transferred the small package I'd had sent down from London to my carry-on bag. I made sure that it was securely locked before I grabbed my washbag and disappeared into the bathroom. I was hoping that Leah would also want to clean up and to my delight, she was waiting as I emerged drying my hair on a towel.

The moment the door closed and I heard the water run, I lunged for her bag and removed the letter. It was short and to the point. Leah was to collect a packet from the locker at the train station and wait to hear from him again. There was no name on the bottom, and I couldn't swear that the handwriting was Mason's. Had I ever seen an example of his penmanship? I didn't think so. At that time, our affair was more a frantic, clandestine coupling to assuage lust rather than any deep romantic feelings. I would probably have been alarmed if Mason had begun sending me sentimental poetry. He just wasn't that sort of a man. In fact, I doubt lawyers who ran their own practice, wrote much by hand any more. They most likely dictated all their letters to some long-suffering secretary and scrawled a signature at the bottom.

But this letter had to be from Mason. Who else knew where Leah was except the couple of people I had told? Little did Leah know but I wasn't the only person who had booked a last-minute flight to Perth and who right now, was in a room on the second floor waiting my instructions.

Leah didn't take long to shower and I only just managed to slip the envelope back into her bag before she walked back into the bedroom.

"What do you want to do?" I asked her.

"First, find a chemist, I forgot to pack the toothpaste."

"Share mine."

"No, it's fine thanks. There must be a chemist near here, or a supermarket."

I wanted to scream at her. I'd have thrown on the first outfit that came to hand and raced to the train station and ripped open the packet. All she wanted to do was buy toothpaste. What was wrong with the woman? It reinforced my determination that she did not deserve a financial windfall. It would be wasted on her.

I smiled and suggested we take a walk and have a look around.

When we knocked on Belinda's door there was no

reply. Leah banged louder and louder but no one answered. "I don't believe she's gone off on her own. Where can she be?"

"Stop fretting Leah. She'll be seventeen soon. Some girls are married and have babies by now. She can take care of herself."

"I don't know how you can be so casual Andrea. Really I don't."

I caught the edge in her voice and backed off. "Oh, darling I'm so sorry, I didn't mean to sound callous. I guess it's not having children of my own. I don't understand."

"No, I guess you don't."

"I'm sorry, I was only trying to cheer you up." I attempted to give her a big hug but she shrugged me off. The problem with Leah was she could blow hot and cold.

I followed her to the lift and immediately the doors opened on the ground floor she asked the receptionist if they had seen her daughter leave the hotel.

"No, I think I saw her heading for the bar."

Leah scooted round the corner and sure enough, Belinda was perched on a stool, sipping what looked like a cocktail from a tall glass, chattering to the young barman. She looked up at Leah and her face fell.

"Young man," Leah addressed the barman. "Are you aware that my daughter is only sixteen…"

"Almost seventeen…" hissed Belinda glaring.

"And I believe it is illegal to serve alcohol to anyone under the age of eighteen in Australia. Am I right?"

"This is just fruit juice," Belinda snarled and wrapped her hands protectively around the glass. But before her stepmother could grab it to check, the barman shot out his hand, removed it and emptied the contents down the sink behind the counter.

Belinda went bright red. Her eyes glittered, her eyelids lowered as she slid off the stool and marched off out of the hotel. We followed.

We had only reached the gatepost when the barman came running after us. "You left this behind." He thrust a backpack at Belinda and she grabbed it with both hands.

"What have you got in there?" I asked.

"None of your bloody business." The teenager turned and stalked back into the hotel and made for the lift.

"That looked really heavy."

"Yes, it did and it might explain why she brought such a large suitcase. Certainly not clothes."

I agreed with her. Not knowing how long Belinda was going to be or if she was going to follow us, we decided not to wait for her but go in search of a chemist. Turning right at the end of the road, we walked down a steep hill. We could see the train station at the bottom.

"Mason must have chosen the hotel because it's so near to the station." I hoped Leah might take the hint and make for the lockers, but she turned left and we dawdled along peering in all the shop fronts. Leah only nodded, intent on hunting down the toothpaste she needed.

Despite it being winter it was not that cold, and I felt comfortable in a light jersey. There was a buzz, plenty of pedestrians, constant traffic but it lacked that frenetic feeling you get in London. The sky was blue with just the occasional white fluffy cloud. I noticed that most of the people were young. Men and women in business suits, twenty somethings pushing prams, crowds chattering in the eateries and trendy coffee shops.

We walked quite some distance before Leah dived into a small grocery shop and pounced on her favourite brand of toothpaste. I peered along the shelves while she queued at the till to pay.

"Wow that was expensive," she remarked as we walked outside and made for the nearest coffee bar.

"Looking at prices in general, they do seem high." I glanced at the tags on the mannequins in the window and winced.

"I guess most stuff is imported and that adds to the cost."

"It will help if we remember the exchange rate too. We get about one and a half Australian dollars to the pound."

"Ah yes, I'd forgotten that."

We pushed our way in between the closely packed tables and found two seats. A waitress came over and placing two glasses on the table poured water into both.

"Uh, we didn't order…" Leah began.

"Ah, you're English. I can tell from the accent."

"I can't place yours," I replied.

"South African. Perth is full of immigrants. Not too comfortable living over there now, not for us." She didn't need to elaborate. "The water is free and it's served everywhere, it's the law."

"That's a nice touch," Leah sipped from her glass. "A coffee for me and a doughnut if you have them."

"Sure." She moved off back to the counter.

"Strange, it's like home but it's not home, if that makes sense."

"I agree." I looked round and glared at one of the other patrons. Yes, he was supposed to follow us but not this close. I flipped my hand urging him to leave but he pretended not to see me and turned his back on me. I felt the anger push my blood pressure up but managed to keep my face neutral.

When the doughnut arrived, Leah was disappointed. "Not as good as the ones at our local café," she observed. "Are you sure you don't want something to eat?"

"No, not after the food on the plane and then again at Changi. I need time to let my tummy settle." I sipped my coffee as she ate her doughnut.

Leah stirred in her sugar while staring into space.

"Leah, what are we, uh you, going to do now? What did the letter say?"

"Only to collect what's in the locker and hold on to it."

"Aren't you curious?"

"Andrea, I can tell you are. Me, I'm a bit frightened. I can't help feeling that whatever it is, it can't be anything good. Mason is on the run you know." She sighed and put her cup on the saucer with a clatter. "I don't know why I'm here. I'm not sure it's too wise. Maybe I should have gone to the police instead."

"But why would you do that? The police never came looking for him, did they?"

"Goodness no."

"Then all you could tell them is that he skipped out on you, happens every day in every country in the world. All you know is he legged it because some of his disgruntled clients were after him. And do you remember who told you that?"

"Leo."

"Exactly. And while you trust him, I don't. He wouldn't know the truth if he fell over it."

"It was in the papers. 'Local businessman goes missing'."

"Yeah and the reporters probably got that from his firm or maybe one of his clients. No clients came knocking on the door trying to find out more either?"

"I have no idea. I wasn't there, I was locked up."

"Ah, of course. Did it ever occur to you that Mason may have driven you there for your own safety?"

Leah gasped. "No, never."

"If they were after him, and they couldn't find him, what better way than to hurt him by bumping you off?"

She sat still lost in thought. I wished I could read her mind. She shook her head a couple of times and then polished off the rest of her coffee and ordered another one. She grabbed my arm.

"Oh, Andrea what did I do? I moved away and then lived with another man and all the time my husband loved me enough to protect me?"

Personally, I didn't see it that way. But if it helped persuade her to meet up with him and stop her getting cold feet, then I'd support the theory I had just planted in her head."

"At the very least, you should collect..." I broke off as the waitress dumped two more coffees on the table and scribbled on the bill. "... what he's asked for and meet him.

Let him explain himself. You owe him that much."

"If only I knew who was really behind the trouble before. At one time you got the blame, then it was Leo and Belinda mentioned that her father asked for her help too. But that was months before he ran off."

"Mason had probably been planning it for some time. What you need to do now is collect whatever it is from the railway station, and then wait at the hotel for further instructions."

Leah glanced at her watch. "You're right. And I must go and check on Belinda. I think I have a right to know what she is up to."

"Of course, you have. Demand she show you."

"As we left the café, I appeared to stumble giving me the opportunity to elbow the man I'd glared at previously. Making sure Leah was not looking I hissed, "Keep your bloody distance you cretin."

He only grinned at me and concentrated on his meal.

I blinked as I walked outside into the bright light and caught up with Leah as she walked briskly back towards the hotel.

"Uh, the station? Had you forgotten?" I pointed across the road.

She stopped, flustered. "Oh yes, I had. I'm so tired of all this stress, I'm sure every brain cell has deserted me."

I squeezed her hand. "That's why I'm here, to take all your troubles away."

Leah gasped. "Don't, don't you dare start dancing in the street. I'll disown you." She walked on ahead and I skipped along to keep up with her.

"I'll behave, or maybe I won't," I laughed. "Cheer up Leah, no harm can come to you. I'll protect you."

Or maybe not.

She smiled and pushed the button on the traffic lights to cross the street to the railway station on the other side of the road.

It was not the biggest railway station I had ever seen but it was quite spread out. By unspoken agreement we were not going to ask where the lockers were, so it took us some time to find them.

Leah fished in her bag and looked along the rows of numbers. There were maybe three hundred lockers but certainly not two thousand. We stared at the key, the numbers 2406 showed quite clearly.

"Now what?" Leah's shoulders slumped. "Do you think it could be another set of lockers? Say for the bus station?"

I looked at the map. There is one the other side of Yagan Square, but I can't see there being that many lockers there either.

"I have an idea but we need to pick up a couple of things and go back to the hotel."

Half an hour later we perched on Leah's bed, and peered at the key. The magnifying glass I had purchased, enlarged the numbers so it was easy to see that two extra ones had been added, one at the front and one at the end. When I dug out the gold colouring, I discovered it was a little deeper in the two middle numbers.

"I don't understand," Leah muttered.

"I think whoever used the key added more numbers so, like us, they'd think they had the wrong station. I suggest we go back and try to open box 40."

"That's clever. I would never have thought of that."

"It's an excellent way of disguising a key." I agreed. "So, shall we go back?"

Leah groaned. "Not looking forward to tackling that hill again."

"Me neither, but I don't think it wise to take a taxi. Not if we are to remain incognito."

"Uh?"

"Like spies, remember?" I wound a scarf round my face and pulled a hat down low. "See now you'd never know it was me!"

Leah burst out laughing. "Oh Andrea!"

"Shall we go?"

She heaved herself off the bed but as she opened the door, she paused. "I'd better check on Belinda first."

"Leave her for now. Don't let's get side-tracked. Come."

Like a lamb, Leah followed me to the lift and down the hill to the station. It was time to discover what Mason was hiding.

To my annoyance, just as we reached the road at the bottom, my phone rang. When I saw who it was, I declined the call, but it rang again. "I'm sorry I can't take your call right now. Please leave a message and I'll get back to you as soon as I can."

"Who was that?" Leah glanced at the phone in my hand. "Do they know you are out of the country? Calls overseas cost a fortune."

"Only the dry cleaners." I thought that was quite clever, even if I do say so. "I expect they are wondering why I've not gone to collect my coat." Leah accepted that as the truth.

This time we knew exactly where the lockers were and I held my breath as Leah inserted the key into box number 40.

"If this doesn't work, then I'm giving up. I'll just have to tell Mason when he contacts me. It's ridiculous that he can't just go and get whatever is in there himself, but drags me half across the world to open some stupid box." Each time Leah got angry it was always a surprise.

The key turned on box number 40. We looked at each other and smiled, then frowned as we peered inside. It was empty. I leaned in and felt around, stretching my arm right to the back.

Leah tried too, running her fingernail along the metal seams top and bottom, but all we disturbed was the dust.

"Someone must have taken it before we got here."

"You didn't leave the key anywhere did you?

"No. It was in a pocket in my bag zipped up. No way someone could have grabbed without me knowing. And then they would have had to return it."

"Wait I've got an idea." I crouched down and peered at the roof of the small box. Stuck to the top was a very small envelope. "Yes!"

Before I could look at it, Leah's hand shot out and slid it into her pocket.

I was about to complain, but we had been hovering around the lockers too long and attracted the attention of a station official who came over to ask if he could help.

Leah got all flustered and it was left to me to make up some idiotic excuse. I'm not sure he believed we were working for a local law firm and looking for evidence, but relaxed when we walked away, leaving the key dangling on the open door to box number 40. I didn't look back but I heard him slam it shut and the click of the key as he locked it.

We hurried back to the hotel. Leah was fretting big time about Belinda worried where she was and what she was up to. But as soon as we were back in the hotel room Leah threw her bag on the bed and ripped the envelope open.

"He wants to meet."

"Mason?"

"Who else?"

I filled the tiny kettle with water from the bathroom and plugged it in. "Are you going to take Belinda with you?"

Leah paced back and forth over the industrial quality, brightly patterned carpet. "I should. She is his daughter. But he doesn't mention her."

I was through being coy, as I removed the letter from her hand and read it.

"King's Park. Let silent contemplation be your offering. Six three zero. What the hell does that mean?"

"I don't know." Leah nibbled her lip.

"Not a secret code for something you had when you were married is it?"

"I'm still married to him. He's my husband."

"Uh yes, sorry."

Leah mechanically tore open the sachets and poured them into the cups. "Those are the kind of words you might put on a war memorial. Is there one in the park?"

I checked the map. "Yes. It has a cenotaph overlooking the lake. Wait, I'll google it on my phone and maybe Trip Advisor has pictures."

Leah peered over my shoulder as I flipped past the views. "There, the exact words. And it's not a lake on the other side of the monument it's the Swan River."

"And I suppose the six three zero is the time?"

"Six thirty, I guess."

"But Leah, it will be dark by then."

"Maybe it's not in the evening. Maybe it's early morning."

More googling, as we discovered times for sunrise and sunset for Perth in June. It was dark for both. Daylight lasted from 7.17am to 6.15pm."

"This is nonsense. Parks close at night. Does Mason expect you to hide out when they close? Stay in there all night?"

Leah was tapping away on her phone in between taking sips of coffee. "Amazing, but some areas of the park are open all the time."

"Feeling nervous?" I could tell she was.

She nodded then glanced at her watch. "I must go check on Belinda and find out how to get to the park."

I stopped her before she got to the door. "I should come with you. I'm not happy about you being out there alone in the dark."

"I won't be, not if I take Belinda. I'd prefer it if you waited here Andrea. Then if I don't come back there is someone to raise the alarm." She closed the door behind her.

A lot bloody quicker if I raised the alarm if I saw her being assaulted, but it made no difference, she could want all she liked, I was going anyway.

I opened the packet I'd brought from England and turned the tiny black buttons over and over in my hand. It was difficult to believe they were as powerful as I'd been promised, but I had to hope they would work.

I waited until after five, then went to knock on Belinda's door. When she opened it, both she and Leah looked guilty and I could only guess what they'd been talking about. Full of apologies for disturbing them I handed Leah her coat, insisting that it would be cold in the park once the sun went down. She thanked me for being so thoughtful.

"Are you leaving soon?"

"Yes, in just a minute." Leah shrugged into her coat.

"And you're not invited," Belinda added rudely.

"No, no I'll wait here," I lied. As the youngster picked up her backpack, I helped her strap it on while inserting the smallest black button. She pulled away from me and I almost dropped it, but to my relief it slid down a side pocket and out of sight.

I waved them goodbye and watching to see they got into the lift, I slipped back into our room and returned the earlier call.

"Listen," I said, "if I cut your call off do not call me back. Do you understand?"

"Yes. How is it going?"

"They are on their way now."

"To meet up with Mason?"

"Yes. But I'll follow them. Just giving them time to walk out of sight. It's dark here at the moment so it should be easy."

"Did you fix the bugs?"

"Of course I did. We may be luckier than we expected.

Belinda is carrying a bag which I think might have what Mason wants. Her suitcase weighed a ton and I can only think that Leo brought something down from London. Mason had told Leah to empty a locker at the station, but there were only instructions for the meet up."

"Have you got a number for him?"

"Not yet, but if he takes the bag with him, I'll be able to find out where he is staying. Just sit tight and keep an eye on Leo."

"You don't trust him, do you?"

"I don't trust anyone but myself. And if you try and cross me your life won't be worth living either. You'll be watching your back for the rest of your life, if you can see of course."

"Understood Sis."

"And don't bloody well call me Sis!"

"OK keep your hair on."

I disconnected the call. How I hated having to rely on other people. So often they let you down.

I ruffled up the sheets and duvet on my bed and pushed my nightclothes under the cover, then slipping on my coat and pulling my hat down over my face, I turned off the lights and left the hotel room. I took the stairs to the ground floor and breathed a sigh of relief when I saw the desk was unmanned. I slipped out into the night.

The streets were brightly lit, so the walkway over the main road leading to Kings Park left any pedestrian exposed. I hunched down, glad to see there were a few other people about. I glanced occasionally at the GPS directions on my phone, shielding the bright screen in my hand. It would take me to the nearest entrance but from then I would have to follow the tracking device in Belinda's backpack.

The overhead trees made the walkways feel sinister as I kept to the shadows. Then I heard them talking.

"Told you Leah, we should have turned right, not left, but oh no, you insisted."

The clarity of their words made me jump back into the bushes and I quickly inserted the earpiece to cut out the reverberation. I smiled. The devices worked better than I could possibly hope for.

I waited before trailing them towards the river. I could see the tall stone monument and the path leading to the circular memorial to the brave soldiers who had fought in the First World War.

When the two of them reached it, they stopped and looked around. There was no sign of Mason.

"Where the fuck's Daddy? You sure you got the right place?"

"Yes. Those are the words described in the note, you can just make them out."

"Maybe we're too late. You didn't walk fast enough."

"Belinda, give it a break, will you? It's not yet 6.30 and we left in plenty of time."

Belinda's next words were conciliatory. "Yeah, well I forget sometimes you've only got one leg. We could have taken a taxi though."

"Remember your father is on the run from some nasty characters and maybe even the law. I have explained that to you. It's wiser not to leave a trail behind us."

"You still protecting him then?"

"What do you think?"

"You still love him then?"

"Let's just say the jury's still out on that one."

I broke out in a cold sweat when I heard that. Leah and Mason getting back together would ruin everything.

Leah leaned forward and pointed to the backpack on the ground at Belinda's feet.

"What's in the bag?"

"It's for Daddy. Leo gave it to me."

"Do you know what it is?"

"Nah. It's all sealed up. Papers." Belinda paused. "Was supposed to give it to you, but then you might have left me at home."

"No wonder your case was so heavy," Leah murmured.

A dark figure came out of the gloom and I breathed a little faster. But it wasn't Mason. It was an old man looking for a handout.

"Shove off," that was Belinda. Leah dug in her pocket and gave him some money. He thanked her profusely and shuffled off.

"What you do that for? He'll only go buy booze and get drunk."

"Precisely. It was the quickest way to get rid of him."

The minutes ticked by and I wondered how long they were going to wait. They both sat down on the low wall, whilst I remained hidden in the shadows, ready for a quick getaway the moment they set off back to the hotel.

Mason appeared so suddenly he made all of us jump. Belinda noticed him first and with a squeal of delight she threw her arms around him. He hugged her back rocking her to and fro. "How I've missed you, both of you."

Leah stood but didn't move.

Mason let go of his daughter and held out his hand to Leah. "What can I say?" His voice was husky and I could almost imagine he was close to tears.

"What can you say Mason?"

"Can you ever forgive me?"

"I don't know, I really don't know."

"Bill is living with us now," Belinda chipped in.

Well done kid.

"In my house?"

"No, we moved to Weston-super-Mare. It's quite cool living by the sea."

"Who's in the London house?"

"I dunno, probably Leo. He's got to live somewhere right?"

My mind was full of questions. What was in the papers in the backpack. Would the contents clear Mason, allow him to return to England safely? I had to hope Belinda would hand it over.

Leah turned to go but Mason stopped her. "Leah, Leah please listen to me. I'm sorry, so sorry about all this. I want to explain."

"All I know Mason is you dropped me off at a mental institution and then walked away and disappeared."

He pulled her arm and guided her to the wall and they both sat down. Belinda hovered nearby, listening.

"It was for your own safety. I was worried they would come after you if they couldn't get to me. I knew no one could hurt you in there."

"And you never thought to tell me, explain?"

"Can you honestly say that you would have volunteered to go into a place like that? And to be fair, you were falling apart."

"And why? Because you were driving me insane, with that dammed rabbit, the noises, things moving around the house. It was enough to send anyone mad and your attitude didn't help either."

"I had nothing to do with any of that. As far as I was concerned you were not making any sense and I put your behaviour down to your imagination. I thought you were attention seeking when I was frantically trying to hold everything together."

"Attention seeking!" Leah sprang to her feet. "How dare you. Have you any idea of what I went through? The fear, the uncertainty? No, all you cared about was keeping your business going, maintaining your reputation in the community. You cared more for your status and standard of living than you did for me."

Mason stood and held on to her wrist. "I admit that's true. I don't deserve your forgiveness but I hope in the future you will understand why I did all that. Now I have what I need to clear my name and put everything right. I'll prove it to you, but it might take time."

He reached over and grabbed the backpack. I thought for a moment Belinda was going to stop him but he tugged it sharply off her shoulder and tucked it under one arm.

I couldn't see Leah's face too clearly but I could see her wavering. Did she believe him?" I guessed not for her next words surprised me.

"Mason, I want a divorce."

"No Leah. No. I won't agree. Give me time, please darling? I still love you so much."

I thought I heard Belinda grunt. What was her take on this? Who would she support?

A party of young people was approaching along one of the paths and Mason looked up in alarm. "I can't stay, it's too dangerous. Please give me a second chance. I'll make it all up to you both." He pulled Leah towards him and wrapping his one free arm around her kissed her hard on the lips.

Leah didn't pull away. She was always so indecisive. Dear God that woman had no backbone. I'd bloody kill a man who'd treated me that way.

"Hey you two, what about me?" Belinda whined.

Mason turned to her, but kept glancing at the raucous group who were now a lot closer. "Be a good girl and I'll keep in touch, promise. Look after Leah for me and keep her safe. Don't let her trust anyone."

"Phone me. Once a week, please." Belinda called after him plaintively. But he had melted away into the darkness.

Leah sank back down onto the low wall, head in hands.

"Come on, I'm cold." Belinda whined and began to walk back towards the park entrance.

I glanced down at the little black box to see the red light blinking. Mason had no idea I was tracking him. I didn't need to hear what Leah and Belinda said on their way back, so I switched off the microphone and raced around the bushes intent on getting back to the room and into bed before they returned. I'd not run far before I realised how unfit I was. I needed to get over the bridge before they reached it. I could probably talk my way out of following them but matters were complicated enough. I also needed time to think and plan my next move. Strange Mason didn't mention the station locker, I thought as I hurried back. Was that just a blind to see if we had been followed? He may have been watching us. A shiver ran down my spine.

JUNE   LEAH

Dear Diary,

I have just come back from meeting Mason for the first time in months. I'm sitting in the hotel bathroom so I don't disturb Andrea, who bless her, is fast asleep. I'm not sure it was a good idea to even come to Australia but I did and I don't regret it, but now I'm wondering how much danger I may be in and Belinda too. Is Mason's story believable? He may have had me locked up but Belinda was a sitting duck for anyone who wanted revenge. I'm not sure who to believe anymore. Mason? Leo? I know I'm not the bravest of people but however awful she is, I need to protect Belinda.

And do I still love Mason? I honestly don't know. Bill is so sweet and comforting but there isn't quite the same spark. Yes, I felt something when Mason kissed me. If he can clear his name and we are a family again and Belinda grows out of her agro behaviour then life could be wonderful. So many questions, so few answers. Please, someone give me a sign.

JULY ANDREA

July is usually one of my favourite months, but here I was in the middle of an Australian winter, and it was decidedly chilly. It's not all sun, sand and sea down under that's for sure.

Leah was very subdued the following morning so I didn't press her about her meeting with Mason. I wasn't to know she'd seen him at all of course. I had only just flung myself into bed before she returned and pretended to be fast asleep.

There was no sign of Belinda when we went down to breakfast, but that didn't bother me. A few extra minutes without her whining and complaining suited me fine.

I was extra gentle with Leah, offering to fetch her a second coffee and went to ask the staff when I saw they had run out of marmalade. I checked the app on my phone surreptitiously and was relieved to see that the tracker in the backpack was still transmitting. I had no idea how long the signal would last so I would have to find an excuse soon to wander off on my own.

"Leah, I guess you met Mason last night?" There it was out in the open.

Leah plastered her toast with butter over and over, lost in thought. She nodded.

"I need a few bits and pieces, so I'll give you time to think." I dropped my serviette on the table and stood up. "See you back here at lunch time?"

She nodded again and piled huge globs of marmalade on top of the butter. She was far away and if I'd told her I was going skiing in the Alps she would have responded the same. I didn't care one bit about giving her any time to worry herself to death, but I had urgent errands of my own to run.

I squeezed her shoulder and I could feel how thin she was despite all the food she ate. "I'll be here to listen when you're ready to talk," I whispered then I left the hotel and walked briskly down to the shopping area looking for a quiet place to phone England. The open area at Forrest Chase was as good as anywhere. It was deserted at this time in the morning with few pedestrians and even the water jets lay silent. I sat on one of the benches and tapped in the number I knew by heart.

Leo answered on the first ring. "I've been waiting for your call," he snapped.

"I'm sharing a room with her, it's not as if I can say, 'Hey, I'm calling the man I'm not supposed to be talking to.'"

"OK don't get your knickers in a twist."

"Don't be crude Leo. What news? Did you go down to Weston?"

"As instructed. I had to hang around all day, forgot he's at work."

"A few of us do that, you know, leave home in the morning, go to an office, perform tasks then…"

"Don't give me that crappy nonsense Andrea."

"Tell me what happened."

"He wasn't going to let me in, but I was too quick for him." Leo laughed. "The old geezer was so intent on not dropping the pizza and the bottle of wine he was carrying it was a piece of cake."

"Very clever," I snarled.

Leo sniggered. "Anyhow, I frightened the life out of him."

"No violence I hope."

"Not much."

"Leo! I told you to be careful. Bill is not that young and at his age he could have a heart attack."

"Stop worrying. I know how far to go. Scared him shitless though." Leo couldn't stop laughing. "I could see he was about to piss himself. Silly old codger. Threatened him with the police for having drugs on the premises, said I knew Belinda had a stash in her bedroom. Boy did that rattle him. He didn't know which way to fucking turn. Was quite a laugh."

"I see you picked up some new pastimes inside."

"You got to blend in to survive."

"Well I'm not one of your inmate buddies. You'd do well to remember that. It wouldn't impress your father either."

"Heard from him?"

"Not personally, but Leah met up with him last night. She took Belinda."

"And?"

"Those voice things worked brilliantly. You can thank your mate for them."

"Having low friends works both ways. Untraceable too, an extra perk. So, don't keep me hanging on, what did he say?"

"He was contrite with Leah. And Belinda handed over a backpack."

"Great. Those were the files I gave her."

"You could have told me. I hadn't the faintest idea what was in there."

"You don't need to know everything."

"Sod that, I'm a major part of this team and don't you forget it. I demand you keep me in the picture."

"Oh shit!"

"What now Leo?"

"Didn't you tell me that Leah has a sister in Australia?"

"You can rest easy. She's not in Perth. Leah told me she's in Brisbane, miles away. Maybe you don't realise how big Australia is. It's as far as Spain to Moscow or maybe even farther from one side to the other. Since you've never been here, you wouldn't know."

"That's a relief."

"I can tell you something that will wipe the smile off your face. Mason was talking about getting back together, a cosy little family again."

"Balls to that. She didn't fall for it, did she?"

"She did ask him for a divorce, but he can be very persuasive."

"Yeah, well, work on her. The last thing we need is for them to…"

"I know what to do, trust me. It's Mason I don't trust. Whose side is he on?"

"Guess we'll find out sooner or later."

"That's a great comfort. Still this call will be costing me a fortune on roaming. Keep an eye on the flat in Weston and make sure he moves out."

"Will do. When you due back?"

"At the weekend. I don't want to find him there, got it?"

"Loud and clear. What you going to do now?"

"Stop wasting my time with you and go track Mason down."

I disconnected the call. While I trusted Leo, I had little time for him. He could be useful on occasion. I deleted all record of my conversation off the phone and checked the location app again. The red light was still blinking, but it didn't flash as brightly as before. I needed to move fast. I called it up on Google maps and was relieved to see it was not that far away.

I walked to the end of the square and grabbed a taxi which dropped me off in a residential area closer to the university and government offices. There was a row of shops on the street level with flats above. Mason could be in any one of them. The little red indicator beeped louder at the far end of the street but it could not pinpoint which of the entrance doors was harbouring the transmitter. I dithered, walking back and forth thinking. There had to be a way to find the exact location.

I hesitated outside one of the doors leading to the apartments above peering at the names on the doorbells. It was unlikely Mason would have labelled his, so I took a chance and pressed the only one which did not have a label.

I thought I heard a click on the other end and some

heavy breathing before it shut off again and then fate rewarded me as a young couple opened the door from the inside and even held it open for me to enter. I took the stairs, preferring not to alert Mason who might hear the lift working. He might be on his guard after I rang his doorbell

I was sweating by the time I reached the third floor and paused to take a few deep breaths. The day was warming up a little and my heavy coat clung to me.

The little light on my phone blinked stronger, I was in the right place. I didn't ring the bell in the hallway but thumped heavily on the door, pressing my thumb against the spyhole. Nothing moved inside, but I had a sense that someone was there. I banged again, louder this time.

Mason opened the door a little and peered out then flung it wide open.

"Good heavens Andrea what are you doing here? Come in."

The apartment was small and dingy, little more than a bedsit, with flimsy cotton curtains in a dull orange shade. There was one brown couch which I guessed doubled up as a bed, a small shag carpet on the floor and two doors which I guessed led to a bathroom and a kitchen.

Mason had been working on his laptop, papers from the abandoned backpack scattered on the coffee table and the floor. He had not shaved and looked unkempt. He was jittery. I noticed a half empty bottle of whisky on the sideboard below a small television set fixed to the wall. It was a depressing and dreary place to hole up and I wasn't going to hang around.

When I left him an hour later, my ears were ringing, full

of his promises that he was still on board and his loyalties had not changed. I was still not convinced. He was confident that he now had the paperwork to get himself out of trouble with the clients who were threatening him, but he was cagey about who they were or what they were after. He did check my mobile number and promised to get in touch the moment he was clear to return to the UK.

Before I left, he tried to take me in his arms, but I pulled away.

"I'm not in the mood Mason, not now. Let's wait until all this is settled. I'm not going to rush into anything. Who knows how we'll feel once we have our hands on the money?"

He dropped his hands and gave me his puppy dog look. I almost laughed but reminded myself it was always good to have the upper hand. I'd keep him dangling on a string a little longer.

As I retraced my steps back to the hotel, I could feel the fury rise at the work we still had to do. It should have been so simple and then Mason had to stuff it up by getting himself into a mess and then running away. I was so lost in thought as I walked back to Leah, that I almost forgot to buy a few items to explain my absence.

I found Leah fully dressed lying on one of the loungers by the pool. She was the only one there.

I hurried over. "Leah, are you all right?"

She opened her eyes and peered up at me. "As all right as you might expect."

"You poor darling." I pulled the closest sunbed next to

hers and held her hand. "What can I do to help?"

"What can anyone do?" She sighed.

I'd promised not to pry or at least wait for her to talk, but I couldn't hold back any longer. Would she give me an accurate description of her meeting with Mason? She wouldn't have a clue I'd heard every word.

"How was Mason last night?"

"Jittery. Contrite. Almost humble."

"Is that why he wanted to meet, to apologise and make it up?"

"Only in part. I think he was more interested in what Belinda had brought him."

I frowned pretending not to understand. "Belinda? She went with you?"

"Of course. He is her father."

"So, are you getting back together?" I held my breath.

"It's not as simple as that. He can't leave here and I'm not staying here. Maybe once he's cleared his name and comes back to London, well we'll see."

"Oh darling, can you forgive him? Do you want to?"

"He said it was all done to protect me."

"I guess that could be true. He was mixed up with some unsavoury characters." I stood up pulling on her hand. "Come. Let's have a stiff drink at the bar and let Aunty Andrea cheer you up. You will have to decide which of the two men in your life you're going to choose. Exciting Mason or boring old Bill. I'll help you forget both of them and after a few drinks you won't even remember Mason and his crooked clients and their threats. They can't get to you here."

Leah had no option but to scramble to her feet and let me lead her back inside. I'd ask nothing more about the meeting but let it rest.

I carried the drinks back from the bar to a table next to the window. Leah sat watching the dust motes float through the air.

"Just one more question. Are you meeting up with him again?"

"Mason?"

"Who else?" Leah could be so pedantic at times.

"No, nothing planned."

"So, that leaves me to entertain you the rest of the time we are here. What shall it be? We can go for a walk in Kings Park." I watched Leah shudder. "Or a trip to the Mint to watch them pouring gold, or how about the zoo? It's not only for the kids you know."

"Pouring real gold? That sounds cool." Belinda's voice behind me made me jump. I needed to work on my nerves.

The kid plonked a large glass of bright green juice on the table and sat down. "We should do something in Perth. Seems such a waste. Any clubs with some decent music? Or are they still in the dinosaur era down under?"

"Do shush!" Leah looked around fearful. "Remember we're guests here so keep it down."

"Yeah, yeah whatever." Belinda's waving hands sent her drink flying, flooding the table and dripping onto the carpet.

Leah groaned. "I just don't need any extra problems today."

"Huh, you think you got problems? You have it easy. In

the old days parents stayed together for their children. Not selfish like today."

"You really think that?" Leah was mopping up the table with serviettes, doing her best at damage control.

"Leave it," I hissed. "They have staff here to take care of all that." I tossed back the rest of my drink and stood up. "Let's go upstairs, freshen up and take Belinda to see the gold pouring." That attracted her attention.

I stalked off to the lift, leaving the other two to trail behind me.

The tour around Perth Mint was interesting and even Belinda didn't grumble or complain. She stood for ages watching the liquid gold as it flowed from the ladles and was transfixed by the displays, especially the largest gold coin in the world.

"Did the Guinness Book of Records people really fly all the way here just to check this was the biggest?" she asked one of the officials.

"Oh yes. It's 99% pure gold."

"Wow!" Belinda then wandered on to the shop and gazed at all the jewellery for sale. "Hey Leah you can sell your gold here. Bet they'd give you a decent price."

Leah smiled. "I don't own that much, only my wedding rings and a pendant. I'm sure Andrea owns more jewellery than I do."

Not yet, but give it time.

We meandered into the café for a full Devonshire cream tea.

"What now?" Belinda asked as she mopped up the jam

and cream with the last bit of her scone. "Shall we hit the shops? That's if you're not going to buy me some fabulous bits of gold Leah."

"I wish I could but…" her stepmother flapped her hands.

"Not many young ladies get flown to Australia." I reminded her.

"Yeah well got to miss school so that's gotta be a plus."

"Isn't there anything you like about school?" I asked her.

"It's naff. Teachers are dozy, the other kids just babies. Nah, ready to leave. I would if I'd not promised Dad."

"He expects you to go to uni?"

"Yeah and then go and work in his boring old office. Yeuk. Not for me some small dusty room with piles of paper working out how to get slippery clients off the hook. Well that was before, before all the fuck up."

I saw Leah's eyes open wide and she didn't even bother to complain about the language. Belinda had a better handle on Mason's nefarious dealings than his new wife.

I suggested that hitting the shops before they closed was not a bad idea and then maybe a stroll around Elizabeth Keys.

Belinda knew how to twist Leah round her little finger as she succeeded in charming her into buying two tops, a skirt and three pairs of leggings. She was all sunshine and light a regular Pollyanna as she wheedled her stepmother into paying for it all.

We had two more days left before flying home, so we took the train down to Freemantle where we visited the

Roundhouse and the prison. Belinda had been chattering non-stop, asking the guide one question after another, but even she fell silent when we walked into the execution chamber and observed the noose hanging over the empty pit beneath. Even I gave a shiver and gave thanks that few countries retained the death penalty. Not that I had as yet broken the law to any great degree, but I couldn't be sure that might not be the case in the near future.

Walking back out into the bright sunshine we caught the bus back to Perth and had supper at a pizzeria not far from the hotel.

Leah did not say much when we got back to our room and I decided it was because she was tired. To my surprise she slipped out into the corridor and I heard her knock on Belinda's door. Since she'd not taken her coat off, the little black button I had slipped into her inside pocket was still working.

I listened in for a while until I got bored. They were discussing Mason and Belinda was all for forgiving him and welcoming him home. She could not see he had behaved badly in any way. I could tell by the tone of Leah's voice she did not agree. They didn't argue or shout at each other. The conversation was more a debate and it was not likely to reach any conclusion. It would be up to me to drop hints to ensure that Leah didn't change her mind and I might also drop the odd comment to Belinda to poison her mind against her father.

JULY   LEAH

Dear Diary,

I can't think. I can't concentrate. Part of me refused to believe that Mason would materialize out of the darkness in Kings Park. It's been so long since I last saw him and there are days when I never think of him at all. Yet there is still that charisma and I can sense the strength in him, even when he's fighting for his career and maybe even his life. Do I believe him, or is it all nonsense? The biggest question is, did he have me committed to keep me safe, or to get me out of the way? Leo says he had me locked away to get his hands on my money, but surely two insurance payments can't be worth all this bother? I'll hardly be that well off after the financial stuff is settled.

And then there's Belinda. Should I deprive her of time with her father? I would hate to be the reason the family is split. But then she will soon be leaving home and it will be up to her to decide how much she sees her father, and her mother, come to that. I've asked her several times if she ever talks to her mother but she has never given me a straight answer.

The only thing I can do is to take one day at a time. We leave for home soon and maybe things will seem clearer there. I think it's time to talk this over with Bill, get his take on it. Maybe we can make sense of it together. Thank you for Bill, he is such a comfort. I am looking forward to seeing him. I've missed him.

AUGUST   ANDREA

The flight home was uneventful. Belinda was extra
irritating. She hardly spoke to either of us. Was it because
she wanted to stay with her father? Or the dressing down
Leah gave her for disappearing the last two nights to who
knows where? She really is a little shit, totally out of
control. What she needs is a boot camp for a couple of years,
that would lick her into shape. If she was going to ignore us
then two can play at that game. Wish she'd wandered off in
Singapore and missed the flight, but no such luck.

We took a taxi from the train station, and I got the
driver to drop me off first. I'd had a gutful of the pair of
them and needed time alone.

The flat looked even more drab after the comfort of the
Perth hotel, but I was now counting weeks rather than
months before I could leave.

I checked in with Malcolm my contact at the insurance
company to catch up. I wanted him to send Leah a letter
with a couple of hundred thousand pounds to suggest that
was the total due. She'd be happy with that, she doesn't
need more and she wouldn't be expecting it.

Malcolm promised to see what he could do, but he
wasn't very optimistic that it would work.

I'd only just emptied my suitcase and loaded the

washing machine when Leah was on the phone. She was frantic. Bill had gone! I was sympathetic, made all the right noises and said I would be with her as soon as I could get there.

Leo had done something right for once. I admit he can be scary when he wants to be.

Belinda let me in and I found Leah huddled on the sofa in the TV lounge, curled up in a ball, crying her eyes out. I resisted the urge to shake her and put my arms around her.

"Come on, it can't be so bad. So, Bill's gone out? I'm sure he'll be back later."

"I don't think so. He's pushed off. Taken all his clothes and moved out." Belinda loomed over the sofa, hands on hips. "Good riddance too. Doubt we'll see him again," she added.

While I agreed with her, Belinda could do with a lesson in tact.

"Leah darling. It's not the end of the world. How many times have I told you we don't need men in our lives? Look at me, deliriously happy on my own."

"I'm not you Andrea," she sobbed. "It's not having a man, it's what's wrong with me? First, I'm a widow, then my husband runs out on me and now Bill has gone too."

"They're all shits," Belinda added. "Girlfriends are the best any day."

"See? For once Belinda agrees with me."

"I wasn't referring to you." She grabbed a large plate from the cupboard and began to liberate food from the fridge, piling it so high it was in danger of falling off the edges. The chair screeched as she pulled it out and sat at the table shovelling chunks of cheese and ham into her mouth as fast as she could.

I ignored her and turned back to Leah. "Did he leave you a note? Tell you why he was moving out?"

She nodded.

"Show me."

I could have guessed his handwriting would be the script we all learned in school, all those curly letters we were forced to keep between the lines.

Dearest Leah,

By the time you return from Australia this letter will be waiting for you. I think it wise to give you a little space for now as I cannot be the cause of bringing you more grief and unhappiness. Forgive me, it's for the best.

Love

Bill

Well that was short and to the point. I breathed easier to learn that he did not mention Leo and his threats, even if it gave Leah no real reason for his abrupt departure.

"Darling, did you have a fight before you left?"

"No, nothing like that. He was so understanding about the trip. Wished me the best and said it would either provide closure or I would decide that Mason was the right man for me."

"Good riddance," the words floated across from the dining table where Belinda was still munching her way through the mountain of food.

I glared at her. "Try to be a little kind for once," I

snapped at her, but she only shrugged her shoulders and carried on eating.

"I cannot understand why he's not given you any real reason. Did you phone him from Australia?"

"No. Only one text to say we had arrived safely. Roaming costs so much I switched my phone off."

"It's all water under the bridge. Time to start afresh." I sat up. "Tell you what, I'll move in, keep you company, so you are not alone."

"Oh yeah and what about me?"

"You're not any bloody help Belinda. Leah needs a friend, not more grief."

"Charming I'm sure." She stood, brushing the crumbs off her hands onto the table. "Don't mind me, I only live here. What do I matter? Nobody asks me what I want. No one cares about me. It's as if I didn't exist for all anyone cares." She stalked off into her bedroom slamming the door behind her.

I gave Leah one last hug and told her I would go straight back to my place and collect my things before she had time to think about it. As I got to the front door, I remembered the bug and dived into her coat pocket and retrieved it. I didn't want her finding that and asking awkward questions.

I moved in the same day and made myself at home but living with Leah strained my patience to the extreme. I had not realised how pernickety she was. My house in London was always clean and tidy but that was due to the cleaner who came in three times a week. If you don't count the stay in Perth by the end of the first whole day in Leah's flat, I was ready to tear my hair out. She was just so neat and tidy it was enough to make anyone scream.

As a reminder of our friendship, I placed the friendship teddies side by side on the shelf near the television. I'd had to nag Leah to find hers which she dragged out of a cupboard in the lounge.

Belinda kept out of the way, appearing at meal times consuming large quantities of food and then disappearing back into her room. Most evenings I heard her creep out, leaving a trail of perfume along the hallway. I didn't mention it and I don't think Leah even noticed.

We heard nothing from Bill. Leah was tempted to go and see him at the college library but I managed to persuade her she would look pathetic and desperate. If he wanted to return to her he would. They would soon be breaking up for the long summer holidays and then there would be no way of knowing where he was. I knew he didn't like me and I hoped we'd seen the last of him.

All hell broke loose on the third night. It must have been about three in the morning when we were woken by loud bangs on the front door. I sat up in bed, rubbing my eyes, fumbling for my dressing gown. If someone didn't open it soon it wouldn't withstand the force. I heard Leah open her bedroom door and shuffle past. I tiptoed across the room and peeped out.

The moment Leah turned the knob the door flew open and three large men came flying into the hallway. One pinned her hard against the wall. She managed one shriek before her attacker covered her mouth with his hand. Her eyes bulged, she began to slide to the floor, with his other hand he grabbed her round the throat and held her up.

The other two stormed into the lounge ripping open the cupboard doors, sweeping ornaments off the shelves, the china and glass figurines tinkling as they smashed onto the floor, exploding into a sparkling shower as they flew into the air before settling like ice crystals on the wooden floorboards. They flipped back the curtains, flung the cushions off the sofas, ripping them apart with knives and pulling out all the stuffing.

I kept well back in the shadows, watching Leah as she whimpered, her eyes wild and unfocused, I don't think she really understood what was happening, or how her home was being destroyed.

The thugs returned to the hallway, kicked open the door to Belinda's room took one look at the cult posters and left it alone. They moved on to the open kitchen / dining / TV area, wrenching open drawers and letting them crash onto the floor. They upended the television, which landed on the dining room table the black screen cracking down the middle before they yanked the cables from the wall. The taller of the two threw open the fridge door and swept all the food off the shelves, half a pie landing on a carton of milk which poured out onto the floor mingling with a jug of fresh orange Leah had squeezed that afternoon. The liquid seeped under the cupboards and over to the table.

The crockery and cutlery fell into the orange puddle, together with the vegetables from the upended rack. Not content with that, the intruders unscrewed the tops off the herb and spice jars and sprinkled those over the mess around their feet. One had a high-pitched giggle which ran straight though me. Like unsupervised schoolboys let loose for the first time, they destroyed everything they could see.

The shorter one, dressed in a well-worn parka and chukka boots, stormed off into Leah's bedroom but reappeared a moment later. He caught my eye as I shrank back into my bedroom and nodded as he joined his fellow intruder still pinning Leah to the wall. I could see the tears running down her cheeks as she was struggling to breathe. It took all my strength not to tell her to knee him in the balls but she was paralysed with fear.

The third man finished in the kitchen and all three loomed over my friend. The leader slid his hand into his pocket and brought out a lighter. He flicked the wheel against the flint and waved the flame close to Leah's eyes.

"We will be back. You better pay up what you owe us or next time we won't be as gentle."

Leah was flung to one side as they marched out slamming the door shut behind them.

The silence was deafening. Leah slid to the floor staring straight ahead, her prosthesis at an odd angle, reminding me of a rag doll I once owned. I rushed to her side.

"Leah, can you hear me? Leah are you all right? Talk to me."

"Andrea, who were they? What did they want?"

"I don't know darling," I found myself shaking. For once I had no idea who had sent the intruders. Had they come on the instructions of Mason's disgruntled clients?

Were they Leo's prison mates who decided to frighten Leah near to death? Had I pre-empted Belinda if she was taking drugs and owed a local dealer? I had no idea and no way of finding out.

I helped Leah to her feet and we shuffled through the debris and sank onto the couch. The one cupboard they hadn't touched was the cocktail cabinet. I fetched a couple of plastic tumblers from the kitchen, careful not to step on the broken glass and shards of china and poured us both hefty slugs of brandy.

Leah's hand was shaking so much I had to hold the beaker so she could drink. She gulped a huge mouthful and coughed violently, her whole body shuddered and her eyes watered.

"Another one," I urged her, supporting her hand to stop her from spilling it. "Hey, we've enough mess to clean up without you making it worse."

She stared at me for several moments before breaking into fits of giggles. I wasn't sure if she was laughing at my joke, or was in the grip of hysteria but my attention was diverted by a sound from the front door. I stiffened. Had they returned?

It was Belinda's key in the lock. She blinked as she walked in, expecting the apartment to be in darkness. She saw us and was about to say something when she noticed the puddles on the floor and the broken china.

"What the fuck!" She disappeared into the lounge and looked around then checked out her bedroom before walking into the open plan kitchen area.

"Fuck! Did you two have a fight or something?"

"Don't be so bloody stupid, Belinda. We had uninvited visitors, who were not particularly careful."

"Sheesh." If Belinda was drunk when she opened the front door, the chaos around her had sobered her up. That was not enough to stop her searching for an unbroken glass and helping herself to a generous portion of the brandy.

"So, these uninvited visitors, friends of yours or hers?" she pointed at Leah before taking another slug of her drink.

"I have no idea why they were here or who sent them – neither of us do."

Leah struggled to sit up. She turned to Belinda. "Did they come from your drug dealer?"

"My what!" Belinda sat down suddenly on a dining room chair. "My what!" she repeated.

"The person who sells you your drugs." Leah enunciated each word slowly and carefully.

"I don't take no fucking drugs," Belinda shouted. She rose and pressed her face close to her stepmother's. "No, not ever so you can get that crap idea out of your head right now."

"Then who do the drugs Andrea found in your room belong to?"

"You..." for a brief moment Belinda was lost for words as she turned to glare at me.

"Only because we cared," I said quickly. "Your dilated pupils, your moods, huge appetite, sleeping half the day." My words tumbled out one after the other.

"You went through my room?" She rounded on Leah.

"No, Belinda, I did. Your stepmother tried to stop me, she has these antiquated ideas of privacy, and respect. I have no such qualms. And yes, I found drugs, Xanax and Ket.

And if you don't believe me, I took a photo on my phone. I have proof."

She frowned. "I don't understand. I've never taken drugs ever. They do your head in. Drink yes, never drugs."

"Maybe one of your friends?" Leah's voice was low and hesitant.

"I ain't brought that many back here. It might have been…" she paused, not about to give us a name.

I shook my head. "None of this makes sense. These guys were professional, they knew what they were doing."

"You knew them then?" Belinda reacted quickly.

"No, don't be stupid. They were heavy duty. Look at all the damage, who would order that for a few hundred pounds of overdue drug money?"

"Never a dull moment living with you is there Leah? Never know what to expect any time I come home."

"And what time is this to come in? Where have you been?" I'd ask even if Leah didn't have the guts.

"Down at the Club in town, as if it's any of your business." She looked round and wailed. "Oh shit, they've totalled the telly." She picked up one corner but the outside frame twisted and the screen broke into even more pieces. "Why did they leave my bedroom alone?"

"They didn't bother with the bedrooms, just the lounge and in here."

Leah stood, gave herself a good shake. She tossed back the rest of the brandy then bent over to tighten the straps on her leg. "I'm going to bed. I've had enough excitement for one night, and if they come back then they will have to knock the door down because I won't answer it."

"Surprised the neighbours haven't been round," was Belinda's contribution.

"If you'd seen them you would understand." Bed was a great idea, but before I closed my door, I was surprised to see Belinda slip into Leah's room. Perhaps the girl had feelings for her new parent after all.

I couldn't sleep. Thoughts whirled round and round in my head. Who'd ordered this? The only clue was the look given to me by one of them when he walked past my bedroom door. If they were sent by Leo would he have told them to leave me alone? No, that didn't make sense as he wasn't aware that I was now living with Leah.

I tossed and turned until the early morning when I must have fallen asleep because the next thing I remember was waking to Belinda's screams.

I threw on my robe and rushed into the kitchen.

"What's going on?"

Belinda was sitting on a chair with her leg up in the air, while Leah was holding a bowl of water in one hand and attacking her foot with a pair of tweezers.

"Someone walked barefoot and got slivers of glass embedded in her feet."

"Ouch. Careful!"

"I'm being as gentle as I can, but for heaven's sake keep still."

"Who were those people?" Belinda tuned to me. "Friends of yours?"

"Watch your tongue young lady. Do I look as if I knew them?"

"Yeah well, Leah's not exactly the type to consort with

guys who'd smash stuff." She waved her arms to indicate the damage.

"Keep still. There's more in here." Leah attacked her foot again.

I swept then vacuumed the floor and turned on the coffee machine. "Would you believe this is the one thing they didn't break. There's always a silver lining."

"Yeah and I guess I get to be grateful they didn't smash up my telly either." Wasn't that thoughtful of Belinda?

"Oh good, then Leah and I can come and watch our favourite programmes in your room." I scrabbled around picking up the coffee pods which had scattered over the floor in all directions.

"You wish. Dream on."

"That's kind of you," I replied.

The rest of that month saw no further incidents. There was no way to replace the ornaments the family had collected over the years. A few, I knew, belonged to Mason and some to his ex-wife Caro which she had left behind before her mad dash to South America with her boy lover.

Leah shed silent tears over her precious dinner service, not a single piece had survived. She would never be able to replace it she said as she swept the pieces up and flung them in the bin. I was amazed to see that several pans from her stainless steel cookware set were dented and the handle had come off one saucepan. It must have taken quite a battering; the advertising companies tell you those are indestructible.

The Friendship Bears had survived, our visitors had not

ripped them apart and I picked them up and placed them back on the empty television shelf in full view.

It had taken less than half an hour to wreck the flat but it took us three full days just to clean up the floors and walls where the flying chips had scuffed the paintwork. We had long discussions on what to salvage and what to throw out. Leah reasoned that it would cost more to have the lounge suite re-covered and stuffed than it would to buy a new one.

My suggestion of claiming on the insurance was shot down the moment I mentioned it.

"We don't want the police here!" Leah exclaimed. "What could we tell them?"

"Case of mistaken identity? Tell them the truth, you have no idea who they were and what they wanted or who sent them."

"We've been over this before, we've talked and talked, trying to answer those questions and we've got nowhere. I can't claim on insurance without a case number and that's an end to it."

For once, Belinda was subdued but she was also helpful. It was the school holidays and she stayed in most of the time. I tried to chat to her, to discover if she was hiding anything but she blocked me every time I opened my mouth.

The big fear, none of us mentioned, was the men returning. It made Leah nervous cleaning and replacing. We couldn't help worrying that the moment we got things back to normal they would reappear and reduce the flat to chaos again.

I accompanied Leah on the shopping trips to buy cutlery and cookware. I was curious to know if she was choosing cheap items because she didn't have the money to buy expensive replacements or she wasn't taking a chance on having them smashed a second time.

The atmosphere in the flat was uncomfortable. We were all jittery and jumped at every little noise, creak and bump. The neighbours, in typical English fashion, didn't say anything, but now they didn't smile or wave but avoided us and scuttled away every time we went out. It was awkward, but what could we tell them? It was amazing they hadn't called the police.

To escape the oppressive atmosphere, I took myself off for long walks on the promenade, or wandered aimlessly around the shopping areas. It was frustrating that I couldn't get hold of Leo or Malcolm. Why weren't they answering? I had sneaked into Belinda's room when she was taking a shower and copied Mason's number off her phone. It was the only chance I had, that phone was permanently welded to her hand.

When I tried the Australian number, I got the disconnected tone, so I guessed he'd used a burner phone and it was no longer in service.

I had no idea what to do and that made me so angry. I needed to be in control of events and I was now left just to babysit Leah. Nothing was moving forward and September was fast approaching.

AUGUST LEAH

Dear Diary,

I promised myself I would not sink into another pity party and allow life to beat me down like it did before. I cannot understand why I'm facing one disaster after another. I'll ignore the car crash and losing a leg, that can happen to anyone. People lose their lives every day on the roads the world over. But ever since that damned dog Zeus died my world has been turned upside down. If I had an ounce of strength, I'd walk away from all of them, even Andrea. Much as I love her, I find living with her stifling. I can't laugh all the time. I don't want to laugh all the time. Her jokes are becoming tiresome, her fussing over me, is driving me insane – ha, there I go again. I know I shouldn't be ungrateful, not everyone has such a good friend but I'm longing for some me time, time alone.

Belinda has been a lot quieter as well. She's also super-attentive but there are only so many cups of coffee I can drink in a day and I'm going to scream if she brings me one more bar of chocolate, or another bag of doughnuts. Soon, I'll be the size of a house.

I'd love to go away for a few days, by myself, to a hotel in the Lake District. Dare I leave Belinda with Andrea? I wish I didn't feel so responsible. I'll suggest it tomorrow and see what the other two say

SEPTEMBER ANDREA

My nerves can't stand this any longer. I need to speak to Leo and find out what the hell is going on. I'm not about to discuss it with Leah either. I need a break from her. I admit she has not been as clingy as I expected, even I was shaken by the home invasion – what neat words they use these days for thugs tearing your house apart. But I can't remain upbeat all the time watching brave little Leah attempting to hold it all together. A quick trip to London, as a refresher, should set me right.

I packed my overnight case, scribbled a brief note to Leah, left it on the hall table and was gone long before she got up. I left the car at the station and jumped on the first train heading east.

As I got off at Paddington I smiled. It was refreshing to be surrounded by the hustle and bustle of the capital. I stood and watched the crowds pouring out of the station. Businessmen making for the city, mothers with prams hauling more brats behind them, out of work artists in bizarre outfits, every day office workers and young teen shoppers, early talented buskers playing for pennies. I even appreciated the heavy flow of traffic, each vehicle adding to the sense of importance, rushing from one point to another on urgent business. I filled my lungs with the carbon monoxide fumes from the exhaust pipes as they passed.

For the first time in weeks, I felt alive. Perth had been tame, laid back and spread out with its wide roads, SUVs and huge shopping malls. In contrast Weston-super-Mare was a sleepy backwater, home to retirees, who never moved faster than a tortoise with sore feet.

It was so pleasant to walk along my own familiar street, the small mall where Leah had those coffee dates with Bill, the tree lined street where Mason used to walk Zeus and the dark brooding house sitting between the Brand family home and my house. I paused to read the 'For Sale' sign planted next to my gate post, then whirled around to look behind me. There was an identical sign outside Leah and Mason's house – though who it belonged to now was debatable. To the man who had disappeared, his wife who was miles away, or his son?

A cloud of musty air from the hallway greeted me when I opened the door, pushing it against the pile of mail that had fallen on the inside mat. I picked it up and flicked through it as I waited for the coffee maker to brew my favourite Java blend. Mostly bills, circulars, even a few cheeky invitations from estate agents assuring me they had a list of cash buyers just desperate to buy my property. As if one For Sale sign wasn't enough, put them all up and you advertise yourself as desperate.

A peep into every room told me that nothing had been disturbed. I wouldn't have put it past Leo, or Malcolm for that matter, to break in and make themselves at home at my expense.

I carried my coffee and rest of the mail into the lounge and sank down onto the sofa. It was going to be hard to leave, how many days dared I stay away? Two, three or more?

I kicked off my shoes as I walked up the stairs and threw myself on my bed for the best sleep I'd had in weeks. My last thoughts on closing my eyes were that I hoped Leah would understand.

When I woke up, it was well after lunchtime and my stomach reminded me that I'd only had a coffee and early snack on the train, since yesterday. I stumbled downstairs still half asleep, alarmed to see a shadow framed in the glass in the front door.

The chimes of the doorbell echoed around the hallway but I decided to ignore it. No one knew I was here and I wasn't expecting anyone. I slipped into the kitchen and rooted around in the cupboards for something to eat.

Whoever was standing on my doorstep was persistent, holding a finger on the button, creating a constant jangle which echoed in my ears. I marched to the door and flung it open. Malcolm stood there with Leo bouncing up the path behind him.

"What the fuck are you doing here?"

Malcolm grinned. "Can't hide from me Sis. My radar's always working." He pushed past me and strode into the kitchen.

"Don't call me Sis!"

"Only do it to annoy you. Fun, see?" He leaned his face next to mine and I could smell the liquor on his breath.

"And you can put those away too," I pointed to the cigarettes and lighter he drew out of his pocket.

"Spoilsport," he grumbled, tossing them from hand to hand.

"I've never allowed smoking in this house and the last thing I need is cigarette fumes greeting any prospective buyers they might bring round."

Malcolm sighed as he turned the key in the back door and stood just outside before lighting up.

I turned to Leo. "I want some answers from you."

"What have I done now?"

"The heavies."

"What heavies?"

"Don't pretend. Those thugs you sent round to scare Leah. Old prison mates?" I couldn't tell from his face if he knew anything. "Come on, don't act the innocent with me. It had to be you."

"I haven't the faintest idea what you're talking about. Tell."

Malcolm stubbed his fag out and came back inside. "You can tell me too. What the hell you on about?"

I described the threats and destruction at the flat. As I spoke, I glanced from one to the other but neither gave me any indication they were involved.

"Must be Dad's clients. They have plenty of undesirables on the payroll who excel in little visits like that."

"Then what was in the files you gave Belinda to take to him?"

"She tell you that?"

"Yes. Is it true?"

"I only followed the Old Man's instructions. He called me, from Brazil I think. He told me to pack up certain papers that were in his desk and give them to Belinda. He didn't know she'd moved to Weston, but before I could explain he'd rung off."

"Did you keep the number?"

"Tried to. Caller ID was blocked. I pressed the recall button immediately but I only got the disconnected tone."

"You and me both. He's in Perth."

"His dad's in Scotland?"

"No, Western Australia. He was there, who knows where he is now."

"Gets around doesn't he? For a bloke who's got no money." Malcolm pushed past me and ferreted in the fridge. "No beer?"

"No, you'll have to make do with white wine."

He pulled a face and poured himself a coffee instead.

"You knew where we went, you promised to shadow us," I turned to Leo.

"Yep, my mate told me you fingered him on the plane. As instructed, I told him to stay there and keep an eye on Mason, if he showed up. He saw you visit the flat."

"Ah, so, you know where he is?"

"Uh no. He gave my guy the slip."

"You lost Mason? That's bloody great. Can't trust you to do anything right."

"Hey that's not fair." Leo ducked and moved round the central island as I threw the sugar jar at him. It crashed against the wall.

Malcolm looked startled. "I hope you remember Andrea you only brought me on board to check out the insurance claim? All I had to do was tell you when they were ready to pay out. Leo may have got one of his mates to shadow you overseas and spy on your old boyfriend, but I was the one with the contacts to source listening and tracking devices.

It's adding up to a larger share of the loot. I hope you bloody realise that."

I sighed. "Yeah you're right. It's all got a lot more complicated than we planned. We hoped you'd be able to divert the money to us, leaving enough so Leah wasn't suspicious."

Malcolm pulled up a stool. "The compensations start next month when we begin paying into the bank accounts or posting the cheques."

"Oh shit. And we don't know where Mason is. What the fuck are we going to do?"

"I can try and buy us a little time."

"How?"

"I said before, I can push her name to the bottom of the list but that's as much as I can do."

Leo drummed his fingers on the table. "Can't you just make out two cheques, one to us directly and one to her, enough to keep her happy and shut her up?"

"Leo, don't be so fucking stupid. You have no idea how insurance companies work. There are too many checks and balances and we're talking millions here man. It would never work."

"Send millions my way and they'd never find me. If my old man can disappear so can I."

"Yeah right, with the cops on your tail. We always follow up with every client, to make sure they've received the money and are happy with the settlement. If your stepmother learns how much her pay-out is, she will be screaming to the police before she's read the letter."

"We're screwed then." Leo covered his face with his

hands and slumped onto the counter. "All this bloody work for nothing. Months of moving furniture, wiring up the house, hiding out in that mausoleum next door, tracking them down to Weston, it's all up the shoot."

I watched the two of them. How easily men gave up. "Look, if we have to take a hard line then let's do it. Leo's right. We've put too much into this to let it fail. It's OK for you Malcolm, you've got a steady job, but Leo's existing on benefits, and I'm down to my last few pennies. I'm prepared to do whatever it takes."

"So, are you suggesting we cut Mason out?" Malcolm asked.

"If he doesn't pitch up before she gets the money, yes."

"Dad will go ballistic."

"Yes, he will, but that can't be helped. You can do what you like, but I won't be hanging around to find out. He doesn't know about Malcolm and once you get your share, Leo, it's up to you what you do with it and where you go. Wait here for Daddy if you want."

"No bloody way! If he's stirred up enough shit to get those guys to put the fear of god into Leah, then I'm not hanging around."

"Let's leave it at that then. How many days do we have Malcolm?"

"About a month at most. The courts just turned down the final appeal so as soon as my company access funds and balance the books, we'll be ready to pay out."

* * *

I breathed a sigh of relief when I let the two of them out. While I kept a smile on my face, and made all the right noises, they had no idea I wasn't planning to share a single penny with either of them.

I ordered in a few groceries, cooked myself a simple meal and was settling down to watch a film when my mobile rang. I glanced at the number, it was Belinda and she was beside herself.

"Andrea, where are you? Why aren't you here?"

"I just needed a few things from home darling, so I popped up to London to get them."

"You've got to come back now, immediately."

I sat up. "Calm down. What's the matter? What's happened?"

"It's Leah, she's leaving."

"What!"

"Yeah, she's packing right now and leaving in the morning and I can't stay here on my own. I'm too scared. What if those men come back?"

"Where, where is Leah going?" My mind was racing. I jumped up, sending the supper tray crashing onto the carpet as I began pacing the floor.

"Up north somewhere. Her mother has died and she has to go and bury her or something."

I gave a sigh of relief. "Is that all?"

"What do you mean, is that all? It's enough, isn't it? She's leaving me alone. She says I'm not to miss any more school. She says that if she's not here then I'll be quite safe. I don't believe her. She's falling apart Andrea, not thinking straight."

I agreed with Belinda. Leah was acting irrationally. Leaving the kid alone was not a good idea. "Keep it together kid. I'm on my way back and we can all go north together. Stuff school, your safety is more important. In fact, it might be wiser to move all together. I'll see if I can persuade your mother."

"Stepmother." Belinda never missed a correction.

"Stepmother," I agreed.

I was in a filthy mood by the time I got to the station, dragging my hastily-packed bag behind me. I needed time to think, re-group and now this. I needed a bereaved daughter like I needed a hole in the head.

As the taxi dropped me off at the gate, I noticed Belinda watching out for me from the lounge window. She had both doors wide open before I closed the front gate. I found Leah in the kitchen cooking meals ready for the freezer. She had spooned mince into a foil tray and was spreading mashed potato over the top. She looked up threw down the spoon and flung herself at me, wrapping her arms so tightly I could barely breathe.

"Thank god you've come back. I thought you'd disappeared as well."

"Don't be such a daft duck. You know me better than that. BFF, remember?"

Belinda stuck her fingers in her throat as if to throw up. She was such a drama queen. I glared at her.

"My mother died last night." Tears welled up in Leah's eyes.

I couldn't understand it. That woman had been a total bitch to Leah, made her life hell as she was growing up and now the stupid woman was crying because she'd kicked the bucket. I'd never understand her, I'd be dancing in the aisles cheering.

"We are coming with you tomorrow so we can all face this together." Behind Leah's back I saw Belinda pumping the air and prancing up and down.

It took all my patience to calm Leah down and I even got her to laugh a few times that evening. The care home phoned again to confirm we were coming, and assured us all the arrangements had been made. In her more lucid moments, Leah's mother had left exact instructions as to what she wanted, had a paid-up funeral plan and there would be little to do besides attend the service and collect the few possessions she had left behind.

It was a solemn drive north. I couldn't think of anything to say. Once or twice, Leah tried to recount a few pleasant memories she had while growing up, although there were not many.

Belinda sat quietly in the back not saying a word. She'd not been too impressed with her one and only stay in Leah's childhood home and it always hits the young when they are faced with death. I remembered how I felt as a teenager in a similar situation. It would be the first time she had been close to a death.

The staff at the home were kind and caring. They treated Leah gently and asked if she wanted to go and say goodbye.

"What the fuck does that mean?" Belinda whispered to me. "She's dead, isn't she?"

"The funeral home will have collected her and dressed the body and then put her in a casket for people to see before they close the lid. It's a chance for relatives to pay their last respects."

"Oh gross!" Belinda pulled a face. "And will Leah go? And, ug, will she kiss the dead body?"

"She may do. It's up to her."

The girl suddenly clutched my arm. "She won't make me do that will she?"

"No, don't be silly of course not. But," I paused for effect, "it might do you some good to see a dead body. We all have to go at some time or another."

Belinda began to tremble so violently I thought it was some kind of fit. She staggered back to the car and flung herself on the back seat and sobbed. Her behaviour was more than strange. I was torn between supporting Leah or finding out what was wrong with the teenager.

I drove to the undertakers. Leah could hardly see for the tears streaming down her face. After a couple of wrong turns, I parked between the white lines outside and helped Leah out of the car. I looked back at Belinda but she shrank down in the back seat so we left her there.

A small bell tinkled above the door as we went inside which I thought was inappropriately cheerful. Church music, low and soothing, played in the background as our feet sank into the deep pile, fluffy, maroon carpet. The sofas and chairs were an unremarkable grey, and the pictures on the walls were scenes of hazy figures walking towards a bright light in the far distance. The coffee table held brochures of funeral plans and coffin designs.

No sooner had we walked in when an impeccably dressed young man appeared and asked how he could help. It was easy to guess his profession from the black suit, highly polished shoes and the faint odour of formaldehyde that clung to him. He ushered us into one of the viewing rooms where Leah hesitated before creeping towards the coffin.

I had never met the woman lying there but I loathed everything I had heard about her. It was beyond me why Leah was grieving. Good riddance I would have thought. She never had a kind word to say to her daughter and that was long before the dementia had set in.

The weather mirrored Leah's sorrow the following morning as a handful of mourners gathered in the local crematoria. Besides Leah, Belinda and myself there were two staff members from the care home. Five people left to say goodbye, one who hardly knew her and one who had never met her. What a sad end to a wasted life.

Leah had contacted her brother Martin in Canada and her sister Daphne in Australia but both said they were unable to travel so far and there wasn't much they could do when they arrived. They had both sent large wreaths, which along with Leah's, now balanced precariously on the simple pine coffin.

We sang one hymn and our voices wobbled and echoed thinly in the empty chapel. Leah continued to weep, the tears continually rolling down her cheeks, her mascara leaving black streaks resembling a clown escaped from the circus.

We drove back to the care home where they invited us in for tea and cakes. They reminded me of Leah clones, as I watched them bustle around the lounge, whispering kind words to the old crones who sat staring into space like breathing mannequins. Quiet, respectful, caring women who were devoting their lives to caring for these oxygen thieves whose relatives were probably paying a fortune to keep them fed, sheltered and out of sight. Those with the money could salve their consciences by transferring their family duties to these underpaid skivvies. Is this the best they could hope for in life? Did these overworked carers ever dream of hitting the casinos, buying satin dresses and dancing until dawn on some tropical island? I guessed they had come to accept their lot in life.

Before we left, they handed Leah a black, plastic bin bag which she packed into the boot before we drove away.

"What's in the bag?" Belinda asked as we turned out of the driveway.

"Mother's things," replied Leah, wiping yet more tears from her eyes.

"Shit is that all? Everything? One sodding bag?"

"We can't take it with us," I reminded her.

"Only one bag," she repeated.

"It is sad," Leah's voice was a little above a whisper.

"I guess you don't need much living in a residence. Couple changes of clothes, few pictures and ornaments and so on." The moment I said that I shivered. I was just past forty, not so many years left and I was damned if I was going to let this final opportunity pass me by.

This trip had been good for me, it hardened my resolve.

From the way Leah rushed into her bedroom pulling out the drawers and looking in the wardrobe, I think she was checking to see if Bill had returned. If she had heard from him, she had not told me and I wasn't going to ask her.

Belinda also disappeared into her room, slamming the door behind her. When I put my ear to the keyhole, I thought

I could hear her sobbing but decided not to get involved. Teens are very unpredictable.

Leah called to tell her supper was ready several times, until eventually she came and sat at the table. She toyed with her food, pushing it round and round her plate taking no more than a couple of mouthfuls.

I shook my head when I sensed Leah about to question her and not one word was spoken before Belinda abruptly left the table and dived into the safety of her room again. For once, we were not deafened by the raucous cacophony she calls music.

"I think the whole funeral thing has shaken Belinda." Leah said as she carried two glasses and the wine bottle, to the table in front of the television.

I noticed the friendship teddy bears were now on different shelves, so I moved them next to each other linking the arms together. I glanced back and smiled at Leah before sinking down next to her on the sofa.

I flicked through the channels with the remote desperate to find something to watch. "I'm not sure it upset her that much." I suspected Belinda was worried about something quite different to Leah's deceased relative.

"Poor kid, she's had such a rough ride."

"Come on Leah. She's got a home, food, shelter, education, health facilities. More than the vast majority of the world."

"Yes, the practical stuff, but mentally she must be suffering. Absent parents, thugs trashing the flat, uprooted to a new town."

"You're too soft Leah, always making excuses for her.

Kids are tougher than you think. She's got the confidence to go out clubbing and get drunk. She's been brought home by the police more than once."

"I know all that Andrea. All hallmarks of unhappiness."

"Did you do that?"

"What?"

"Get drunk, take drugs, mix with unsavoury types?"

"No."

"Then there's no need for her. Let's forget all that for now and find a decent film to watch. Stop worrying."

Over the next few days Belinda's mood didn't change. She was jumpy, spent hours in the bathroom and barely exchanged more than a couple of words with either of us. Once again, the atmosphere in the flat was oppressive and depressive. I took every opportunity I could to escape.

On Friday, Belinda stayed out all night. Leah was beside herself. I could hear her pacing the hallway outside my bedroom well into the early hours. I was still in my nightclothes the following morning, munching on a piece of toast in the kitchen when Belinda walked in the front door. Leah was waiting for her.

"Where the hell have you been?"

"Out." Belinda tried to push past her to the fridge.

"Out where? That's not an answer. Where and with who?"

"None of your sodding business." She pushed Leah to one side and opening the fridge removed a bottle of milk.

"Do you realise how worried I was? I've been up all night, waiting for you to come home."

"Yeah well I'm back now so why don't you go back to

bed?" She poured the milk over a bowl of cereal and sat down at the breakfast bar.

"Anything could have happened to you. Why do you do this to me?"

Belinda flung her spoon down, it bounced on the counter top and clattered as it hit the floor. "It's always about you isn't it? You! You! You! What about me? Ever think of that? No, you're too selfish!" She swept her arms wildly from side to side sending the cereal bowl crashing to the floor to land beside the spoon. Then she stalked out and slammed her bedroom door behind her.

Leah stood gazing at the mess for a moment before bursting into tears. I thought about going the comfort route, then decided I couldn't be bothered. It was about time she stopped allowing the child to upset her.

Leah blubbered on about how and why she had gone wrong with Belinda which was a good time to remind her about the drugs. I asked if she wanted me to search her bedroom again, but Leah shook her head firmly and told me not to put a foot in there. I shrugged, went and got dressed, put my coat on and gathered my bag on my way out to the hairdressers. Once there I threw caution to the winds and booked to have my nails done, a pedicure and highlights. To hell with the money, I'd put in on the credit card.

I didn't hurry back to the flat, but dawdled, gazing in the shop windows before stopping off for a coffee. As I stirred in a heaped teaspoon of brown sugar I wondered if Leah would be worried. I'd been out all afternoon and she was nervous and jittery on her own. To hell with it, she wasn't my responsibility.

My phone buzzed. I guessed it was Leah wondering where I was, wanting to know when I'd be back. I dragged the handset out of my bag and glanced at the screen. No caller ID, my heart beat a little faster as I pressed the green button.

"Hello."

"Andrea?"

"Yes. Mason?"

"Listen carefully. I'll be back next month. Everything under control?"

"As best as I can tell."

"Keep it on the boil and don't call."

"You know she's in Weston, but I might be at my home?"

"All in hand."

He rang off. No goodbye. No encouraging words, but he was coming back. Had he sorted out his problems? Did he plan to stay in England? So many questions, so few answers.

Leah was waiting for me in the hallway when I got back. "I didn't find anything."

"Leah, give me a moment to get my hat and scarf off and put my slippers on." I didn't hurry, as she followed me from room to room bursting to tell me her news. I sauntered into the kitchen and liberated the wine bottle from the fridge door. I poured myself a large glass, and perched on a kitchen stool and turned to her. "Now, what is this urgent news?"

"I didn't find anything in Belinda's room. Not one pill, not one grain of powder. She's not into drugs Andrea and I'm so relieved."

"That is good news." I watched as she helped herself to the wine. "She may be going cold turkey, would explain her weird behaviour."

"No, I can't believe that. I would know if she was high."

"Would you?" I raised my eyebrows and then shook my head. "Name me the symptoms."

Leah struggled to remember. "Pupils enlarged?" She fell silent.

"There see. You're not sure. Just ignore it all Leah and stop fussing." I spoke too sharply and I saw Leah wince, but I was past caring. My patience was wearing thin and I wasn't sure if I could keep up the charade for, how long would it be, the next four to six weeks?

We sat in the TV lounge and watched a film in silence. It didn't have much to commend it, one of the many that Hollywood churn out one after the other. Totally unrealistic though, the baddies got caught in the end, seldom happens in real life.

I stood up and stretched, I'd been sitting too long curled up and rubbed the cramp in my leg.

Leah glanced at her watch. "Belinda's not home yet, it's late."

"At one of those clubs for sure. She's got her own key so you're not going to wait up for her again, are you?"

"No, but I doubt I'll sleep."

I offered her one of my sleeping tablets but she refused and after tidying up in the kitchen she wandered off to bed. I slept like a baby. When I got up the following morning Leah was pacing the kitchen in her dressing gown.

"What's up?" I made a beeline for the coffee maker.

"Belinda didn't come home again last night."

This was the second or third time I'd lost count. I shrugged. "Maybe she spent the night with friends." That was one of many suggestions I made but Leah wasn't having any of it. She continued to fret even when I told her to phone the hospital, the police station and if she was that desperate, the morgue.

The colour drained from her face and I could see her beginning to descend into the same spiral of panic she'd followed only a couple of years ago. She refused to go to her water aerobics class, even when one of the other amputees phoned to meet up with her.

She buried herself in her usual domesticity, and after promising to make phone calls for her later, I stepped out of the flat in an effort to stop myself from screaming.

We drew a blank with the police. Belinda had not been picked up. She had not been taken to hospital either and despite me suggesting she was probably shacked up with some boy, Leah got more and more hysterical.

"For heaven's sake Leah, she's almost an adult. She's old enough to look after herself."

"She's still at school!"

"Yes, but only because she's taking A levels. Thousands of children her age have left and are out there working. Stop trying to smother her."

"I'd be just as worried about you if you were out all night without saying where you were going and when to expect you back." She stormed off feather duster in one hand dragging the vacuum behind her with the other.

She had a point but I was not going to agree with her.

* * *

Another day passed and by now Leah was quite frantic. She filed a missing report but admitted to me on her return that she did not mention the visit we'd had from persons unknown in the middle of the night.

"Leah you think they have taken her don't you, our night time visitors?"

"Yes, and that's what scares me. I'm going out tonight to the clubs. Someone may know where she is."

"That's the craziest idea I've ever heard of. Don't ask me to come with you."

"I won't."

SEPTEMBER   LEAH

Dear Diary,

My hands are shaking so much I have trouble holding this pen. Everything, just everything is falling apart. Where to even begin. Belinda has disappeared, and I just know they've kidnapped her. Why don't they phone and tell me what they want?

How I miss Bill, but it's for the best. I couldn't put him through this. He's better off without me. I care for him too much to make his life miserable. He texted me every day at first but I didn't answer and now he doesn't contact me anymore. I guess he's somewhere in Weston but if I think I see him in the street I duck into a doorway. Everyone whose life I touch suffers. I'm a harbinger of disaster.

My one true friend, who has been my rock, is increasingly distant and if I'm honest, she suffocates me. I can't laugh at her jokes anymore I've heard them all beforeand her platitudes are beginning to grate on me. I've caught some odd expressions on her face, usually when she thinks I'm not looking or reflected in the mirror when she doesn't realise that I can see. I'm beginning to wonder why she puts up with all this chaos. Does she really like me that much, or is she putting on an act? I can't describe in words this feeling of unease I have but it gets a little stronger every day.

This year is flying by, yet so much has happened. It will be October tomorrow. I've decided to go and search for Belinda at all the nightclubs. I wonder how many they have in Weston? I'm not looking forward to it but the police are not taking her disappearance seriously. The friendly sergeant told me that over three hundred thousand people go missing every year in the UK alone, and many of them are never seen again. I can understand the police not being overly concerned, it's not as if she was a really young child. I promised to inform them when she came home. They are convinced she'll come crawling back. They hinted teens returned when the drugs wore off, or the boyfriend threw them out. The most they would do was circulate copies of the photo I'd given them and ask the patrols to keep an eye open. At her age she is legally allowed to leave home, so there's no crime to follow up. Should I have told them of the threats the intruders made? It took a lot of courage to even go to the police station. I've not forgotten I was a person of interest when my mother fell down the stairs. If it hadn't been for Belinda lying to them, they would have arrested me for assault or attempted murder. I still have nightmares about being locked up. Prison terrifies me.

It will take every bit of courage tomorrow to go searching for her, but I'll do it. I owe her that much and I won't sleep if I do go to bed.

OCTOBER ANDREA

I watched Leah put her coat and scarf on by the front door and stuff money and keys into her pockets. She had spent the afternoon researching every club and dive in town and was hell bent on her quest to visit them all. I could sense her dithering but I looked the other way and turned up the sound on the late evening news. She was just waiting for me to change my mind and go with her, but I didn't even glance back when I heard the front door close behind her.

I must have dozed off for the next thing I remember was a frantic banging on the front door. Much more of this and the neighbours would have us evicted.

I peeped through the spyhole. If it was the same crowd as last time, I would be phoning the police but when I saw who was on the other side, I flung the door open in a fury.

"What the fuck are you doing here?" I snarled as Leo barrelled past me and made for the fire to warm himself.

"It's bloody freezing out there."

"You didn't come here to give me a weather report. I expressly told you to keep away."

"Yeah, I know, but it was getting on my nerves sitting at home waiting to hear. The payout should be any day…" He paused. "She's not here is she?"

"No, she's out clubbing."

"What?"

"Not what you think, Belinda's gone AWOL so she's off on a mission of mercy."

"Shouldn't you be with her?"

"In theory, yes." I scowled as I watched Leo make for the cocktail cabinet and run his eye over the line of bottles. "But I've had her up to here, I'm sick of her. She can get herself mugged, for all I care."

Leo poured himself a hefty glassful of vodka and knocked half of it back in one go. "Naughty, naughty. It's your job to babysit the goose that lays the golden eggs."

"I can't see you being that patient."

"I can take over if you like."

"Over my dead body." Did Leo seriously think I would let him keep tabs on Leah? I didn't trust him an inch. "Well now you've had a drink, you can bugger off."

"Come on, it's cold out there."

"If you don't leave, I'll have you thrown out."

"Oh yeah, you and whose army?" Leo smirked and turned away to top up his glass.

"Leo, have you taken Belinda?"

"Have I what? Don't be so bloody stupid."

"I wouldn't put it past you. She's never stayed away this long before. Even mousy Leah braved the police station." I was pleased to see the alarm in Leo's eyes. With his criminal record he had no desire to get involved with the law.

He slumped down onto the sofa leaned back and put his feet on the coffee table. With one kick I sent them skidding off.

"Read my lips. I do not want you here. Get out or I will

call the police and lodge a complaint of harassment, or rape or whatever it takes."

His face went white and he froze. "You can't mean that," he spluttered.

"Try me and see."

He pulled himself to his feet and swallowed the last of the vodka before slamming the glass down. "I thought we were partners in crime. You wait till I tell Dad."

"Tell him whatever you want. I don't trust you Leo. I don't know that you've not stashed Belinda away somewhere. I don't trust those heavies didn't come from you. And when I tell your father how you've been harassing me, he won't trust you either."

"Why you little bitch." Leo took two strides towards me his eyes blazing, his whole body shaking, but I was too quick for him. I darted back into the hall, grabbed an umbrella from the stand and drove it into his stomach.

He screamed and doubled over clutching his belly.

"If you want more then hang around."

Leo got the message. He shuffled towards the front door which I obligingly opened for him, and still bent in two, he fell against the lift door and pressed the button.

I slammed the door and fixed the chain across. Belinda would have to wake me to let her in but that was a small price to pay.

I overslept the following morning and it was after nine when I opened my eyes. I stretched, imagining the feel of real satin sheets, a jacuzzi at the end of my bed and a sun with real heat.

It wasn't until I was brewing the coffee in the kitchen that I remembered the chain on the door. I checked and it was still in place. So now both of them had stayed out all night. Should I worry? The goose that was about to lay the golden egg was missing. I had no idea where to go and look for either of them, I could hardly report it to the police and I thought it unlikely either had got into any serious trouble. I'd wait a few hours.

It was pleasant to have the place all to myself. I had a leisurely bubble bath, washed my hair and settled down with a murder mystery. Doubtless the alcoholic detective and his young, pretty, female sidekick would nail the miscreant before the final page, but I knew it wasn't going to be realistic.

I lay back and had a good think. All of us had failed to research as carefully as we should have. When we thought that having Leah committed would be sufficient to deprive her of her compensation, we'd been wrong. Leo and I believed that having Malcolm as a contact in the insurance company, he would be able to divert the funds to us. Wrong again. I had the uneasy feeling we'd behaved like amateurs. Maybe it was time to realise the only way we could legally benefit was to remove Leah altogether.

I'd never considered murder before, wasn't sure I was capable, but I was beginning to change my mind. It can't be too terrible. One quick knife stroke, that's all it would take. There was one loose end to tie up first. I'd just have to be patient a few more days. In fact, if there was nothing much I could do here, as soon as Leah came back, I would take off and stay at home in London for a few days. It was the only way I could think of to keep my sanity.

I got very nervous as the day passed and neither Leah nor Belinda returned. There had been no ransom call and I'd kept the phone with me, even carried it into the kitchen and bathroom. It didn't ring once, not even some poor schmuck trying to flog double glazing or a sun room extension. I didn't dare leave the flat just in case there was a call on the land line.

It rained at lunch time, and the grey clouds hung low over the sea, and the afternoon dragged on. The book held little interest, and the news on the television was depressing with more politicians squabbling.

It was six o'clock and dark. I went to make myself a cup of coffee. I'd polished off one bottle of wine today and needed to keep my head clear. There was nothing I could do but wait. Where the hell were they?

For once I did not sleep well that night. I tossed and turned for hours. Every little creak from the contracting floorboards, every car that drove past had me wide awake and sitting up, ears straining. I was tempted to take a tablet or two to knock me out but I needed to stay alert.

By lunchtime I couldn't stand it any longer. I'd paced the flat from one end to the other, desperate enough to haul the vacuum cleaner over the carpets. I'd changed all the sheets, had a good poke around the bedrooms, spying in all the cupboards and drawers. It was when I discovered Leah's diary that I got the biggest shock. She was having doubts about me? I was getting on her nerves. I'd overplayed my hand.

How could I put this right? The old saying 'absence makes the heart grow fonder' popped into my mind. We had been living too close for too long. Moving in with her had been a mistake. The answer was to leave, at least for the moment. When she came home, as of course she would, she'd expect to find me here. It would throw her off balance to find me gone. No shoulder to cry on, no one to share her experience.

With both of them missing for all this time, the police were bound to get involved. It would not be wise for me to remain here. I needed to be as far from Weston as possible. I could always get Leo to say I had been in London the whole time. If the wheels were about to come off, then I wanted nowhere near the train wreck.

I made up my mind, dragged my suitcase off the top of the wardrobe and began to pack. I would leave enough stuff behind to show her I would be back and I'd write a note with some excuse about sorting affairs in London so she'd know where I was. I'd give her time and space. It was the perfect answer. It would also give me time to get my head together. I began to pack feverishly, eager to leave before she returned.

Once back in London, I breathed in the polluted air and wondered if all my plans to say goodbye to England forever had fallen apart.

OCTOBER LEAH

Weston took on a whole different face at night. The friendly streets I enjoyed during the day, took on a dark and sinister feeling as I hurried past darkened doorways and threatening alleyways rubbish piled high at the entrance. I looked at the map, I would start with the clubs in the main streets first.

I clutched copies of Belinda's photo, ready to show to the youngsters queuing outside. My first impression of the crowds was the tenacity of the young girls waiting in the freezing cold with barely enough clothes on to keep them warm indoors. I guessed that frenetic dancing and a few drinks would warm them up, but they were prepared to suffer the cold to show as much flesh as decency allowed. Of course, they were in hunting mode.

The first line of youngsters all shook their heads, some barely glanced at the photo. When I walked to the front of the queue, the bouncer, at least I guessed that's what he was, refused to let me inside.

"Not a good idea love. It's packed tighter than a tin of sardines in there."

I explained I was searching for my stepdaughter and he was sympathetic, but suggested that if she'd been missing for hours, she was most likely with a boy in his place, or living rough at one of the drug hangouts.

I asked for directions but he refused to tell me where those were. "Ain't safe lady. You'd be best going home and waiting for her. She'll turn up eventually."

"And what if she doesn't?" I was close to tears.

He shrugged and turned to sort out an altercation where a spaced-out youth was trying to gate crash the front of the queue.

It was the same at the other three most popular clubs, but one young girl did take my arm and whisper a couple of addresses where the druggies hung out.

You can't tell on a map if an area is upmarket or dangerous, but as the taxi pulled up at the address I'd given him, it was obvious this area had seen better days.

"Will you wait for me?"

"Not on yer life. I ain't hanging round here. Must be mad. You take care of yerself now." He grabbed the bank note and was gone. I could have kicked myself. If I had not paid him, maybe he would have waited, but it was too late.

As I walked up the front steps to one of the terraced houses, the rank smell of urine and sweat hit me like a brick wall. The hall was narrow with a concrete floor and the walls were covered in graffiti, lurid pictures of devils and mythical creatures liberally intertwined with swear words.

In the first room, I could see six dead bodies. I jumped when one of the corpses asked what I was doing.

I leaned towards the voice, trying not to breathe in the drug induced fumes and showed him Belinda's photograph. He shook his head. I backed out. It was pointless asking the others, they were out for the count.

The area which had once served as a kitchen, was

deserted, so I picked my way up the stairs, trying not to brush against the rubbish bags and the soft, brown piles I could only think were excrement and tried all three rooms. No one either knew, or admitted to knowing, Belinda.

I was glad to escape back onto the street but nearly jumped out of my skin when a voice behind me asked "What's her name then? What's she to you?"

I spun round to face a teenager about the same age as Belinda. She had short, dark, spiky hair shaved very short on both sides of her head. Her mini skirt barely covered her butt and her lacy top was practically see-through. Her eyes reminded me of a bush baby, large and black, but her cheeks had shrunk inwards like those of an old woman. Even in the dim glow from the street lights, I could see darkened marks on her arms. She swayed slightly and clutched the gatepost to steady herself.

I told her I was looking for my stepdaughter and pushed the photo under her nose.

She took a long and careful look and then shook her head. "Nah, don't know her. Try the squat round the corner, fifth house along. More people there." She leaned in against me and I tried not to cringe as the smell of her unwashed body invaded my nostrils. I put both arms out to steady her and propped her back against the gatepost. She nodded and smiled. "Ta. An' when you find her tell her how bloody lucky she is. You thump the daylights out of her. Not many of us have anyone bothering to find us. Just written off and forgotten. Well, fuck the lot of them." She turned and laboriously climbed the steps and disappeared inside.

The next house was little better. It was larger, with three

rooms on the ground level. Several of the inhabitants were awake and aggressive. I began to wish I'd never come. One young man scrambled to his feet, lurched towards me and slammed me against the wall. He rested one arm across my chest and wanted to know why I was there. Was I the fuzz? No, not the police. I was looking for my daughter. If he let go of me, I could show him her photograph.

He backed off just far enough for me to slide a copy out of my pocket. He snatched it from my hands and circled the room kicking anyone who didn't take a long hard look at Belinda's picture.

Leaving me in the doorway, he bounded up the stairs and I heard him shouting at unseen people to tell him if they knew this slag. I winced at his description of Belinda, but I didn't react.

He came tumbling down the stairs and thrust the crumpled paper at me. "No go. How much you got?"

"Pardon?"

"Pardon? Pardon, oh how posh. Here that everyone? 'Pardon'."

Several of the reclining bodies rose to their feet and joined us. It reminded me of a zombie movie I'd watched years ago. I was scared, very scared.

"I said, how much you got? I ain't done all that work for you for nothing."

I let out the breath I'd been holding. Now I understood and I felt in my pocket for the notes I'd put there before leaving the house.

They were gone.

I thought back, I had paid the taxi driver and – it was

the girl! She had leaned against me. How could I be so stupid? She would probably kill herself with a couple of hundred pounds to spend on drugs.

I searched every other pocket in the hope of finding even a few coins, but there was nothing.

The young man scratched his unshaven face, exposing the split in his torn leather jacket. I sensed his impatience.

"I've lost it. I haven't got any money." I knew I sounded weak and frightened. I cleared my throat. "A girl round the corner, she must have mugged me. Come, help me get it back."

"Yeah right, a likely story. Think you can come round here, nosing where you've no right to be? Disturbing folks having a quiet night at home."

I nearly laughed at that it was so incongruous.

"Accusing them of hiding your precious daughter?"

That wasn't so funny. I tried to step away but my back was against the wall and there was nowhere to run. I had a brief flash of terror and somehow, I knew what was about to happen. The youth kicked out at my calf but unfortunately for both of us, he hit my prosthesis and it threw him off balance. He roared in fury and that's when they all piled in, raining blows on my arms, legs and any part of me they could reach. It was a wild, animalistic attack and it went on until everything went black and I remembered no more.

I woke sometime later in a hospital bed. From the familiar decor I guessed it was the same one I'd been in a few months ago. I tried to move, but every inch of me hurt. I attempted to lift one arm and broke out in a sweat. My movements were enough to alert one of the nurses.

"Ah good, you're awake." She fussed over me, taking my temperature, blood pressure and pulse. She was so wholesome, so clean and kind such a contrast to those of roughly the same age I'd been with, was it last night? Yet we all lived in the same town.

"What day is it?" my voice came out in a whisper.

"Thursday."

I tried to think. What day had I gone out?

"You've been here two days," she read my mind. "Can't say too much, that's for the doctor, but nothing's broken. We had to wait for you to come round to check you out for concussion or any other damage."

I lay back. It was too much effort to concentrate. The nurse handed me a pill and held a plastic cup of water. The darkness greeted me like a warm blanket.

The hospital food was surprisingly good and I wolfed it down. I could see it was dark outside, the street lights reflected on the other side of the thin cotton curtains drawn over the windows.

"Still Thursday?" I asked the orderly who removed my tray.

"Still Thursday," she repeated with a smile.

They left me to sleep, but the next day they wheeled me downstairs and subjected me to a battery of tests. I was able to walk, although I was stiff and sore. Before climbing back into bed, I leaned over to the locker searching for my clothes. My skirt and top and underclothes were there but my coat was missing.

I had heaved myself back onto the bed when a lady, clip

board in hand, approached the bed. "Feeling better?" she asked, as she pulled up a chair.

"I'm still aching all over."

"It'll take a while," she agreed. "I've come to find out who you are."

"Pardon?" I cringed. The last time I'd used that word it did not turn out well.

She consulted her notes. "You were brought in by ambulance the night before last, with no identification on you. So, you need to tell me all about yourself."

Of course. "Where was I found? Do you know?"

"Bryston Street, not the best area of town. Not your usual stamping ground I suspect?"

"No. I was looking for my stepdaughter." From the corner of my eye, I saw a middle-aged lady pause nearby. She was listening intently to the conversation. I was a little annoyed that she hovered as I recited my name, address, and the reason I was in that part of Weston.

"I'm in Weston General?"

"Yes."

"Then you'll have hospital records on me. I was in here in January with a real broken leg and I'd smashed that one too." I pointed to my prosthesis leaning against the bed.

"I'll check that out. Thank you, that's all for now. I'm sure they'll let you go home soon."

"One more thing. I was wearing a coat, and there should have been a phone in the pocket and other bits and pieces?"

She paused and checked the file again. "No, no coat, no shoes and certainly no mobile. Do you know the exact house number where the attack took place?"

I did, but I was not about to share that information with her or the police for that matter. I expected they would be visiting soon to ask the same questions and I didn't need to upset any more people.

"Sorry, I don't."

I was pleased to see the lady who had been hovering nearby had disappeared, but the moment the hospital administrator left the ward she came back.

"You are Leah? Leah Brand?" she asked.

"Uh, yes. And you are?"

"Caro, Caro Brand."

I couldn't help staring at her. This was Mason's wife? His first wife that is. She was nothing like the dizzy blonde bimbo I'd imagined. The classic, pale blue wool suit fitted her to perfection and toned in with a matching blouse and scarf. She was at least five foot ten and carried herself well. Her whole demeanour screamed 'well-bred' with her open and honest face, her beautifully cut blonde hair and the same blue eyes as her daughter.

I'm not sure who was more nervous, but all I could do was stare at her. "But you're in Brazil," I stammered at last. "What are you doing here in Weston?"

She came closer and stood next to my bed. I admired how she moved so gracefully and I could easily picture her on Mason's arm at official functions, the perfect elegant couple. So different to Mason's second wife, the one with the false leg who was not quite dumpy, but was not willowy either.

"May I?" she asked.

"Uh, of course."

The tea lady hurried over with a tray. "Here you are love, nice cup of tea, and I'll bring one for your visitor."

Caro settled herself in the plastic chair and sipped the lukewarm tea before she continued.

"I heard you mention Belinda and I'm sorry I eavesdropped, but this is such an amazing coincidence."

"Yes."

"Belinda's here, down the ward."

"Belinda is here, in hospital? Why? How is she? Is she going to be alright?" I struggled to sit up. "Can I see her?"

Caro put out an arm to stop me struggling to get out of bed. "No, she doesn't want to see you. Not yet. I'm sure she will explain, later."

"But is she going to…"

"Yes, she'll make a full recovery."

I sighed with relief and sank back against the pillows.

"But why are you not in Brazil?"

"I was coming to explain that. I need to start at the beginning, tell you the full story. You need to know."

My head was buzzing with questions and I couldn't take my eyes off her.

Caro continued. "It was Ecuador, not Brazil. Lost in translation I expect. What did they tell you?"

"This is a little embarrassing." I pulled myself farther up the bed and sat up straight plumping up the pillows behind me. "I understood you had run off to Brazil with your boyfriend. And he was, uh, half your age?"

Caro put her head back and laughed. "Not even close."

I shook my head. "Even Belinda believed it. She said he was only a little older than she was."

Caro was now shaking with laughter. She gathered herself together and keeping her voice low, told me her version of events.

She had met Mason at university. He was studying law and she was taking a history degree. They did all the usual student things, and after the graduation ceremony he had asked her to marry him.

Her parents were not happy about the match. There was nothing obviously wrong with Mason, his background was impeccable from what he told them, but her father never warmed to him. Her mother too was uncertain but neither could tell Caro exactly why they felt uneasy about the match.

"Looking back now, it must have been a sixth sense. Anyhow," she continued, "the wedding went ahead."

It was a grand affair, several hundred guests, many of them powerful with a sprinkling of a few celebrities. While Caro's family were well connected, having farmed in the county for several generations, and with contacts in the City of London, Mason seemed to know everyone.

"There were very few members of Mason's family there. I didn't think about it at the time, as he explained, they were all overseas in Australia, South Africa and Singapore."

Caro looked down at the floor lost for a moment in thought. "How naïve I was in those days. That's what happens when you grow up in a niche. Same friends at prep school, on to boarding school, few months playing around Europe and on to uni." She sighed. "We thought we owned the world, knew it all. I had no idea there were layers of society I wasn't even aware of."

I drew in a breath, she wasn't the only innocent one,

except my background wasn't landed gentry and boarding school.

"And after marriage?" I prompted her.

"It was all smooth sailing to start with. We had a great social life, I became pregnant with Leo almost immediately, so I wasn't working. And when he arrived, he was a handful. I had Belinda nine years later, so there's a big gap between them and they never got on. Leo resented having to share my time and he attacked her more than once. On one occasion she ended up in hospital but she learned to defend herself and they settled to a love / hate relationship. When Leo left home, I could finally relax."

"He went to Australia?"

"Uh, no, the law removed him and he served time for drug dealing and assault. In fact, he was in trouble more than once. First as a juvenile, he got sent down from his boarding school, then later, he ended up in adult prison." She sat silent for a while as she drank the rest of her tea and nibbled a biscuit.

"And then?" I prompted.

"I discovered, by chance, that Mason had taken out a very large life insurance policy on me, for millions. It made me nervous because by then his behaviour had changed. His true colours showing at last. My parents were not wrong after all. He was behaving like a typical narcissist. Everything I did was wrong. Everything I said was criticised. He was dictatorial, made me feel as if I was losing my mind. He wanted his own way all the time, my feelings weren't even considered. He had no empathy, even for Belinda. He took credit for everything."

I picked up my tea, wishing it was coffee instead. Why does everyone assume because you are British you have to like tea?

"I recognise the behaviour."

"Once I landed in South America, I did a lot of research on personality disorders and Mason is definitely deficient. The strange thing, for all his bombastic ways, deep down, like all narcissists, he is fearful and has a low self-image. Strange isn't it? He alienated all my friends they were all too scared to come round to the house."

I nodded, casting my mind back to Mason's furious outbursts which were not unlike those of a two-year-old having a temper tantrum. "You went to Ecuador because you were frightened of Mason?"

"Yes. He had me so confused I was beginning to doubt myself. I thought I was going mad. He was telling me I'd said stuff I knew I hadn't. That I forgot to do as he asked, or be ready for an evening out I was sure he'd not told me about."

"Oh heavens, that all sounds so familiar. I lived through exactly the same. Only it was worse. Objects moved around the house. I found the television in the garage, my clothes were re-arranged, and a stuffed toy bunny appeared in the strangest of places. It haunted me."

"I didn't experience weird stuff like that. But the day I discovered the life insurance policy was the last straw. I began to fear for my life. I hired a lawyer to begin divorce proceedings and he arranged for one of his paralegals to travel with me. I bought two tickets, but Belinda refused to go with me. I tried everything to persuade her but she wanted to live in England. I changed my mind, I would stay. Then one night, Mason came home very drunk and more or less boasted about his plans and what he was going to do with all the money he'd get when I was dead. That was the night I knew I had to leave."

"But now you are back. Why now?"

"Two reasons. Once the divorce went through, I wrote to the insurance company and under the terms and conditions, Mason wouldn't receive anything on my death if we were not married. And, I discovered he had also stopped paying the premiums, so I was safe.

"I wrote to Belinda regularly, but she never replied. I didn't know if she received any of my letters. Mason could have so easily intercepted them. It was snail mail I'm afraid. I didn't have an email address for her, though I'd asked her time and again for one. Then, out of the blue, two weeks ago I heard from her. She was in trouble and didn't know what to do. She was close to suicide, she said, so I jumped on the first plane and here I am."

Belinda had never let on she heard from her mother and knew where she was. And suicide? I sat stunned. I had failed her. Much as I had tried, she'd not trusted me or bonded with me but preferred to turn to the mother she accused of abandoning her. I choked back a sob.

"Please don't feel bad Leah. She was too ashamed to tell you. You have no idea how much she admires you."

"Me? No. What nonsense."

"She's told me how you coped with losing your family and your leg. How you suffered, how Mason tried to get rid of you. How you stuck by her when he skipped the country.

Believe me, she worships you. And that was before you went looking for her in the most dangerous area of Weston, wait until I tell her that."

"No need, really," I murmured. "She's in this ward? I want to see her." I pulled back the sheet and reached for my prosthesis. Why is she in hospital?"

Caro looked at the floor before rising to her feet. "That is her story to tell, if she decides to. I'll let her know you're in here and why. I'll be back later." Caro left me to my thoughts.

Had Mason taken another life insurance policy out on me? I should have listened. Leo warned me, Andrea warned me and Belinda had been so friendly and welcoming when I went home. But then Andrea also warned me about Leo. She'd told the truth after all.

I made up my mind. The first thing I was going to do when I got back to the flat was to find a good lawyer. It was time the Brand family and I parted company. I'd cut loose and somehow find the money to start over in a new town, maybe in a new country.

For whatever reason, I did not see Belinda in the hospital. Caro said her daughter needed time to find the courage to tell me her story. When she was discharged, she would come home and explain.

I could only think that Andrea was right and she had been on drugs. Why had I not noticed? Why had I not been more observant? Typical Leah, always falling short.

The flat felt cold and damp when I walked into the hallway. I'd expected to see Andrea, wine bottle in hand, feet up on the coffee table, binge watching a Netflix series, but she was not there. I peeped into her room and noticed her weekend case was missing. Had she run out too? No, her large case was still perched on top of the wardrobe and her clothes were still in the drawers. She'd probably gone off for a few days, angry with me, this was a typical Andrea punishment. I couldn't blame her, I'd been gone for a few days and hadn't thought of her once. I used the house phone to call her and she answered on the first ring.

"Darling! Leah! Where are you my love? I've been frantic. Days and days and not a word from you. I had you hauled off for the slave trade, or run away to join the circus, or kidnapped at the very least," she screeched down the phone. "I even came back up to London to see if you were here. I rang both phones, dozens of times and you didn't answer. Were you cross with me darling?"

I had to laugh. Andrea the drama queen. "Nothing as exciting as that. I was in hospital."

I heard a gasp on the other end of the phone. "And where are you now sweetie? I'm going to jump in the car, and I'll be with you in a couple of hours. I'm coming to hug you and make it all better."

"At the flat. But I'm on my way out to get another mobile."

"Only you could lose another phone Leah! Now, you must get them to give you the same number, that's so important. Don't forget. And they will have your contacts and stuff up in some cloud. You know what a techie idiot you are so promise Aunty Andrea you'll do that?"

It was the old Andrea again. I'd missed her, well the old

version. I promised to do exactly as she told me and she said she'd drive down and be with me before supper.

I would take a taxi into town. It wasn't far, but I was still aching and sore. I was covered in an interesting variety of yellow, orange, blue and green bruising. Those bastards must have kicked the hell out of me and I was lucky to have passed out so quickly. My head was also still a bit fuzzy and the hospital wanted me back for a check-up in a couple of weeks.

They had of course reported the case to the police, and I'd received a brief visit from them while I was still flat on my back. I didn't have to pretend to be vague. All I could remember was being in the wrong part of town, looking for my stepdaughter. I was unsure which houses I had entered and I certainly couldn't identify my attackers. It had been dark and the only memory I had was the splits in that black leather jacket. I had no idea who had called the ambulance nor did I remember it arriving and carting me off to Weston General.

I sensed the law was not that interested in one attack on a middle-aged housewife who was unlikely to put herself in that situation again. They took my statement, asked me to sign it, wished me a speedy recovery and bid me a good day. I could see the other patients looking at me fearfully and after that no one stopped to chat or ask how I was. Caro had been the first person other than the medical staff to talk to me.

I scribbled a quick list. Phone shop, bread, milk, wine, ready meal for tonight, I wasn't up to cooking, and at the bottom I added 'locate GOOD divorce lawyer'. I added curly patterns round the word good. I wasn't intending to walk away from my marriage with nothing at all. I must be entitled to at least half of the house, or other compensation.

I phoned for the taxi then left the list on the hall table as I hurried to put on my coat when I heard the horn beeping outside. The driver was middle-aged and kept his speed down but I couldn't help noticing that he kept glancing in his rear-view mirror. He saw me looking at him and smiled.

"Just watching that car behind us, he's stayed on my bumper since I picked you up. Just hang on while I try something. He made an abrupt turn into a large parking area for one of the huge hypermarkets and then drove straight out the far exit. "Yup, still there."

I shivered. "Drop me off at the nearest mobile phone shop. I searched in my bag and pulled out a couple of notes. "That should cover the fare. Drive off as soon as I get out."

"You on the run or something?" His chuckle sounded nervous.

"No, nothing like that." I improvised. "I have a few friends who like to play practical jokes."

As I jumped out of the car as fast as possible, I couldn't resist looking round at the car which had pulled up behind us. There were two men in the front but I didn't recognise either of them. I breathed a sigh of relief when they drove off behind the taxi and accelerated away into the traffic. Maybe they were after the driver and it had nothing to do with me at all.

The shop was brightly lit and the array of phones and other electronic gadgets on display made my head spin. I wanted the same model as I'd had last time but they didn't make that one anymore, 'out of production' I was told. I settled for one as close as possible. The young shop assistant asked me if I'd turned on the Activation Lock on my old phone, but I hadn't a clue what he was talking about. Nor, apparently had I installed the 'Find my Phone' app. He gave me one of those pitying looks the young reserve for anyone over the age of thirty. When he learned that I'd only had a handful of numbers in my old phone and had never used it for banking or paying bills he suggested I start over with a new sim card. I really didn't need a device that told me the time in Alaska, or the name of the ships sailing past Weston, but he was kind enough to set up it up with a new ID and password and we keyed in the few numbers I could remember. I'd add the ones I had written down when I got home. As I left the shop, he assured me that from now on, all my data would be in the cloud and I'd never have to worry if my phone was lost or stolen again. As I tottered along to the supermarket, I wondered what he would think if I'd shared with him, I'd had my old phone lifted in a crack cocaine den down town.

I couldn't shake off that feeling I was being watched. Each time I spun round no one was taking any interest in me, but as I walked up and down the aisles in the supermarket, the hairs on the back of my neck were prickling and my back shivered. But no one approached me and I told myself it was another bout of paranoia.

When I arrived back at the flat it was to find Andrea in a state. She had the door open for me the moment the lift arrived on the first floor and glared at me as I walked past her into the kitchen to drop the bags on the counter.

She had worked herself into a fury. Her cheeks were flushed, her bearing stiff and anger radiated from every pore.

I closed the front door and took off my coat and gloves. "What is it now Andrea? What's upset you this time?"

"This." Andrea grabbed my shopping list off the hall table. "What's this about searching for a 'good' divorce lawyer?" She flapped the piece of paper in my face.

"Pretty self-explanatory. I'm looking to get a divorce. I wouldn't want a 'bad' lawyer, would I?"

"From Mason?" I could see the fury drain away.

"Who else?"

She flung her arm around me and walked me over to the sofa, settled me down, plumping up the cushions behind me. All of a sudden, she was sweetness and light. Andrea was a chameleon she could spin her moods on a whim.

"I'm so sorry darling. It was such a shock." She jumped up and grabbed the wine from the bag and poured me a glassful.

"I can't drink all that Andrea" I protested. "I haven't had anything to eat and I'm on meds as well."

"Live dangerously." She clinked her glass against mine and drank. "I'll take care of you. So, what do you fancy eating? I'll knock up an omelette. You just sit there."

As soon as Andrea walked over to the kitchen counter, I was on my feet grabbing my laptop off the shelf. I'd made up my mind and nothing was going to stop me. I could sense Andrea peering over her shoulder as she broke the eggs and whisked them up. Every movement exaggerated and loud. I could hear the oil sizzle in the pan, the clank of the fork on

215

glass, the clatter of the plates as she took them out of the cupboard.

Despite being really hungry, I was more interested in finding the very best lawyer. The problem, the best ones were also the most expensive ones, but I'd face that later. It wouldn't hurt to get some advice.

Andrea bustled back in and whipped the laptop away replacing it with the tray of food. "There, get that inside you."

Even on a good day, Andrea was not known for her cooking. It takes some skill to turn an omelette into hardened rubber, and the salad had been languishing in the fridge for almost a week. I managed to force some of it down, pleading a small appetite and my aches and pains so I could leave half the food on the plate.

Andrea removed the tray but did not hand back my laptop. She sat next to me and grasped my hands. I could guess she had every intention of ensuring I changed my mind. She launched into a long litany of the first two years of my marriage, how happy I had been and it was only the worries from work that caused Mason to be so short tempered. I didn't bother to remind her that she'd told me months ago she'd finished her affair with him due to his unreasonable moods.

As she rambled on and on, I switched off. I had almost fallen asleep when the word selfish penetrated the fog.

"What do you mean selfish? Who is?"

"You Leah. You can't abandon Belinda. You need to find her and look after her. She had no one else since her parents walked out on her."

I have no idea why I didn't tell Andrea about Belinda

being in hospital and Caro popping up out of the blue. Looking back now, maybe I should have. Instead I said "She's got Leo."

"Oh yeah, right, an ex-con with dubious connections who couldn't tell the truth to save his life."

I sighed. "Andrea, I can't put the world to rights on my own. I've done my best, now is the time to accept defeat and walk away."

"How do you think Mason feels?"

"Frankly, I'm past caring how he feels. I raced half way round the world to see him, but I suspect he was more interested in getting his hands on those files than seeing me. If I think about it, he didn't try that hard to entice me back."

"You don't need to rush into anything just yet. Give yourself more time to think it through."

Andrea was beginning to irritate me again. Why was she always trying to control me? I must attract domineering people. I clenched my teeth and hissed. "I don't need more time I don't bloody need any more time at all. I've made up my mind and the sooner I get started the better. Stop telling me what to do."

Andrea shrank back. "Calm down darling. No need to get upset. If you've made up your mind fine, I'm only trying to advise you. I'd hate to see you make a huge mistake." She topped up the wine glasses. "Just remember I'm always here for you."

Quite without thinking I blurted out "That's the problem, you're always here."

She sprang to her feet, hands on hips. "Oh, I know what you think of me. Your diary tells it all."

"You snooped in my room and you read my diary?"

She froze, realising what she'd just said. "I, oh I'm so sorry, Leah. I wasn't prying, I only wanted to find out where you were, so I could come and rescue you."

I didn't believe her. If she was so worried why go back to London? She wasn't going to find me there.

"I have a suggestion." Andrea changed tack. "Why not leave here, leave the flat and you and I go away somewhere, anywhere. Maybe a quiet little hotel in the Lake District? We can just chill out, as long as we get in a few bottles of wine. Relax, sit back and watch the daisies grow."

"It's not feasible Andrea, be sensible. I've got to go back to the hospital next week."

"It's nothing permanent is it? Oh, sweetie you are OK? Nothing long term?"

"No, I don't think so, it's just a check-up."

"Let's take off till then."

"No. I'm staying right here."

Andrea was angry I wouldn't go along with her suggestion. She banged on and on about how it would be good for us, but I stood firm. I wasn't leaving Weston.

From that point things went downhill. We were like two alley cats screaming at each other. I was too angry to even cry. I don't remember now if I told her to go, threw her out, or she decided to leave of her own accord. I do know that a couple of hours later she had flung open the front door, slamming it loudly behind her and stomped off down the stairs. The reverberations bounced round the flat before settling into a threatening silence.

I noticed the friendship bears sitting on the shelf next to

the television. Some friend Andrea was, a friend I didn't need or want. In a fit of pique, I snatched them up, opened the window and flung them out into the rain.

I felt drained and depressed and grabbed the TV remote to create an illusion of sound and company. As I went into the kitchen to switch on the coffee maker, I heard the weatherman forecast grey skies and lots more rain for the whole of November.

NOVEMBER LEAH

The next morning the weatherman's predictions proved correct. A cold wind blew in off the sea bringing with it squalls of sleeting rain which beat against the lounge windows and scattered the last few remaining leaves in swirling patterns along with old, abandoned supermarket flyers.

The scene matched my mood as I stood gazing out across the deserted promenade, cradling my coffee. I watched a group of seagulls squabbling near the shore line over some dead offering, but their shrieks did not penetrate the glass. The rain ran down in rivulets, pooling onto the windowsill before dripping into the garden below.

I turned away and wandered into Andrea's empty bedroom. Her large suitcase was no longer perched on the wardrobe. I checked in the drawers and bedside cabinet but there was not a scrap of evidence that my friend had ever stayed there. She had not left as much as a cotton bud or paper hanky behind.

Belinda's room was as she had left it. The usual teenage mess, clothes on the floor, open drawers, dresses slipping off hangers in the wardrobe. It must mirror her mood because she'd been quite neat and tidy until we went to Australia. Picking my way carefully across the floor I resisted the temptation to clear it all up. I had invaded Belinda's privacy once and still felt guilty.

I stripped the linen off my bed and stuffed it into the washing machine. I sniffed the scented, freshly ironed sheets and remade it, smoothing out the duvet cover I had made to match the curtains. For a moment I was tempted to crawl back in, curl up and go to sleep, but that might spell defeat. I would stay up and face the world, but I wouldn't waste the energy to get dressed. I snuggled deeper into my dressing gown as I meandered back into the kitchen area. Checking the fridge and cupboards there was nothing in there I fancied, so I shuffled over to the sofa and sank into the soft cushions. The interminable hours of the day stretched ahead, and I imagined future days the same.

For a while I dozed, and when I came too, my head was throbbing painfully. I brewed another coffee and broke open a bubble in the pack of painkillers. The hospital had suggested I take things easy, but what would I do when I was fully recovered?

I hadn't thought to ask Caro if she was staying in England, or if she planned to take Belinda back to Ecuador. The teen was infuriating but in a masochistic way she was still company, someone to cook for, wash and iron clothes.

Last night's row had that feeling of finality. I knew with certainty that my BFF – Best Friend Forever – was not salvageable and would never be again. Too many harsh words had been exchanged, too many truths exposed and too many frustrations hurled between us.

Less than a day later, I was having big regrets. Who was left in my world now? A brother and sister on different continents I hadn't seen for years. Our relationship, was never close in childhood, and had dwindled to the annual letter at Christmas. I had not even met their spouses or children. I briefly considered inviting myself to Toronto or Brisbane but I doubted they would welcome me with any enthusiasm.

Had I made a big mistake falling out with Andrea, my only friend? All friends could be irritating and we had been joined at the hip for weeks. And she must have been so hurt when she read my diary. I had been so frustrated at the time it was good to get it all out there on paper. I couldn't even remember what I'd written and I couldn't be bothered to go and check. The damage was done. I've alienated everyone one, or they had deserted me.

Now I really was alone.

The minutes passed slowly, the hours dragged. I alternated with pacing the empty flat, my slippers thumping on the polished wooden floors, and I vegetated on the couch staring sightlessly at the current book I wasn't reading.

I went into a self-imposed lockdown. I ordered in groceries and anything else I needed online and only went downstairs to collect the deliveries. I didn't go to my swim classes, the book club, charity shop or the hospital to play with the sick children. I sank into a deep depression. I had never felt so alone and so helpless.

I didn't bother going to bed but slept on the couch at night, with the television droning quietly in the background. I stayed in my nightclothes all day and wandered aimlessly around the house. The only thing I marked up was my return check-up at the hospital.

It was early evening almost a week later, when I was woken with a start by the sound of the doorbell. It wasn't the intercom buzzing from the panel at street level but here, in the hall, outside my front door.

I swung my feet off the sofa and was about to rush and open it when I remembered and froze. Were the visitors the same thugs standing just inches away? I shuddered and wrapped my arms tightly around myself as I crept into the hallway. I could pretend I was out. Neither the television nor the radio was on and I hadn't turned on any lights in the early evening gloom.

I held my breath, as I inched towards the spy hole and peered through. I couldn't see anything, the uninvited visitor had blocked it on the other side. Then I heard voices, female voices. If they were female enforcers that would be a first, I drew back the chain and opened the door to Caro and Belinda.

I relaxed and smiled. "Come in, I'm so happy to see you both."

Belinda hesitated in the hallway, unsure where to go or what to say. She stared at the floor and wriggled the edge of the mat with her foot.

"Belinda wasn't sure you would want her back here in the flat."

My mouth fell open. "Why ever not, Belinda? This is your home, or as much a home as I can make it. We can go back to London if that's what you would prefer, but of course your mother is here now…" I trailed off.

"I think we all have lots to talk about." Caro's face relaxed and she smiled.

"What am I thinking, come on in." I led the way through the kitchen into the television lounge. "It's not the smartest lounge but it's the warmest." I reached out to take Caro's coat and hung it up in the hallway. "Now, what can I offer you? Tea, coffee, something stronger? And you Belinda, Time to treat you as an adult. Please excuse me still in my dressing gown but…"

"You're still convalescing, quite understandable."

To cover my confusion, I bustled about brewing coffee, pouring wine and slicing cake.

"Is there anything you don't like to eat, before I begin supper?" I asked Caro. "Of course, I know what Belinda prefers. Pasta?"

The girl nodded, but she continued staring at the floor and her hands never stopped twirling bits of her hair around her fingers.

"Hey, relax," I reached out and squeezed her shoulder. "You look so sad."

Caro took a small bite of the fruit cake. "This is nice. Did you make it yourself?"

"I enjoy cooking," I was never sure how to receive a compliment. In fact the cake was shop bought but to admit that would only highlight my inactivity and depression.

"Belinda tells me you're an ace at keeping the house running. She knows how hopeless I am."

"Oh, I'm sure you're…" I stopped in confusion. I couldn't choose between feeling thrilled at the company and the embarrassment of sitting with Mason's first wife and his daughter, the same daughter I'd tried to bond with and failed.

An awkward silence fell. Two adults concentrating on our drinks and cake and one teenager fixated on fiddling with her hair.

At last Caro broke the uncomfortable silence. "Leah, we came to explain Belinda's absence and to talk about the future."

"Yes, of course, that's understandable, sensible I mean." I found it hard to keep still and shuffled from side to side in my chair. I gripped my plate so hard my knuckles showed white. While I'd wished so many times to be shot of Belinda, now I was going to lose her, I felt part of me die. It was another bereavement. My two babies and now this recalcitrant teenager who'd caused me so much grief. I wondered how much of a masochist I was, but I genuinely loved the child.

"At the hospital, I told you my version of past events, and I can promise you it's the truth. I hope you believe me?"

"Of course, I do," I would not have thought otherwise. "Now that I've met you, I can't imagine you running off with a toy boy."

"That was Mason's version, of course. The one he repeated frequently to Belinda."

"How was I to know he was lying? You told me you'd bought a ticket for me and then you ran off without me." The first words Belinda had spoken since arriving and she still had that edge in her voice.

Caro sighed. "You refused to leave with me, if you remember."

I rushed in to deflect any argument.

"We always believe what our parents tell us, Belinda,

it's instinctive. It's not until we're oh, twenty or thirty, or maybe the day we catch them out in a lie that we discover they are just people with all the faults and failings of very ordinary human beings." I ran out of breath.

"Things are not always what they seem."

Another silence fell, but it was less tense than before. Then I spoke up. "Then it's only fair I tell you my history with Mason and Belinda."

Belinda looked up in alarm, then crossed her arms tightly around her chest. With her head down and hair hanging over her face it was impossible to read her expression.

The light faded in the sky outside and the street lights came on and twinkled as I shared my life experiences with Caro. We both agreed that Mason's dog Zeus, breed unknown, was a pain and laughed together over the animal's antics and Mason's slavish devotion to the animal. I left nothing out except for my trip north to stay with my mother. I caught a brief look of relief on Belinda's face. I didn't go into detail either about Belinda's skipping school and her late-night trips to the clubs and I mentioned nothing about drugs.

Caro sat for a moment. "I firmly believe that Mason never loved either of us. It's tricky for narcissists to love anyone other than themselves. I think he chose us for what he could gain. I'm an only child and when my parents passed on, I stood to gain a great deal of money, from our farms and business interests in the city. Mason went to my dad once too often trying to borrow money when he was setting up his practice. They saw through him even if I didn't. It got to the point when dad wisely changed his will and tied up all the assets in such a way that Mason could not use a penny for himself. You can imagine how furious he was when he found out after the funeral."

I nodded, I had experienced the rages and temper tantrums often enough.

"And that's when he took out the life insurance policy on me," Caro said.

"I'm not sure the end results would have been the same. I had no money when I met Mason and I only discovered there were a couple of small insurance policies. One on my life and another for the car accident. Nothing to compare with land and high finance. Unless Mason also insured me, but he would never try that twice surely?"

"It would look very suspicious." Caro agreed. "And, I think I read somewhere that you can't take out insurance on someone else's life and name yourself as beneficiary without telling them. And there are terms and conditions about not being allowed to benefit financially from the death of that person. By that time, I couldn't get away fast enough, and desperate to divorce him."

"I don't blame you." I stood up and disappeared, first into the bedroom to get dressed and then into the kitchen to prepare the supper. I could hear the low murmur of voices behind me, but I didn't even try to hear what they were saying.

"That was excellent, thank you." Caro replaced her coffee cup on the table. "I have not eaten that much for weeks. It was a lovely meal." She glanced at her watch. "Time to get back to the hotel. It's been a long emotional day."

"No, you must stay here," I insisted. I didn't want to be on my own. "There's a spare room but take mine, it's got an en-suite, it will be more comfortable."

Caro looked doubtful, until Belinda said "Please stay, Mum."

"I'm outvoted. Let me go and collect my luggage and check out." She went to get her coat then paused. "Belinda, it will give you a chance to chat to Leah. I think you owe her an explanation, don't you?"

Belinda nodded. She looked so forlorn that I wanted to sweep her into my arms.

As soon as the door closed, I pulled the child over to sit beside me on the sofa. "Now, tell me all about it and I promise not to say a word until you have finished."

It all came tumbling out. At some point over the summer, at one of the parties, held at one of the clubs, she got blind drunk, as on so many other occasions, had sex with boy or boys, unknown, and got herself pregnant.

It took all my self-control not to blurt out 'for heaven's sake why weren't you on the pill?'

That was not the worst part. Too embarrassed to tell me and too scared to approach the local doctor, she took a friend's advice from school and visited a back-street abortionist.

Now that shocked me. I had no idea that such people still existed. Early termination was quite legal in Britain and all the privacy laws kept your secrets even from parents.

I couldn't help myself. I threw my arms around Belinda and rocked her like a baby. What if my little daughter Henrietta had survived the car crash and grown up and got herself into the same predicament? I wanted to weep.

"Oh, my love, you could have come to me."

"Couldn't."

"Why not?"

"Cos you never do anything wrong. You're just so good."

"Oh no, believe me I'm not. I'm a mousy, boring little housewife, while you, you have the ability to go far. I admire your personality, your ability to say what you think and the confidence I'll never have."

"Even with Dr Cromptom's help?"

"You've heard of him? Read his book?"

Belinda giggled. "Only because I saw it on your kindle. Load of rubbish if you ask me."

"I have to agree. It didn't do me much good. Are you going to be OK now? Healthwise I mean. No permanent damage?"

"I'm not sure. I had an operation and they stitched me up and I've got to go back in a few days so they can take another look. I can't believe how stupid I've been."

"We all do daft things. You'll get over it."

"They told me I may never be able to have any children." Tears flowed down Belinda's cheeks.

"Oh, my poor dear." I had no idea what to say to comfort her. It was a heavy price to pay for one very stupid mistake.

We sat in silence until Belinda asked. "What's going to happen now?"

"I have no idea. Did your mum mention if she was going back to Brazil, no it's Ecuador isn't it?"

"No, she didn't. I wonder what it's like living in South America?"

It hit me again that I really would be on my own if Belinda left. I had no idea if Mason would ever contact me again and wondered how long it would take to divorce him if I didn't know where he was. It was all so complicated and I was still having problems focusing and concentrating.

The next couple of days passed without incident. I enjoyed having people in the flat again and my depression lifted. I began to feel like my old self and I found myself humming as I stacked the dishwasher and fussed around my guests. I didn't want to look too far into the future and I didn't have the courage to ask Caro what her plans were. With the follow up appointments booked for Belinda at the hospital, they were here for another few weeks. I'd face the worst if and when it happened.

With the resilience of youth, Belinda bounced back. It was almost a relief to hear her backchat and swearing and her constant raiding of the fridge.

She raced into the kitchen and threw the post on the table.

"There. See, never say I don't help around the house!"

I looked at the pile of envelopes. "I've not even thought to check the mailbox downstairs."

"Saw the postman trying to stuff more letters in and gave him a helping hand." She smirked as she made for the fridge.

"Nooo." I snatched the frankfurters from her. "Those are for the hot dogs at lunch time, and it's only ten o'clock."

"But I'm hungry now," Belinda whined.

"Then have some fruit, it's much better for you."

"Boring, yeah, one of your five a day, I've heard all that propaganda too." Belinda stalked off into her bedroom.

Everything back to normal, I thought, as I thumbed through the pile, slit open the first envelope, and gasped at the contents.

My cries brought both Caro and Belinda running into the kitchen.

"What's the matter?"

"Look, read it!" I passed the letter to Caro who ran her eye over the contents.

"Is this for real?"

"I guess so. I heard something on the news about a major class action against the motor company for faulty manufacture and a claim for compensation. I think they lost and then appealed, but it says here they've been ordered to pay out."

"It's millions" screamed Belinda who had no qualms about whipping the letter from her mother and reading it herself.

"Leah, we told you months ago you were going to be rich, but this rich, Wow!"

"That was the life insurance pay-out, and that goes into my bank account monthly, not in one chunk."

My head was spinning. Strange, now all my money worries were over, the rest of my life was likely to fall apart.

"Where's the cheque?" Belinda peered into the envelope.

"If you read it again slowly," her mother smiled "you'll see they need Leah's bank account details so they can pay it straight in."

"I think this calls for a celebration." I picked up my phone. "I'm going to book a meal in the best restaurant in town."

It was late when we returned to the flat, giggling from too much wine and food. Even Belinda had taken full advantage of the occasion to top up her glass again and again, despite her medication.

It took me several attempts to find the keyhole as I tried to open the door. We were so drunk we bounced off each other as first Caro and then I raced to the bathroom. I remembered thinking that neither adult had been a good example to the teenager, but it wasn't every day you were given millions of pounds. I still couldn't get my head around what kind of lifestyle I could afford in the future.

In an alcoholic haze we tumbled into bed.

The person lurking in the shadows was desperately trying to keep warm. As the hours passed, the car got colder and colder and the once hot coffee in the polystyrene cup, was long gone. There was no activity in the quiet suburban street, the majority of the elderly residents exhausted by ten in the evening. One by one the lights went out, except on the first floor flat, the only one of interest. Then at last those lights went out too. Time to move? No.

There was movement as a pedestrian crossed over behind the waiting vehicle and walked along the pavement, and in through the same gate. Who was that? None of the lights in any of the block of flats, went on. It was probably some teenager sneaking back after curfew.

The low hanging clouds obscured the new moon as the

driver slipped out of the car and crossed the road. Keeping to the shadows, the driver crept along the hedgerows, opened the gate and tiptoed up the short path. It took a moment to unlock the lower door, slip medical scrub boots over shoes and creep up the stairs. The front door opened without a sound, and creeping down the middle of the hallway the intruder entered the last bedroom on the right.

It took less than five minutes to complete the task, leave silently and jump back in the car, and drive off in the direction of Bristol.

Went off without a hitch. No problem.

Wrong. Someone had been watching. The act had not gone unnoticed.

She never knew what woke her up. It was probably too much of that wine, but she needed the bathroom urgently. She was surprised to see the other bedroom door open and went to close it, but paused. The woman in the bed was lying at an odd angle, one leg hanging over the edge, her head too far back to look natural.

She slipped inside to lift her back into the bed and make her more comfortable, but the body felt wet and sticky and there was a strange coppery smell. She bent down to lift the leg back onto the bed when her foot gave way and she lost her balance, pitching her onto the sleeping figure. Her hand shot out to steady herself and closed round something hard and sharp. The light reflected in the room from the street lamps outside, was too weak to let her see what she was doing, but then the overhead light flashed on and Belinda was standing in the doorway, with her phone in her hand.

She began to scream and the high-pitched screech went on and on.

The woman looked down and screamed too. Her hands were clasped around a bloody knife and she had fallen onto the body on the bed. It was still warm, but the eyes, were wide open, staring, accusing and lifeless. It was the huge, red gash on the throat that transfixed both of them. The blood was still trickling from the wound, as the heart pumped for the last time and the body jerked as the nerves reacted and the screams increased.

The woman holding the knife, didn't move but her bladder gave way and a stream of warm urine pooled on the carpet by the bed, to mix with the blood spatter.

"You killed her! You killed her!"

The screams went on and on.

It was a quiet weekday night and the police station in Weston-super-Mare responded quickly to the call from the ambulance service to attend a serious incident.

The scene that greeted them suggested an open and shut case. Victim deceased in bed as a result of having her throat slashed, perpetrator in situ still holding knife, apparently in a catatonic state. They would bring her in and notify the morgue. It was a good thing one of the responding officers had seen it all before, as the young constable with him, fled into the bathroom and donated his supper to the plumbing system.

He could just hear the words "… I am arresting you on the suspicion of the murder of …" There was a pause "um, the deceased who has yet to be, uh, identified. You don't have to say anything but it may harm your defence if you do not mention when questioned, something which you may later rely on in court and anything you do say may be given in evidence."

Would that caution hold up, the young constable wondered if you didn't name the deceased? She'd probably be cautioned again when they had a name for what remained in the bed. He leaned over the toilet again as his stomach contracted into another spasm.

As they processed the accused at the station, she didn't respond to any questions. She stared straight ahead, but followed their instructions as they handed her the paper suit to wear and removed her clothes for forensic investigation. She held her hands still when they fingerprinted her and then stood rigid by the chart as they took her photograph. She didn't cry, or show any emotion. She was one of the most unemotional, hard-boiled criminals they had ever seen. Every other murderer they had apprehended had deafened them with protestations of innocence. This one neither admitted nor denied her actions.

The only information they had recorded was given by the other two people in the flat at the time. The younger one, moody, silent, and prone to weeping. The police had to drag every morsel of information from her by asking her the same questions over and over again.

The other witness was polite and helpful. The police described her as a real lady. She was able to fill in all the details, the names and their relationships with each other together with a cast iron motive for the murder.

"Hell hath no fury like a woman scorned," muttered the desk sergeant as he closed the file.

"It's your knock off time. You go keep your little woman happy Sarge," his colleague teased.

They put her in a holding cell for the night, with one concrete shelf that served as a bed and a thin plastic-covered foam mattress on top. A couple of blankets and a wafer-thin pillow, added little to the comfort. A portion of the cell was walled off to hide a toilet without a lid and a wash hand basin. She made no comment when they escorted her in, and locked the door.

She said neither please nor thank you when her food was pushed through the door at mealtimes, although she ate every scrap of the food they gave her.

Since she was not co-operating in any way, they assigned a Duty Solicitor and the lot fell to the newest arrival to the team, the nervous young man who was at a total loss with his very first case.

Eric Chamberlin consulted the notes. They had sent a doctor to check her out and he'd confirmed she was not catatonic, nor in a stupor. He had to look that up to learn the difference but to him, her behaviour didn't make sense. Nor had he heard of anyone accused of murder accepting years in prison without pleading some mitigating circumstances. Who knows what might have driven her to act the way she did? That she had committed the murder was beyond question, yet there was that niggling doubt at the back of his mind. How much strength did it take to slice a throat open with a knife, even a very sharp one?

He'd not been able to find the answer to that even after hours on Google.

She was scheduled to appear before the magistrate in the morning, so he didn't have much time to prepare.

Someone had brought her clothes to wear in court. They had not returned her blood-spattered nightie. She was handcuffed and transported in a van to the local magistrates' court, a modern stone and glass building, and left in a holding room.

Her first court appearance lasted less time than it had taken to drive from the police station. She was led into the court room and stood silently next to her lawyer as the charge was read out and her name and address confirmed.

The magistrate raised his eyebrows. The woman before him did not look the type for such a crime, but then you could never tell these days. "Do you understand the charges against you?" He asked.

The woman nodded.

"I need you to answer yes or no."

"Yes." The response was barely a whisper.

"Has application for bail been lodged?"

"Yes Sir. Mrs Brand has no previous record, is an upstanding citizen and unlikely to be a flight risk, we'd like to request bail...."

The magistrate's waving hand cut off the rest of the sentence. He rechecked the papers in front of him and shook his head. "This, is a murder case. Bail denied, accused remanded in custody for trial at the Crown Court."

They led her back the way she had come but this time

the ride in the van took much longer. When it finally stopped, she was led up some steps into a reception area where they put her through the whole processing procedure again. The staff were much kinder than she expected and suggested she contact family and friends to ask them to bring her some clothes and toiletries. She had nothing with her other than the one outfit that had been delivered to the police station. She'd not enquired who had brought it in for her. If she had no one on the outside, they said, then they could source clothes for her from the prison shop. Prisoners on remand were not forced to wear prison uniform. She listened but did not respond. They led her through several doors, electronic locks clicking open and locking as they passed through each one. She would be on the remand wing, separate from the convicted prisoners, served meals in her cell and allowed exercise each day. There would be an association time for a couple of hours each evening where she could meet others also awaiting trial. They guided her into a cell and locked the door, leaving her to read the graffiti scribbled on the walls.

NOVEMBER ERIC

Back in the office, Eric Chamberlin listed all the people who had been in the flat at the time of the murder. Leah Brand, Belinda Brand and Andrea Coe. What was their relationship to the deceased, Caro Brand? Why did he have this feeling that his client was innocent when all the evidence proved she was a murderer. He picked up the phone.

Andrea arrived on time for her appointment and settled herself opposite him, rearranging her skirts and hanging her bag on the back of the chair. She was conservatively dressed in a classic suit with matching accessories and if the woman he was defending looked naïve and innocent, Mrs Coe projected an air of healthy living and model behaviour.

She was more than willing to help her dear friend and spoke so fast it was impossible to keep up with his note taking. He was relieved when she agreed to the interview being recorded. He'd get one of the juniors to type up the transcript later.

"We've been friends for a number of years," she said, leaning forward to give him a glimpse of her cleavage and he felt himself responding to the aura of sexuality she exuded.

"I think it's true to say we've been what the children call BFF, best friends forever. We first met in London, we lived next door but one to each other. She was in a very unhappy marriage, even though most women would have envied her. OK, I know having a false leg can't have been easy, but besides that her husband was very generous. She had a beautiful home, foreign holidays and the freedom to do what she wanted. I can't tell you why she was so dissatisfied. Her stepdaughter is a sweet teenager, a little grumpy on occasion but then they all are these days, aren't they?"

He made no comment but sat silently waiting for her to continue.

"Then she grew a little strange. It was more than normal depression. She began to have hallucinations, she accused people of behaving weirdly, and it got so bad, her poor husband was forced to have her placed in an excellent private mental clinic."

"And how long was she there?"

"Only a few weeks. Her husband was overseas on business and the stepson she'd never met, returned from Australia, He had never got on with his father and he wangled her release. Much too soon in my opinion."

"And how did her husband react to that?"

"He was completely unaware as far as I know. Still overseas he's a high-powered lawyer and very well respected in the community. As I said, she had the perfect life until she began falling apart – that's the only way I can describe it. Such a shame."

She paused, stretching out to pick up a pen off his desk. She twirled it between her fingers and sighed.

"I can't tell you why it all went so wrong. When Mason

met her, she was just a poor little disabled mouse, and he gave her the world."

"And what was her relationship with the deceased?"

"Caro? She was Mason's first wife and Leah was insanely jealous of her. She told me that Caro had run off to South America with a toy boy. I always thought that Leah was terrified she would return and Mason would dump her and take up with Caro again. I mean she doesn't have a penny to her name, and Caro inherited a fortune from her deceased parents."

"And where is Mason Brand now?"

"I have no idea. I believe he's keeping his distance. It's his second failed marriage and he doesn't need that in his life. Of course, his work takes him all over the world, his clients are based in many different countries, and Mason looks after their interests in Britain."

The lawyer sifted through the papers in the file on his desk, and brought out a passport. He flipped it open to the Australian visa and showed it to Andrea. "Just recently, my client travelled to Perth. Have you any idea why?"

"She said it was somewhere she had always wanted to visit. To be honest I have no idea why. I'm sure the opera house in Sydney or Bondi Beach or even the Great Barrier Reef, would be more attractive. But she decided on a whim and off she went."

"On her own?"

"No, she's not that brave. Her stepdaughter Belinda and I, went with her. She insisted. But I paid for myself," she added hastily.

"Just a sightseeing trip then?"

"Pure tourism. Most of the time she's quiet and pliable but occasionally she gets an idea and then follows it through. She can be very strong willed when she wants to be."

"Now the night of the murder. What can you tell me about it?"

She sat and thought for a few moments.

"I had been staying in her flat in Weston for several weeks. She had been living there with a man called Bill, but he'd walked out on her. Poor dear, she's not had much luck with men."

"Mason was her first husband?"

"Oh dear no. Her second. Her first was killed in a car accident, along with their two children, hence the false leg, you know. He left her broke and she can't even afford a proper lawyer now that she is in so much trouble."

Thank you, he thought. Was Mrs Coe deliberately tactless?

There were more layers to Leah Brand than he suspected. "That night?" he prompted.

"Oh yes, the murder. Well I can only be honest, and admit that we had a bit of a tiff earlier in the week. She could fly off the handle on occasion for no reason at all. So, to give her a little space I took off for a few days, back to my home in London. Once I'd calmed down, I felt so sorry for her, she is my best friend after all, so I jumped in the car and drove back down to Weston. All the lights in the flat were out, but I had a key of course so I let myself in. I was planning to slip into bed in my own room, but there was a body in there already, I mean someone sleeping in the bed. I didn't stop to check who it was. I grabbed some cushions and a blanket from the hall cupboard and curled up on the couch in the television lounge."

"And then?"

"The next thing, I remember, were loud screams coming from the hallway. Belinda was standing by Leah's bedroom door and when I rushed to look, I saw Leah, drive a knife into the person who was sleeping in her bed. I had no idea who it was, no idea what was going on. It was so awful, blood everywhere and Leah, like a wild creature in her bloodstained nightie. I'll never get that picture out of my head."

Andrea covered her face with her hands, a rather dramatic performance that did not endear her to the solicitor on the other side of the desk. He sat and waited sad he could see no way out for his client. Not with an articulate witness like this one once the prosecution put her on the stand.

"Her motive for the murder? Do you have an idea why she would do it?"

"Darling, I told you," Andrea fluttered her eyes at him. "I already told you, she was insanely jealous of Caro. That was even when she was supposedly still in Brazil or wherever it was. To see her here in Weston must have been the final straw. Enough to push her over the edge."

The young solicitor drew out a plan of the flat and got Andrea to identify who slept in which bedroom. "Why then," he asked "was the deceased sleeping in the bedroom which had belonged to Leah? Why in fact was she even staying in the flat at all, if Mrs Brand was so antagonistic towards her?"

"Darling I have absolutely no idea. I can only suggest that Belinda persuaded her. Caro was her real mother after all."

Andrea gazed briefly at the ceiling and smiled shyly at Eric and re-arranged her skirt before she continued.

"After things had calmed down, I looked around the room I had been using only now it was full of Leah's things. I had only been gone a couple of days and in that time, she had got rid of anything that had belonged to me. Absolutely everything. Maybe she was clearing me out of her life as well. Such a shame, we'd been so close for so long."

She reached for a tissue from her bag and dabbed at her eyes.

While she was eye candy, especially for her age, and radiated sexuality like a cat on heat, the young man had had enough of her theatrics." He stood. "I think that will be all for today Mrs Coe."

"Oh." She looked disappointed.

"I appreciate you coming in to see me and for your time. You may well be called as a witness when this comes to trial."

"How long will that be? Goodness, I've never been in a court before. How exciting." Realising what she'd just said, she bit her lip and covered her confusion as she rescued her bag and straightened her jacket.

He saw her out, and breathed a sigh of relief when the door closed behind her. He deserved lunch before he talked to Belinda, the sweet teenager. He'd be gentle with her, she must be devastated at the loss of her mother, murdered by her stepmother. What a sad scenario.

Fortified at the local pub which dispensed real ale and an excellent Ploughman's lunch, he returned to his office for his chat with Belinda. What did the sweet teenager have to tell him?

His first impression was a neatly dressed young lady still in her school uniform. He decided that her skirt was a little on the short side then gave a mental shake. There was less than ten years in age between them, who was he to judge?

"Please sit down." He indicated the chair on the other side of his desk and she plonked herself down and dumped her school bag on the floor beside her and kicked it farther away. She crossed her legs and swung her top leg to and fro. If she continued with that it was going to irritate the hell out of him.

"Eric Chamberlin, I'm the guy defending your mother, uh, stepmother and your stepmother is Leah Brand. Correct?"

"Yeah, guess so." She fixed her eyes on the floor.

"So, I'd like you to tell me a little about your family."

She shrugged and remained silent.

"I'm really sorry for your loss."

She shrugged again. Her head was down he couldn't see her expression.

"Belinda, I know this must be painful for you."

She looked up. "Yeah, well these things happen."

Murder didn't happen every day, but he put her callous response down to bravado.

"I think you're being very brave and I imagine it can't be easy, but tell me about your mother, Caro."

"She was OK I guess."

"Were you close?"

"S'pose so."

"How did you feel when she moved to Brazil?"

"Ecuador."

"Pardon?"

"She went to Ecuador."

"Oh right." He scribbled in the file.

"Did she stay in touch with you?"

"Yeah."

It was like pulling teeth. "In what way? I mean by letter, or text on your phone?"

"When she left, I didn't have a phone."

"And did you reply to her letters?"

"Not often."

"Can you tell me why?"

"Nothing to tell her."

"I see. Do you know why she came back?"

Her body language changed. She went rigid and she twirled her fingers round the buttons on her blazer. She breathed a little faster and shrank back a little from him. She was hiding something.

He changed tack. "Do you know the date she arrived in England?"

"Last month."

"And did you know she was coming."

"Guess so." More shoulder shrugging.

"And did you meet with her?"

"Yeah."

"Where was that?"

She froze reminding him of a rabbit in the headlights. She didn't answer.

He tried again. "Did your stepmother know she was coming?"

"No." It was almost a shout.

"Maybe because she was so jealous of her?"

"What? Leah jealous of my mum? I don't think so."

"She may have been worried that the first Mrs Brand would come and displace her?"

"Fat chance. My mum ran off cos my dad..." she fell silent.

"Your dad?"

"Nothing."

He took a deep breath. "Belinda, I can call you that right? You want to help Leah?"

"Yeah, course."

"You can, by answering my questions. I'm here to help her. If she's found guilty of murder, they will lock her up in prison for the rest of her life." He wasn't sure his law professors would approve of the shock tactic approach but the child was hiding something and he needed to find out what it was.

He sat and waited. Even difficult teenagers rushed to fill pregnant pauses in conversation.

When she burst into tears, he took the opportunity to pass her a box of tissues, popped his head round the door and ordered two coffees. "And some of those nice custard creams," he whispered to his junior. The warm glow of his real ale had worn off.

There was silence until the coffees and biscuits were on the table and they were alone again.

"Shall we start at the beginning?"

Her sobs subsided, and she glanced at him through the veil of the long hair hanging over her face. She pushed it away and like flood gates opening, she told him the Brand family history. It all tumbled out without a pause. He could not keep up with his note taking so he put his pen down and listened.

She was remarkably honest. Her brother had been in jail, nowhere near Australia. Her father's clients verged on Mafia dealings and her mother had run off for her own safety. She told of Leah's haunting and her insanity and how she was due a huge sum of money in compensation for the car accident. The letter had arrived that day. No, her father had not been that loving to her mother, but then most families were not 'Little House on the Prairie' copycats.

He tried not to smile.

"Leah was dead scared of the police," she stopped.

"Do you know why?"

"She had this stupid idea they thought she pushed her mother down the stairs. She was an old crone anyway and if she'd been my mother, I tell you I'd have been tempted. She gave Leah a real hard time. So, when she fell and the police came Leah kept muttering about being 'a person of interest'. Soon put them right though as I saw it and she tripped. The old bag wasn't even dead she was still breathing when they carted her away in the ambulance.

As Belinda recounted the incident with dramatic arm waving, he wondered if he dared make another attempt to find out why Caro had returned.

"How did you get on with Leah? Wicked step mother?"

"Nah, she was OK, I guess. I sort of think she did her

best. She was a bit too fussy about the house, always cleaning and hoovering and polishing. Her food wasn't half bad." She went quiet again.

"I'd like to take you back to that night. What do you remember?"

"What's there to tell? Leah got the letter from the insurance company telling her she was going to get millions so she'd be fuck... rich. Uh, filthy rich. So, we all decided to go and celebrate. You would, wouldn't you?"

"Yes, I'd be dancing on the tables!"

Belinda smiled for the first time.

"When you say all, who was there?"

"Me, my mum and stepmother."

"So, let me get this straight. They were friendly?"

"Well yes, I guess so, they only met a few days ago, but they didn't fight or anything. Not proper BFF though." She saw him frown. "Best Friends Forever. BFF."

Of course, he'd heard that just this morning.

"And you came home when?"

"I dunno, late. We were the last to leave the restaurant. My mum was falling over, pretty drunk and Leah had to prop her up and she's got a false leg you know." Her eyes filled with tears and he waited for her to settle down.

"And when you all arrived home, was the flat empty?"

"Yeah I guess so. I just went straight to bed, didn't look round or anything."

"Then you woke up?"

"Yeah. Thought I heard the front door closing so got up to look and I saw Leah's bedroom door open and I peeped inside and that's when I saw..."

"What did you see?"

"I saw… Leah holding the knife and she was sort of lying on my mum and then I screamed and then Andrea came running in and, and I called the ambulance to come and save my mum. But it was too late." She pulled more tissues from the box and wiped her cheeks. "They wouldn't take her away they said it was too late. Why wouldn't they? They left her lying there." She grabbed more paper hankies.

Eric Chamberlin slipped out of his chair and told his junior to cancel his later appointments. Belinda's view on several things did not match the information Andrea had given him, so who was telling the truth?

As soon as Belinda had settled down a little, he asked her "Why didn't Andrea go out and celebrate with you?"

"'Cos she wasn't there. She did that, get herself into a strop and push off to London. She was always oozing over Leah but if she didn't get her way then she'd get all antsy and then if Leah snapped back, she was all soppy over her again."

"So, if Andrea wasn't there when you got back from the restaurant, when did she arrive?"

Belinda shrugged. "Dunno."

"When you heard the front door, could she have been coming in then?"

"Maybe."

"And where was Andrea when you first saw her?"

"Uh, in the hallway. I uh, could tell she'd been sleeping, her hair was all mussed up and she was blinking like an owl you know like you do when you first wake up."

He noticed that Belinda wouldn't look at him. *She's lying*, he thought *but why?*

"There's one other thing that I don't understand. Wasn't the room where your mother was sleeping, Leah's bedroom?"

"Yeah, she'd been in there when Bill lived with us. It's got an ensuite so when Mum came, Leah insisted on giving her that room. Said it would be nicer for her."

"Belinda, one last question. Do you think Leah killed your mother?"

"No, she sodding well didn't. She wouldn't do that. She's too soft, she couldn't do something like that. She didn't hate my mum or anything." She leapt to her feet, eyes blazing, hands flapping. "You got to get her off, right? She can't go to jail, she can't." She began to sob, wracking gulps of air that shook her body.

He wasn't sure what to do. He stood up and clutched the edge of his desk. Would it be inappropriate to physically comfort her? You had to be so careful these days with accusations of the #metoo brigade.

Belinda solved the problem for him. She grabbed her bag and rushed out of the room.

He sighed, he could see no way of persuading a judge that Leah Brand was innocent, but he'd heard two different stories and one of the witnesses wasn't telling the truth. To make matters worse, one minute the teenager said Leah was leaning over the body with a knife on her hand, the next that she was innocent.

He'd have to talk to both of them again

DECEMBER   LEAH

'Prison', even the word sends shivers down my spine. They have told me that as I'm still on remand, and not convicted I have more privileges than I will have after sentencing. The staff are pleasant and polite but I can sense they believe I'm guilty and it's only a matter of time until a judge sends me down for years.

I can't help them because I can't describe the events of that terrible night. Did I kill Caro? I have no idea, but why would I want to? I liked her we had a lot in common. In the restaurant we were laughing and joking with Belinda. We were all happy, celebrating. What was the occasion, was it a birthday?

I had a nightmare last night. I'd walked into a bedroom and saw and smelled blood and then I was pinned in the car, James' body crushed behind the steering wheel, the whimpering from the back seat when I couldn't reach my babies. Then silence, followed by the screams that went on and on.

My legal defence is very young. Not that it's important. I can't see a way out and I doubt if he can either.

They came to tell me I have a visitor waiting. I don't want to see anyone, but it will help to pass the time. On remand they told me I can have three one hour visits a week, so I'll make the most of them.

More doors unlocked and locked. Thick steel bars everywhere, rows of cells, feet echoing on metal floors. Shouts and shrieks from other prisoners, sobs and wails. I have years of this ahead. Surrounded by people yet so lonely.

An open room metal tables spaced well apart each secured to the floor, two plastic bucket chairs one on either side. As the guard led me across the tiled floor, I could see Andrea. She didn't desert me after all. I went to hug her but the warden warned me off. No touching. We sat, staring, neither of us sure where to begin.

DECEMBER ANDREA

Even the word prison makes my insides curl up. When I saw them bring Leah into the room I wanted to get up and run. Hell, she looked a mess, some shapeless jersey they found for her and a pair of baggy track pants which did not go with the smart shoes I'd taken to the police station for her court appearance. Geez this is going above and beyond, but not for long, oh no, not for long. It sucks. I'll have to sit around waiting for a trial. That really pisses me off. If I do move away, I have to tell them where I am and that won't suit at all. Time to switch on the charm.

I stood up to give my best friend a huge hug, but the warden motioned me back. Bloody spoilsport.

"Leah darling, you look dreadful but I've brought you clothes, and toiletries. I had to leave it all at the reception area but you'll get it later." I chuckled. "Probably checking it for hidden hacksaws, lengths of rope and escape tools." She didn't laugh. "Sweetie, how are you really? How are you coping?"

"OK, I guess."

"It must be so awful for you darling, if I could change places with you, I'd do it in a heartbeat. My poor darling and after all you've been through. Life is so bloody unfair."

She shrugged but didn't answer. This was going to be

an uphill battle. I couldn't wait to get out of there and they said I could stay for an hour. I glanced at my watch. Three minutes down, only fifty-seven to go.

"Darling have you woken up? You were in such a dream state when they took you away."

"I'm living the nightmare." She kept running her fingers along the edge of the metal table, up and down up and down. Maybe she was on the edge of madness again.

"Leah, why did you do it?" I kept my voice low.

"Do what?"

"Kill Caro. What had she ever done to you?"

"I... I don't know, I don't think... I..."

"I know you were insanely jealous of her and furious she ran off and abandoned Belinda."

She sat up straight and stared at me, her eyes boring into mine, her finger pointing. "That's nonsense. Where did you get that from?"

"But you told me so many times."

"Rubbish Andrea! I may not remember the night of the murder, they told me the brain shuts down and forgets traumatic moments, but I haven't forgotten my former life. Mason was as unkind to her as he was to me."

"Oh, I'm sorry I got that so wrong." Damn, I'd hoped she'd believe me. I'd repeat it in court first chance I got. It was the perfect motive.

"We were out celebrating earlier that evening, but I can't remember why."

"How strange. Maybe Caro was going back to Brazil and taking Belinda with her?"

"No, not that, that wouldn't have made me happy." She

started, tapping her nails making an irritating sound on the table. "What's going to happen to Belinda? Who's going to look after her?"

"I have no idea. At the moment we're both in the flat, but Leah, she'd not my child and I'm not the mothering sort. Social Services I guess."

"Oh no. Anything but that."

"Nah, it's not so bad, some foster homes are OK."

"How would you know?"

Whoops, the woman was sharper than I thought. "Oh, you know, tales, stories," I was deliberately vague. "She could opt to look after herself at her age, but as she's still in full tine education, that's when she bothers to go to school that is…" I let the thought hang in the air.

I couldn't stop Leah from worrying about Belinda. You'd think she had enough problems of her own. Not even prison changed her, thinking of other people before herself. How bloody perfect she was.

The rest of the hour dragged slowly. I lied and said I'd not heard from Mason. I plied her with questions about prison life and what it was like and even tried a few jokes to cheer her up, but I didn't lift her depression. I wasn't too fussed, but I had yet to ask her the one big question.

"Leah darling, I know you're locked up in here and helpless but life outside goes on. Bills need to be paid, rent, gas, electricity. I asked the Prisoners' Society for you, to find out what happens. They say it's best to get an outsider to fill in for you." I leaned forward. "What can I do to help? If I can sort out things, then Belinda will have a roof over her head for now. If you give me power of attorney just say the word and I'll keep the wheels turning." I held my breath. This was the pivotal moment. I'd checked out the insurance letter, I'd rifled through her papers and found her bank statements, it was all in place.

She sat for several moments. "Let me think about it. Maybe my lawyer…"

"That child!" I could feel the fury rise inside from my toes to my head. "Leah, you can't possibly trust him! You don't know him. I'm your best friend."

"I know but it will be a burden for you. You've done enough already."

"Darling I could never do too much." I was about to launch into the 'remember when' times when that bloody warden called time. I gripped the sides of the plastic chair to stop my hands shaking. I'd counted on her cooperating and now the bitch was being difficult. I fixed a silly smile on my face as I said goodbye, and watched them escort her out.

Once back at the flat I was relieved to see Belinda was out. I wandered into Leah's old room. The blood-soaked sheets had been taken for forensics, which I thought bloody stupid really as any fool could see it was Caro's blood.

The loud chimes on the answerphone startled me but it was only Mason who barged in through the front door.

He threw his arms around me and pressed his lips to mine. I returned them with a fervour I didn't feel, but I've always prided myself on my acting skills.

"She's safely locked up this time," he chortled, making for the drinks' cabinet.

"Yes, and they can't blame us. Make mine a brandy, a large one."

"So, the money is finally through?"

"May take a couple more days, I had to email them with the bank account details."

"As Leah I hope?"

"Of course." I wandered into the kitchen looking for something to eat. As I suspected there were two meat pies and an apple tart in the fridge and a stack of homemade frozen dinners in the freezer. Good old Leah, we weren't going to starve.

"What do you fancy?" I called back to Mason who was searching through the music DVDs.

"Surprise me. Oh, I have some excellent news."

I chose a cottage pie and turned the oven on. "I hope it's better than the news I have for you." I leaned on the kitchen counter. "She refused to give me power of attorney."

"Damn her! Another delay. I'll twist her arm, say it's for Belinda and she'll have to agree."

I turned back to grab a packet of frozen peas and poured them into a microwaveable dish. "I thought you were going to keep out of sight."

"I'll reappear. Happy family reunion and all that."

"Won't that look suspicious?"

"I can't do anything about border controls. My passport will show when I re-entered Britain. What did you expect me to do? Hide out in a refrigerated truck on the Euro Tunnel like a bloody refugee?"

"No, I guess not." I slammed a couple of plates down and fished for the place mats and cutlery.

"What's your good news?"

"Leo. He's got himself banged up again. Stupid prat. Got in with his ex-con friends again dealing drugs. And one of his charming friends bartered for leniency by shopping him for sending heavies round to scare the life out of Leah. That'll add to his sentence."

I walked over and pressed myself against him, sliding my hand down his stomach to rest at the top of his legs. "That is excellent news, one less to share. We can also forget Malcolm. He's no use to us now. He can scream his head off but it won't get him anywhere. If he goes to the police, he'll only implicate himself."

"Strange how things work out. We targeted Leah, but got Caro instead and now wife number two is going down for murdering wife number one."

"Two birds with one stone."

We laughed.

I felt as high as a kite, like I could fly. I'd soar above those fools beavering away to pay bills month after month, desperate for payday. Not for me a dull, grey life sweating my guts out for some uncaring corporation. So, we'd worked hard for months but look at the big reward. It was all coming together. Good food, good drink and an afternoon in bed. I'd move my things in there later and take advantage of the en-suite bathroom.

We lay in bed planning our future. I was dismayed to read the list of thirty-three countries that did not have an extradition treaty with the UK, I didn't fancy living in any of them. Afghanistan, Namibia and Mongolia were not on my wish list. I'd assumed that the Caribbean would suit me very well, but we had a few weeks to sort out the details.

I was quite relieved to hear Mason say we didn't need Belinda to tag along. She was a big girl now and could look after herself. I suggested he open a bank account for her, but he was non-committal so I'd not pushed it. We decided to go celebrate in style but we'd take a taxi to Bristol where no one would recognise us.

I waltzed into the bathroom to get ready.

DECEMBER LEAH

Dear Diary,

They have allowed me to buy paper and pens from the store here. Andrea had the good sense to leave money I can spend. I treated myself to a large packet of Liquorice Allsorts. I've not had them since I was a kid, but when I saw them on the shelf I couldn't resist. I'll have to go carefully my money won't last long. They don't offer work to prisoners on remand.

I'm starting to remember things. My mind shut down but now its operating at twice the speed. From a book I got in the library this stress is quite normal. Incarceration can swing from apathy to a survival response.

I want to survive, but I'm not sure how.

I had another visitor today. I almost refused to see him, but I'm avoiding all the other inmates, and I'm so bereft of human company, I agreed.

I could see Bill was embarrassed. He wasn't the only one. He looked at me with such love in his eyes, I felt a waterfall of tears rolling down my cheeks. He took my hands in his across the metal table, and today's warden was either more sympathetic or not bothered about the rules.

I didn't know what to say. How could I explain why I'd

cut off his calls and not returned his texts? Only that I was so hurt he'd walked out on me. The second man to do that in a matter of months.

It was then I learned the reason why. Leo had paid him a visit. He had not threatened Bill, but told him he would hurt me if he didn't move out. He'd tried to keep in touch but I'd not responded.

"Leo threatened you?"

"No, his threats were against you, if I didn't stay away. I couldn't risk anything happening to you. He was family after all."

"Why didn't you go to the police?"

"And tell them what? It would be my word against his."

He had a point.

I took a deep breath. "Bill, is it true that you um…" I couldn't put it into words.

"Is what true?"

"You uh, made a pass at Andrea? She told me you forced yourself on her."

Sitting back in my cell later I thought over our conversation. Bill had turned bright red. He was so angry he couldn't get the words out. Much as Andrea had been such a good friend, I'd caught her out in one lie, that I was jealous of Caro. This time I believed Bill. Why had Andrea turned so nasty? I couldn't figure it out.

It was a comfort to have another friend on the outside. I had asked Bill's opinion on giving my lawyer or Andrea my power of attorney, at least for a few months.

He shook his head and looked horrified. Not Andrea, not her. He said anyone in the whole world but her. He was adamant I use a lawyer, or if that would be too expensive, he had suggested Aunt Deidre.

I've deliberately not thought about James' favourite aunt. She was still in the south of France and enjoying life. In her last letter she said she was looking round for property to buy. She'd had enough of the cold, wet winters in Weston and the south of France was the place to be.

I'd been tempted to contact her, but I felt so ashamed I'm now in a bigger mess than before. Whatever Cannes or Nice was doing to her she had no fey feelings about me now.

Our time was nearly up. "One last question Bill. Why did you come here today after you stopped texting me? Because you feel sorry for me?"

"But I never stopped sending them. One every day, just in case you changed your mind, had second thoughts."

"I didn't see them, not after the first couple of weeks."

"They can be deleted."

"I didn't think about that. I wonder if Andrea…?"

"And I never stopped loving you, not for a moment. I just hoped that if I was patient, maybe…? And I'll be here every visit they allow me. I don't believe for a moment you could murder anyone, and if they give me a chance, I'll tell them that in court. Doesn't matter what anyone else says."

I had tears in my eyes when I watched Bill leave. I felt a lot better after his visit than an hour with Andrea. I had such doubts about her and they are beginning to creep in again. How can I be so ungrateful? But there's something I can't quite put my finger on.

Time for exercise. Circuits walking around the yard

outside, or time in the gym on the machines. That's the sum total of the decisions I need to make each day. Strapping on my prosthesis, I can't get the right cream in here to stop it rubbing, it occurred to me for the first time, future hassles from the bullies in real prison.

Oh God, please protect me.

DECEMBER ERIC

I'd had another good lunch at the pub next door. I must watch my waist line, I'm getting too fond of the real ale and today's steak pie was even better than yesterday's ploughman's.

I put one foot in the door to the main office when my junior indicated I had a visitor. No, no appointment.

I was not pleased. I had a full case load, three booked sessions this afternoon and I had planned to leave on time. It felt as if the whole of Weston-super-Mare was on a crime spree. I told her to explain I was too busy and to make an appointment for next week.

"I think you'll want to make time," she informed me and pointed to the figure perched on the chair outside my office.

It was Belinda.

"I'll see her, bring me coffee and biscuits and send her in in five."

I delved into the piles of paperwork on my desk. I needed to remind myself of our last conversation. She had run out of the room in tears shouting that she knew her stepmother wasn't a murderer. She was probably just an over-wrought teenager, but a sixth sense told me I needed to hear what she had to say.

The refreshments and Belinda entered my room at the same time. Without being invited she slumped down in the wooden chair on the other side of my desk and glared at me. "Have you found out how to get my mum off yet?" She demanded. Every fibre of her was taut, her attitude aggressive.

I took a deep breath and leaned back a little in my chair. I'd been wrong, she was just here to make a scene. "No Belinda I haven't and I'm sorry. It is what we call an open and shut case. Caught in the act. The best I can do is to instruct her barrister to present mitigating circumstances to the judge. That means to explain reasons…"

"I know what mitigating circumstances are," she interrupted me. "I watch court cases on telly. I'm not stupid."

"No, I never for a moment thought you were."

"I don't want Leah to spend her life in fucking jail. Isn't it your job to get her off?"

"It's my job to defend her, but if my clients have committed a crime, then there is a limit to what I can do."

"Yeah, you said that, but I told you she didn't do it. Don't you believe me? I'll tell the judge that myself."

"I'm truly sorry Belinda but that will not work. I think it a great idea if you can speak up for your stepmother in court, that could be part of the mitigating circumstances, but courts need proof to be sure a person is guilty."

"Yeah and what proof have you got then, tell me." She was working herself into quite a state and it crossed my mind I should call in one of the other lawyers.

"Please calm down Belinda."

"Don't you bloody well tell me to calm down. It's not your mum that's in jail."

It struck me that she was now calling Leah her mother, when had that changed from stepmother?

"No, you're quite right it's not. Proof? We have a signed statement from a witness that your stepmother was still standing over the body when the police arrived. I believe you called them."

"No. I called the ambulance people to come and save her. The police turned up anyway."

"So, you see my hands are tied."

"I suppose it was bloody Andrea who said she saw the real killing? The knife going in and out?"

I winced at the mental picture that she brought to mind. I'd looked at the photographs of course but that's not quite the same thing.

"That bitch is lying. You didn't believe her, did you?"

"It doesn't matter what I believe Belinda. The case will go before the Crown Court and it will be the jury who decide and then the judge will pass a sentence. Yes, every accused is innocent until proven guilty under the law here, but there is little doubt in this case."

I saw her face redden as she fought back tears of anger and frustration. She jumped to her feet, running her hands over her skirt, and began to pace back and forth in front of my desk. She was wrestling with herself, balling her hands into fists, then flexing her fingers. She picked up my executive toys one at a time before banging them back down on the desk.

I sat and watched her. The child was fighting with

demons, undecided, weighing up, I had no idea what, but I waited, sensing she was about to tell me something I needed to know.

And then she did.

DECEMBER   ANDREA

It's four paces from side to side and ten paces from one end to the other. Shit, farm animals have more space to move around. I'll top myself I swear I will. It's all down to that bitch Belinda. I swear if I ever get out of here, I'll top her, I will.

I tried so bloody hard with her. 'Sweetie this and Darling that' and she goes and drops us in it.

Well, they're going to have fun with this one. I have told them that Mason cut Caro's throat and I'm swearing innocence and blaming him. Either way one of us will be out a lot earlier. They won't lock up an accomplice for as many years, will they?

I still don't know what went wrong. I didn't see her when I crept in, nor when I opened the door to let Mason in. When the London police came and arrested us, Mason totally lost it. All he could do was shout at me for pointing out the wrong fucking bedroom. He can blame me all he likes, but to say he's never been in the flat, is plain stupid. The night we celebrated he left his fingerprints all over the place and his DNA on the sheets. They will lie and say it was that night, not days after. Shit, I hope Mason has good lawyer friends. I don't fancy his chances if he ends up in the same prison as some of his mafia buddies.

I must stop beating my fists against the walls. The wardens get really pissed off wiping up all the blood and dragging me to the infirmary to get them bandaged up yet again.

Think positive Andrea, prison may not be so bad. Lots of opportunity to make money on the side. Leo will be out in a few years and he has the right connections. Think positive and begin planning.

DECEMBER LEAH

The warm December sun wrapped around us like a welcome space blanket as we walked down the steps off the plane. The one-hour flight from Paris landed at Nice airport, with Belinda grumbling that there hadn't been a film to watch on either flight.

I had explained when we took off from Heathrow not all the planes were equipped for long haul.

"Yeah well I wouldn't be me if I didn't make a fuss," she grinned and I gave her a hug as we walked across the tarmac to collect our cases.

Aunt Deidre was on the other side of the barrier and enveloped us both in her arms.

"I am so angry with you," she told me after the drive to her new villa. We had settled on her terrace, in the late sunshine, overlooking the blue Mediterranean Sea. "I'm hurt you didn't call me." She poured real coffee into dainty china cups.

"I was too ashamed. I made such a mess of everything."

"No, you didn't," she snapped back sliding the plate of French pastries towards Belinda who was ogling some boys on the beach. "You got mixed up with a criminally dysfunctional family through no fault of your own. Nice people don't expect to get involved with well…" she paused as she remembered Belinda was part of that criminally dysfunctional family.

"Don't mind me," she grinned. "That's exactly how I'd describe my relatives. They're all a bunch of wank... uh losers. Can I go and walk along the beach?"

"Of course, you can."

Belinda grabbed a handful of pastries and sauntered towards the other teenagers.

"They bounce up so quickly at that age," observed Aunt Deidre.

"A lot of it is bravado. I can tell she's hurting inside. The last couple of months have been a nightmare."

Aunt Deidre settled back in her chair. "I'm waiting. Start after they arrested you."

I paused and watched a bright green lizard scurry along the edge of the brickwork and disappear down a crack in the paving. "I don't remember much of the night of the murder. We had been out celebrating, and for days after I couldn't even remember what the occasion was."

"The compensation on the car accident?"

"Yes. The letter had arrived that afternoon. You can imagine the excitement. We were dancing around making such a racket and planning what to do with it all. I do feel sorry for the neighbours I'm sure they're relieved we've moved out."

Deidre put her head back and laughed.

"When I got back to the flat weeks later, I couldn't find the letter and began to wonder if that was all part of the nightmare too. Then they phoned to tell me the money had been deposited. Apparently, someone, probably Andrea, had helpfully emailed them my bank details.

"The night of the murder? I can't tell you what

happened. I have a vague memory of a man putting handcuffs on me. I never realised they could be so uncomfortable and so heavy. The metal digs into your skin." Whenever I thought of that moment, I couldn't stop myself from rubbing my wrists just like I was doing now. I could feel Aunt Deidre's eyes on me and pulled my hands away and gripped the arms of the patio chair to still them.

I listened to the call of the sea birds, the distant roar of a plane as it began its descent to the airport and the intermittent chatter of the voices on the beach. I cast my mind back.

"There was a young lawyer, a Public Defender. He tried to help, but much as I wanted to tell him I had no words. It was the strangest feeling. I couldn't talk not even to defend myself. They told me I was seen standing over the body, a knife in my hand. I didn't remember any of it." I shivered, and waves of cold air washed over me despite the warm sunshine.

"Maybe tomorrow," Aunt Deidre began to rise.

"No, I want to finish. The psychiatrist advised me it was good to verbalise, get it all out there."

Deidre nodded. "Sounds wise. Never good to bottle things up. Go on."

"Prison was awful, I would not recommend it to anyone. They were kind, but the boredom was enough to drive anyone insane. Locked up for hours on end. I could have spent more time outside the cell, but I was scared witless of the other inmates. I'm frightened of violence."

"Most of us are, that's nothing new." The bangles on Aunt Deidre's arms jangled as she smoothed her long floral skirt over her knees. It toned in with her bright yellow shirt it was easy to see she was a leftover hippy from the flower power days right down to the sensible sandals on her feet.

"You know, Andrea came to visit me in prison. She was still pretending to be my friend and asked me why I did it. She told me I'd been insanely jealous of Caro which was utter nonsense. I wracked my brains later trying to remember if I had ever said any such thing. Now she's the one sitting in prison."

"But the tables turned so quickly?" Aunt Deidre leaned forward, her brow furrowed, the question hanging in the air.

"It was Belinda. She didn't say anything at first. She knew I had a lawyer and I was innocent and she's watched too many legal shows on TV. They always get the bad guy of course and the good guy never has to serve time."

Deidre laughed. "And in the end, it all works out and everyone is happy and they all walk off into the sunset. So unrealistic."

"She woke up when Andrea crept back into the flat that night, and she saw her let Mason in. She overheard them whisper and then creep into my room and stab me – as they thought."

"They had no intentions of killing Caro?"

"No, they didn't even know she was there. All Andrea knew was there was someone in the bedroom she'd used. They were trying to kill me, but Caro was sleeping in my bed. It was a matter of mistaken identity."

"It could so easily have been you."

"Yes. When Belinda realised that the lawyer couldn't

get me off and wouldn't take her word for it that I didn't do it, she was desperate enough to show him the video."

"Video?"

"She used her mobile to record the stabbing. It showed both Mason and Andrea in action – not too clearly as it was quite dark, but the police enhanced it and they were caught in the act."

"But whatever possessed her to use her phone?"

"Belinda's phone is welded to her hand, I'm not sure she puts it down when she showers! She had some idea that it might come in useful. She had a wild thought she could blackmail her dad into staying in England and some unrealistic hope that her parents would get together again if I was out of the way and they would be one happy family. In the heat of the moment she had forgotten that Caro was in my room."

"Good heavens." I'd never seen Aunt Deidre look so shocked. She fiddled with the tea things piling up the plates, cups and saucers leaving them to perch precariously on top of each other.

"A few days later she overheard Andrea and Mason celebrating their success. 'Two birds with one stone – wife one murdered by wife number two and now they were free to spend all my money."

"And could they have done that?"

"I guess so. There was a good chance I would give power of attorney to Mason, and I appeared to have forgotten the payout while I was acting like a zombie. Without Belinda I would still be locked up and they might well have got away with it."

"For once justice is served."

"Yes." I sat and watched as Belinda began to pick her way back along the beach towards the house. "Except Mason and Andrea are now blaming each other. I wonder which one they will charge with murder? Can you prosecute two people?"

"I have no idea, but as long as they both remain behind bars who cares?"

Francoise who kept house for Deidre came out with a tray to clear away the remains of the afternoon tea.

"What time do we need to leave for the airport?" Belinda asked as she bounded over the low wall onto the patio.

Aunt Deidre checked her watch. "In about half an hour."

I felt a flutter inside. I had missed Bill and even Belinda looked forward to seeing him. "We can be a family at last, a proper family. I'll never forgive bloody Andrea deleting his messages off your fucking phone. Honest Leah you are such a techie idiot. I have a lot to teach you."

"True, but that reminds me. We need to go house hunting and tracking down a tutor for you too. You have exams to take and pass."

"Gee why do you have to spoil everything?" Belinda followed Francoise up the path and grabbed the last pastry off the plate.

"Life isn't all fun and games."

"You got that right. I've made a list of stuff to buy." She pulled a piece of paper from the back pocket of her jeans. "I saw one of those new laptops at the airport, and…"

"Not so fast, let's find a place to live first. Somewhere you, me and Bill all love and then we can talk about stuff like that."

As we walked back into the house, the sun was just setting below the headland, turning golden shafts of light over the Mediterranean Sea.

As I climbed the steps back to the house, I prayed that at last, life would be filled with happiness and laughter. It would take time for us all to heal but I had such hope for the future surrounded by the people I loved.

$< < < OOO > > >$

ACKNOWLEDGEMENTS

While a writer spends many hours in mental isolation committing words to paper, to bring a book into the public domain is always the result of teamwork.

My thanks to Mark Nierada for help and advice on the current legal practices in England. I am grateful for his patience in explaining who does what, when and how in the courts. It's more complicated than I had imagined.

David Platt who worked in the prison service gave me lots of insight into remand centres and prison life in general.

All errors are my responsibility.

Grateful thanks to my editor Teddi Adams, Sharon Brownlie for the cover, and I cannot omit my long-suffering husband who has yet again given me the time and space to spend hours at the keyboard during our lockdown in Spain surrounded in silence while we were isolated from the rest of the world.

ABOUT THE AUTHOR

Lucinda E Clarke has been a professional writer for almost 40 years, scripting for both radio and television. She's had numerous articles published in several national magazines, written mayoral speeches and advertisements. She currently writes a monthly column in a local publication in Spain. She once had her own newspaper column, until the newspaper closed down, but says this was not her fault!

Six of her books have been bestsellers in genre on Amazon on both sides of the Atlantic winning several medals and certificates. Lucinda has also received over 20 awards for scripting, directing, concept and producing, and had two educational text books traditionally published. Sadly, these did not make her the fortune she dreamed of to allow her to live in luxury.

Lucinda has also worked on radio – on one occasion with a bayonet at her throat – appeared on television, and met and interviewed some of the world's top leaders.

She set up and ran her own video production company, producing a variety of programmes, from advertisements to corporate and drama documentaries on a vast range of subjects.

In total she has lived in eight different countries, run the 'worst riding school in the world', and cleaned toilets to bring in the money.

When she handled her own divorce, Lucinda made legal history in South Africa.

Now, pretending to be retired, she gives occasional talks and lectures to special interest groups and finds retirement the most exhausting time of her life so far; but says there is still so much to see and do, she is worried she won't have time to fit it all in.

TO MY READERS

If you have enjoyed this book, or even if you didn't like it, please take a few minutes to write a review. Reviews are very important to authors and I would certainly value your feedback. Thank you.

Why not sign up for Lucinda's newsletter for special offers, competitions, news on other authors and new releases. http://eepurl.com/cBu4Sf Subscribers get a free book and the exclusive serialized back stories to the Amie series.

Web page: lucindaeclarkeauthor.com
Facebook:
https://www.facebook.com/lucindaeclarke.author
Email: lucindaeclarke@gmail.com
Blog: http://lucindaeclarke.wordpress.com
Twitter: @LucindaEClarke
I love to hear from my readers.

Also by Lucinda E Clarke

A Year in the life of Leah Brand.

The nightmare began the day the dog died. Leah's cosy new world is turned upside down as inanimate objects more around the house on their own, there are unexplained noises, and slowly she is driven to the edge of madness.

https://www.amazon.com/dp/B07WHJKGXF

Walking over Eggshells

The first autobiography which relates Lucinda's horrendous relationship with her mother and her travels to various countries.

http://www.amazon.com/dp/B00E8HSNDW

The very Worst riding School in the World (free)

Who in their right mind would open and run a riding school when they can't ride, are terrified of horses, with no idea of how to care for them and no insurance or capital? Add to that two of the four horses are not fit for the knacker's yard Yes, that would be me.

Truth, Lies and Propaganda

The first of two books explaining how Lucinda 'fell' into writing for a living – her dream since childhood. It began

when she was fired from her teaching job, and crashed out in an audition at the South African Broadcasting Corporation. In a quirky turn of fate, she found herself writing a series on how to care for domestic livestock, she knew absolutely nothing about cows, goats and chickens. And it all continued from there.
http://www.amazon.com/dp/B00QE35BO2

More Truth, Lies and Propaganda
Tales of filming in deep rural Africa, meeting a ram with an identity crisis, a house that disappears, the forlorn bushmen and a video starring a very dead rat. You will never believe anything you watch on television ever again.
http://www.amazon.com/dp/B00VF0S3RG

Amie - African Adventure
A novel set in Africa, which takes Amie from the comfort of her home in England to a small African country. Civil war breaks out and soon she is fighting for her life.
http://www.amazon.com/dp/B00LWFIO5K

Amie and the Child of Africa
As Amie goes in search of the child she fostered before the civil war broke out, she encounters a terrorist organization with international connections. She is not alone, but one of her friends will betray her.
http://www.amazon.com/dp/B015CI29O4

Amie Stolen Future
In one night, Amie loses everything, her home, her family,

her possessions and her name. She has nowhere to turn, but she has no freedom for other people now control her life and if she does not obey them, they will not let her live.
http://www.amazon.com/dp/B01M67NRG4

Amie Cut for Life
A look and listen mission turns out to be a nightmare as Amie is left to rescue four young girls who are destined for the sex slave trade with a horrifying twist.
https://www.amazon.com/dp/B07545M9DB

Samantha (Amie backstory 1)
A light comedy as Amie's sister ventures overseas for the first time with her boyfriend Gerry – if it can go wrong, it goes wrong.
https://www.amazon.com/dp/B07HVNXV6F

Ben (Amie backstory 2)
Ben's story of his passage into manhood and the beginning of the civil war in Togodo.
https://www.amazon.com/dp/B07K352ZLQ

Unhappily Ever After
The real truth you've never been told before. In Fairyland, Cinderella is scheming to get a divorce with a good settlement from King Charming, and the other royal marriages are also in dire trouble. This year's ball is approaching, along with a political agitator hell bent on rousing the peasants into revolting against their royal masters.
http://www.amazon.com/dp/B01DPVB4M8

Reviews

A six star read, I can't wait for the next one. (**A Year in the Life of Leah Brand - Book 1**)

―――――――――

That Lucinda E Clarke can write and write well is not in question. This memoir left me breathless at times. She writes of her adventures, misadventures and family relationships in an honest but entertaining manner. I wholeheartedly recommend this book, **(Walking over Eggshells)** buy it, delve in and lose a few days, well worth it.

―――――――――

This book was written with such consummate skill. I have enormous admiration for Lucinda E Clarke as an author. She not only knows how to write an edge-of-the-seat, well-constructed story that would make a brilliant movie – she does it using beautiful, spare, intelligent, and amazingly descriptive language. By the time I got to the end of 'Amie' I felt as though I'd been to Africa – seen it, touched it, smelled it, heard it... loved it and hated it. Everything that is the truth of the country is there in this book. Can I give it six stars please? It deserves it. (**Amie an African Adventure**)

―――――――――

Lucinda E. Clarke takes the reader on another fast-paced African adventure full of suspense and twists and turns. The characters are so well developed that I felt as if I was watching a movie while reading this wonderful book. Mrs. Clarke both entertains and educates the reader about the African experience. The story never lags and quickly pulls the reader in this new adventure. (**Amie and the Child of Africa**).

What a great book! I have so enjoyed this and love the tongue-in-cheek, self-deprecating humour with which Lucinda Clarke relates her experiences. It's quite fascinating to read how she becomes involved in writing and broadcasting, and also really interesting to realise how much easier it was to get in touch with decision makers in the days before the digital onslaught. Either that or Lucinda is being overly modest and making it look simple! I loved the descriptions of her early experiences in Libya - both funny and frightening. And of course, there are lots of memories for me here as I moved to South Africa in the early eighties and always listened to Springbok radio. The style is easy and fluid, and I have enjoyed every page, riveted by the quantity of writing she managed to do without any previous knowledge of the subjects. Amazing. For me, this is the best one of Lucinda's yet in terms of keeping me pasted to my Kindle! I've read two of her other books before, and I'll definitely be reading the sequel to this one! (**Truth, Lies and Propaganda**)

I picked this one up purely on the basis of how much I enjoyed reading the first book and I was not to be disappointed. Lucinda E Clarke is one of those writers who can tell a story effortlessly in a way that just carries you along with her adventures. I have to say she is fast becoming one of my favourite authors. The book revolves around a period of her life as she returns to work in Africa and she uses her natural writing ability to not just recount events but to entertain along the way. Her skill is not in telling extraordinary tales but in making often ordinary real life stories come to life and it is in the smaller details of each story that I often found myself most enthralled. I cannot recommend this book and indeed the previous one highly enough. If your next book purchase is from the pen of Lucinda E Clarke you will have made a wise decision indeed. A thoroughly deserved 5 stars out of 5 from me. (**More, truth Lies and Propaganda**)

———————

The author's imagination and humour are combined to create a story that makes your smile or LOL from beginning to end. It is a rollicking pantomime of dry wit and well-described imagery that works exceptionally well. Highly recommended. (**Unhappily Ever After**)

———————

An excerpt from: Amie - African Adventure

Prologue

They came for her soon after the first rays of the sun began to pour over the far distant hills, spilling down the slopes onto the earth below. At first the gentle beams warmed the air, but as the sun rose higher in the sky, it produced a scorching heat, which beat down on the land with relentless energy.

She heard them approach, their footsteps echoing loudly on the bare concrete floors. As the marching feet drew closer, she curled up as small as she could, and tried to breathe slowly to stop her heart racing. No, please, not again, she whispered to herself. She couldn't take much more. What did they want? Would they beat her again? What did they expect her to say?

There was nothing she could tell them she was keeping no secrets. She knew she couldn't take any more pain every little bit of her body ached. How many films had she seen where people were kicked or beaten up? She'd never understood real pain, the real agony even a single punch could inflict on the body. Now all she wanted was to die, to escape the torture and slide away into oblivion.

The large fat one was the first to appear on the other

side of the door. She knew he was important, because the gold braid, medals, ribbons and badges on his uniform told everyone he was a powerful man, a man it would be very dangerous to cross. He was accompanied by three other warders, also in uniform, but with fewer decorations.

They unlocked the old, rusty cell door and the skinny one walked over and dragged her to her feet. He pushed her away from him, swung her round and bound her wrists together behind her back, with a long strip of dirty cotton material. She winced as he pulled roughly on the cloth and then propelled her towards the door. The others stood back as they shoved her into the corridor and up the steps to the ground floor.

She thought they were going to turn left towards the room where they made her sit for hours and hours on a small chair. They'd shouted and screamed at her and got angry when she couldn't answer their questions. This made them angry so they hit her again.

She'd lost track of the time she'd been here was it a few days, or several weeks? As she drifted in and out of consciousness, she had lost all sense of reality. Her former life was a blur, and it was too late to mark the cell walls to record how long they'd kept her imprisoned.

This time, however, they didn't turn left. They turned right at the top of the steps and pulled her down a long corridor towards an opening at the far end. She could see the bright sunlight reflecting off the dirty white walls. For a brief moment, she had a sudden feeling of euphoria. They were going to let her go!

She could hear muffled sounds and shouts from the

street outside. It was surreal there were people so close to the prison going about their everyday lives. On the other side of the wall, the early morning suppliers who brought produce in from the surrounding areas were haggling over prices with the market stallholders, shouting and arguing at the tops of their voices. Not one of them was aware of her, of her pain or despair. Even if they *had* known, they wouldn't give her a second thought. Why should they care? She didn't belong here. Only a few years ago she'd never heard of them or their country. The sounds drifting over the wall that were once so foreign had become commonplace, then forgotten, and now remembered. She was aware of the everyday bustle and noise of the market, goats bleating, chickens squawking, children screaming and the babble of voices. But all these sounds could have been a million miles away, for they were way beyond her reach.

Hope flared briefly. Her captors had realized she was innocent. They'd never accused her of anything sensible, and she still didn't know why she'd been arrested. She knew she'd done nothing wrong. Her thoughts ran wild, and she tried to convince herself the nightmare was over at last.

All the doors on either side of the corridor were closed, as they half carried, half dragged her towards the opening in the archway at the end. The closer they got, against all reason, her hopes just grew and grew. They were going to set her free. She was going home.

As they shoved her through the open doorway, she screwed up her eyes against the bright light, and when she opened them, it was to see they were in a bare courtyard, surrounded on three sides by high walls. As she looked around, she could see there was no other exit leading to the outside world.

Then she saw the stake in the ground on the far side, and brutally they dragged her towards it. She thought of trying to resist, but she was too weak, and there was too much pain. It was difficult to walk, so she concentrated on putting one foot in front of the other, determined not to give the soldiers or police or whoever they were, any satisfaction. She would show as much dignity as she could.

The skinny one pushed her against the post, took another long piece of sheeting from his pocket and tied it around her chest, fixing her firmly to the wood. She glanced down at the ground and was horrified to see large brown stains in the dust.

Not freedom; this was the end. She squeezed her eyes shut, determined not to let the tears run down her cheeks, but the sound of marching feet forced her to open them again. She saw four more men, all dressed in brown uniforms, with the all-too-familiar guns who had lined up on the other side of the courtyard opposite her. They were a rough-looking bunch, their uniforms were ill fitting and stained, and their boots were unpolished and covered in dust.

She was trembling all over. She didn't know whether to keep her eyes open to see what was going on, or close them and pretend this was all a terrible dream. She was torn. Part of her wanted it all to end now, but still a part of her wanted to scream, 'let me live! Please, please let me live!'

The big fat man barked commands and she heard the sounds of guns being broken open as he walked to each of them handing out ammunition, then with the safety catches off, they shuffled into position.

To her horror, she felt a warm trickle of liquid running down the inside of her thighs. At this very last moment, she had lost both her control and her dignity. They had not even offered her a blindfold, so she closed her eyes again and tried to remember happier times, before the nightmare started. Briefly, she glanced up at the few fluffy white clouds floating high in the sky as the order to fire was given.

< < < OOO > > >

Printed in Great Britain
by Amazon